SLEEPER AGENT

JOHN BIRMINGHAM

1

Clem's Bar-n-Grill was licensed for eighty-nine customers. The Saturday night after Gainesville won the Mid States final, totally steamrolling the arrogant toffs from Jacksondale Grammar, more than three hundred supporters crowded in for the party. Clem Dixon, owner of Gainesville's finest eating house, number one ticket holder for the Gainesville Tigers, and captain of the last hometown side to raise the Ol' Jug in triumph thirty-six years earlier ponied up two whole barbecued hogs, half-priced adult beverages, and free soda pop and ice-cream for the kiddies. The revellers inside the bar constituted nearly ten per cent of the town's population. The rest, it seemed, spilled across the lawn of the town square outside, where Clem's locally famous in-house blues band, Rock-apotamus, kicked out the jams in the old rotunda. There were, then, any number of witnesses to vouch for Cooper Fox and to testify that he acted purely in self-defence, even if those witnesses could not quite believe their eyes.

Cooper, who also happily answered to 'Coop', was enjoying a pork slider and the band's foot-stomping cover of *R.O.C.K in the USA* while his girlfriend Mary looked on from the long wooden serving tables. Cooper danced with the same happy abandon as her little ones Matty and Jessica and a dozen or more of their little friends in the loose, parentally supervised mosh pit well away from the grown-ups. Most of the town's adult population was quite drunk and rocking out for reals in front of the bandstand. Everyone who saw Cooper dancing with the children smiled, and if some of those smiles seemed ever so slightly bittersweet, it wasn't because they felt sorry for Mary Doyle and her guy.

She had never looked so happy. And Coop, well, everyone loved Cooper Fox. And everyone in town looked out for him. After all, Coach Buchner insisted he was a big part of why the Tigers had won—as strange as that might seem if you were to meet Cooper Fox just once or twice and you did not have the chance to get to know him well.

The kids all knew him, though, from the pre-schoolers to Gainesville High's graduating class. He was just about their favourite grown-up, and to see him shaking his tail feather when the band slid into the old Blues Brothers classic, you could see why. Cooper Fox was a simple man with a child's innocent soul.

A cruel person would just stop and maybe even sneer a little at 'simple'.

Cooper didn't care. He loved shaking his tail feather. At that moment, he was laughing and marshalling a small but growing chorus line of littluns into a performance of the big dance number from the old movie.

"Bend over and let me see you shake your tail feather," Cooper half-shouted half-sang, pointing at the band and encouraging the kids to play along.

"Come on, and let me see you shake your tail feather," Rockapotamus roared back, pointing at the kids, drawing even more attention to them.

The audience around the children cheered and clapped as they did the twist, the fly, the swim, the bird.

Mary was so taken with the scene, so struck with her feelings for the man who had wandered into her life just a couple of years ago, that she completely vagued out while she was serving a pork-n-gravy roll to Ross Powell, the Tigers' wide receiver. It was his second roll, but he was a big boy with an appetite to match.

"Miss Doyle?" Ross asked when it became apparent she'd forgotten about him.

Mary blushed.

"Sorry, Rosco," she said, hurrying to load up his bread roll to cover her embarrassment.

"No salad or 'slaw, thank you, ma'am," Powell said, sounding almost panicked. "Just more meat if you got it."

Mary apologised again, put aside the roll, which was now hopelessly contaminated with salad, and made Ross a fresh one from the get-go.

Gainesville's prize-winning baker and Rosco's stepmom, Kimmy Thanh, had supplied crusty baguettes, brioche, and plain white dinner rolls, while the school's market garden project provided all the fresh greenery and vine-ripened tomatoes needed to lighten the avalanche of free carbs and protein.

But, Rosco Powell assured Mary Doyle, "Carbs and protein are just fine, ma'am."

"S'okay, girl," Gabby Washington, the town librarian, whispered into her ear when Powell had gone. "That's a fine-looking man you got yourself there. You ain't the only one losin' yo skittles watching that ass."

"Gabby!" she protested, blushing twice as fiercely as before. Mary's lineage was Irish, and her pale skin would burn in the winter sun and blush at the merest hint of embarrassment. She protested way too much now, though, because Gabs had indeed caught her thinking lewd and unmentionable thoughts about what she was going to do with that fine piece of man-ass just as soon as she got him home.

The librarian cackled with delighted laughter at catching her out. Catching folks out was why the good Lord had put Gabby Washington on this earth, and it was a balm to see her spirits run free for just a little while. She had troubles in her life.

The band finished up with the Blues Brothers, rolling right on into Bob Seger's *Old Time Rock and Roll*, the unofficial anthem of the Gainesville Tigers. A great roar went up from the crowd. So loud she didn't hear what Gabby said next.

"I said we all out of lemonade for the little ones," Gabs shouted over the noise.

The line for pork rolls snaked all the way over to the Civil War memorial in the corner of the town square. Seven school moms and Gabs worked the long trestle tables, serving up food and drink, but trade was so brisk Mary didn't think they could spare anybody to run over to Clem's to refill the cooler for kids' drinks.

"I'll get Cooper to do it," she said, pitching her voice over the music and the crowd noise.

It took a few seconds of waving her barbecue tongs at him, but eventually, Cooper saw he was needed and excused himself from the children, who all protested hugely. A couple of the smaller ones held onto his legs, and he carried them over like bear cubs clinging to a tree trunk.

Cooper Fox was a touch over six foot, and he moved with a grace that suggested great strength and agility. But a dancer's strength rather than a linebacker's. And that was the hell of it because Coach Buchner wasn't blowing smoke when he gave Coop a good measure of the credit for the Tigers' pennant-winning year. Cooper Fox was not a qualified coach. As best anyone knew, he didn't even have his high school diploma. And, of course, there was the other thing.

But all that aside, Buchner would tell you, the man had a natural-born genius for strength and conditioning. He was only the assistant to the assistant coach and unpaid at that, but his drills and workouts were acknowledged as the foundation of the Tigers' climb from the second lowest team in the Mid States conference to the championship they had taken off Jacksondale just last night.

"Hey, baby. Hey Gabs," he smiled, gently prising two littluns from his legs and sending them back to their parents with the gentlest of kicks to their tooshies. "S'up?"

"Cooper, could you take the cooler over to Clem's and refill it with soda for the kids?" Mary asked, raising her voice to be heard over the music and the clamour of the crowd. "We've run out."

"Sure thing," he shrugged. "I like Clem."

He smiled, and if you were looking closely, or if you'd been worded up to watch out for it, you'd have seen something in that smile. Or rather, something missing.

Cooper Fox was conventionally, almost anonymously handsome, with thick black hair cut short and grey-blue eyes that would have been striking on anybody but him. His features, once sculpted, had been rearranged at some point with traumatic force; a once aquiline nose broken and reset with a slight crook, and one cheekbone marred by a two-inch scar that was noticeable not because it was livid or gnarled - it was pretty faint - but because with the broken nose, it looked so out of place.

Mary liked to say his scars gave him character. Cooper, who did not care much about them, always replied, "I am a character." Because he'd heard that in a movie once, and it had made him laugh and laugh.

"Here you go, handsome. Fill it up," Gabs said, passing over the family-sized cooler.

"Okay," Cooper said. "I'll do that."

"And bring it back," Gabs added. Just in case.

He nodded seriously.

"And bring it back."

Somebody else might have rolled their eyes or pushed back at Gabs, but Cooper's reply was unaffected. Like him. That's what was missing from his smile: any sense of nuance, or complexity, or the inevitable tensions and contradictions that formed the hidden architecture of a fully grown personality.

Cooper Fox, a man in his late twenties or maybe his early thirties, had the guileless face of a child.

Joe Don Porter had the face of a man who'd spent most of the past fourteen years staring at the bars of a prison cell in Saginaw County Correctional Facility. His skin was sallow, deeply lined, and covered with grey-black tattoos, all of them etched into his hide with a variety of improvised tools and inks. Mechanical pencils, staples, paper clips. Cigarette ash mixed with shampoo, melted plastic and Styrofoam. A barbed wire motif encircled his neck. A spider web covered one elbow. There was nothing Porter could do to hide the dots and teardrops and lightning bolts on his face, but he was smart enough to keep the most noticeable examples of his prison ink covered up.

The night was mild for mid-November but chill enough for Porter to get away with a cheap muffler around his neck and lower face. His companions, Duray McClintock and Warren Lubbers were half his age and probably half as dumb again. He was definitely the brains of this crew. He'd shared a cell with McClintock for a while at Saginaw, and they'd teamed up with Lubbers, a dull, watery-eyed gigantic brute, three days ago across the state line in West Virginia.

Thus, they were interstate fugitives now.

But Joe Don did not imagine the FBI would be getting up a strike team to chase them down any time soon.

Their two-state crime spree was modest. Three break-and-enters, the last of which had turned into a home invasion, with the six-foot-seven Lubbers knocking out the terrified homeowner before he could raise the alarm. Some skinny-ass old coon in a fuckin' nightdress, if you could believe it. They'd robbed a liquor store for a hundred and thirty-six dollars in cash, a sixer of Coors, and a packet of pork rinds. Then, one town up the road, some Podunk shithole called Jacksondale, they'd jumped a school kid with a backpack at the rail siding. Gave him a kicking to think about and stole his pack, which had given up a laptop and an iPad.

They'd sell those a way down the road because Joe Don was calling the shots, and he wasn't so fucking dumb as to try and pawn the stuff anywhere near the kid's hometown.

Gainesville had drawn them like flies to a fresh turd because in Jacksondale, at a gas stop, they'd heard about the big game and the loss to the in-breeds from down the interstate and Duray who'd played one game of high school football had reckoned there'd probably be a big party in town. Morons that they were, McClintock and Lubbers were all for rolling into town to get some drunk cheerleader pussy.

They weren't so fucking dumb as to imagine any self-respecting cheerleaders would give it up for a couple of skeevy convicts like them. "But we could grab some to go," McClintock suggested as they crested a hill and saw the town nestled in the valley below. The square in the centre of the little village was alive with people and brightly strung with festival lights.

"The fuck we will," Joe Don growled. He couldn't think of a surer way to draw the sustained and earnest attention of the authorities.

But Joe Don was intrigued by the other possibilities that suggested themselves. If the whole town was down there, celebrating their win, that meant a lot of houses left unattended and a lot of valuables an enterprising outlaw band could place within their possession before these idiot hicks realised they done been robbed.

They were sat three abreast in the cabin of a stolen F100. The flatbed in back could carry a helluva lot more loot than one school kid's backpack.

"Boys," said Joe Don. "I do believe we have a job of work ahead of us tonight."

Unfortunately, Porter's cunning plan to skirt the centre of town and denude a couple of dozen residences of jewellery and cash foundered on a series of street closures to facilitate the safe and leisurely movement by foot of the town's many revellers to and from their revels. A deputy in a wide-brimmed cowboy hat stopped them at a crossroads and motioned for Joe Don to back up and dismount if he wanted to go any further. The deputy's manner suggested that moving on and never coming back might be an even better idea. Porter would have backed the fuck up all the way to the interstate, having been eyeballed by local law enforcement. By then, however, both of his accomplices had spotted the hand-painted signs offering free barbecue and half-price drinks and free soda, and like the children who'd swarmed around Cooper Fox when the band started in on their Blues Brothers set list, McClintock and Lubbers became somewhat over-excited.

Lubbers jumped out of the truck and ran off into the crowd. Joe Don might have left him, but by then, Duray had also exited the vehicle, and he had the hundred and thirty-six bucks from the liquor store job. And that's how three not particularly wanted criminals came to find themselves in Gainesville on the night of the big street party to celebrate the Tigers' first championship in thirty-six years.

Joe Don parked the stolen pickup outside a pharmacy and locked the doors. You couldn't be too careful, after all. He arranged the muffler to best cover his facial tattoos and the barbed wire inked into his neck and tried to smile with his eyes. He did not belong—none of them did—and it could surely be but a few minutes before one of these yokels started pointing and whispering. Joe Don headed for the barbecue. He would get his dumbass offsiders a free burger, and they would get the hell gone to work before this shit went sideways.

It went sideways less than a minute later.

Joe Don Porter saw it all happen.

Some guy was carrying an ice cooler on one shoulder. You could tell it was full by how careful he was being not to overbalance as he threaded through the crowds. The guy looked sort of thin, at least compared to a lot of the fat asses and dumbos around him, but he looked strong too. If that cooler was full, it'd be a hell of a load.

Joe Don's stomach sort of clenched when he saw McClintock and Lubbers standing in the guy's way, blocking his path.

Dude hadn't seen them yet. His head was down as he concentrated on his footing like some sorta feeb. But they'd seen him, and they were looking thirsty. Joe Don wanted to cry out to them, but he didn't want to draw attention to himself. He wanted to run, to intercept the ice cooler moron before he encountered Duray and Lubbers, or to grab the pair of snaggletooth cons and hustle them out of his way before any CCTV cameras captured video evidence of what now seemed a certainty. There was going to be an incident. Caught between all these options, for a crucial two seconds, he did nothing.

Lubbers—six-and-a-half feet of stupid, unthinking brutality just looking for an excuse to run wild—planted his enormous boots squarely in front of the other man and let the ice cooler hit him in his chest. Taken by surprise, the man was knocked off balance. He might have dropped the burden and spilled everything in the cooler, except that

Lubbers had already laid hands on it, flipped open the lid and was pulling out cold cans of drink.

Pulling them out and throwing them away when they turned out to be soda instead of beer. Duray was jumping up and down like a kid at a candy counter, trying to get a look inside the cooler.

Joe Don was moving now, like really moving, but it was too late. Everything that was going to happen was already happening. He should just run, he knew. Run back to the truck and get the fuck gone. But he knew these two idiots were about to have a whole town fall on them, and an hour or two from now when the local sheriff had finished smashing them upside the head with an old phone book, they were gonna give Joe Don Porter up as part of their blubbering, snot-nosed, bloody-mouth confessions.

Joe Don didn't hear the man with the cooler say whatever it was he said to Lubbers. The crowd, the band, the roar of all those voices and that music, it was too loud to make out the exchange. But he saw the man try to argue with them. Saw Lubbers swing a can of soda at his head. Saw the can connect and explode with the force of the impact. Saw the guy go down like a sack of wet horse shit. Felt his balls crawl up inside of his body.

He heard the first screams. Heard the cries of alarm and outrage. Heard himself swear as he increased his jog to a sprint.

———

MARY WAS ABOUT to fatten up Deputy Dan Ferrucci's dinner roll with extra slaw when she saw Cooper bump into the giant. For the merest second, she smiled. Almost laughed. Gainesville was the sort of town that policed itself and the sheriff's office was only four strong, including Sharon Ferrucci, Dan's wife, who temped as the office manager. Clem Dixon always had security on the door at his place when the band was playing, but apart from carrying Owen MacGilvray home across the square to Sara Stutchbury's boarding house and snorting at the fake IDs the high school kids attempted to pass off as genuine, Clem's doormen earned their money with no real effort. Gainesville was a lucky place. Why, just last year, a big pharmaceutical company had opened a national distribution centre out near the junction with US 44, a development that had brought a whole heap of money into town during construction and left behind more than fifty good-paying jobs when the hard hats were gone. Gainesville was a nice town. The people were good people, and the football team had just won a famous victory. She was so happy when she'd fetched up here with the kids, after getting away from her asshole husband Brian, and happier still when she'd met Cooper, that... well, when she saw that enormous vagrant swing a giant, stiff-armed punch at her man, it just...

It didn't process.

When the soda can exploded against the side of his head, she didn't understand what she was seeing.

As Cooper started to fall to the ground, she was still locked up in that initial confusion.

Wait! What? Huh?

It was only when the cooler full of ice and drinks crashed to the ground and Rosco Powell, still holding a half-eaten barbecue pork roll, flew at the man who'd hit Cooper that Mary started to piece it together.

That guy, that stranger, had attacked her man. Her beautiful, innocent, gentle...

She screamed.

Dan Ferrucci was already turning towards the screams and uproar coming from the fight—because it *was* a fight now, with the giant and some other guy piling into the Powell boy. Dan was so surprised he mashed his barbecue pork roll into his pistol when he reached for the weapon. The band was still playing, and the crowd around the rotunda hadn't yet registered any change in the vibe, but away from the crush at the bandstand, heads turned and arms raised as people pointed the fracas out to each other.

"NO! COOPER!" Mary cried out, stumbling as she tried to get out from behind the serving table.

"Those men!" Gabby Washington boomed out, her voice suddenly hard and loud with authority, "Somebody stop those men."

They were pounding on poor Rosco Powell, their arms flailing in awkward, stiff-limbed caricatures of hook punches and hammer blows. But the fists on the big one were so large that every clout seemed to land like a crude bomb.

Women and children screamed.

Men shouted angrily, uncertainly.

And everything moved in slow motion.

Everything and everyone except her man.

For the second time that night, just moments after being paralysed by confusion and her inability to process what she was seeing, Mary Doyle stared gape-mouthed at her boyfriend.

Cooper, who had never so much as raised his voice with her or the kids, let alone his hand, seemed to flow up off the grass where he'd been knocked down. He leapt like a spark across the distance between himself and the men who were now kicking Roscoe, arriving behind the big one in a blurred wave of colour that seemed to reap the giant's legs out from beneath him. As that one crashed down like a rotten oak tree in a storm, his buddy threw a wild haymaker, and Mary moaned in anticipation of it connecting with Cooper's skull. He'd already taken that one terrible blow. But instead of catching another and almost certainly compounding the head injuries he'd suffered, Cooper moved so quickly that he disappeared in a sort of graceful shimmer.

There was nothing graceful about the effect, however.

Mary saw the man's arm suddenly blocked, extended and snapped like dry kindling for the barbecue. Cooper appeared to pirouette in front of him, dragging the shattered limb across the back of his shoulders. It happened so fast Mary couldn't really tell. One of Cooper's arms was now tangled up in the horribly bent wreckage of the other man's, and his free hand speared into the attackers' throat.

Although to be honest, that guy wasn't really an attacker anymore. He was a victim.

The crowd, which had been surging towards the fight, had stopped. The band had stopped.

But Cooper hadn't. As the giant attempted to get to his feet, in spite of what Mary now saw was a badly broken leg, Cooper pistoned a kick into the side of his head with a single, directed shout that made her jump even at a distance.

Another voice yelled out.

"Fucking stop right there, asshole!"

For one brief moment, perhaps for half a heartbeat, Mary thought Sheriff Andy or Deputy Dan might finally have switched on.

But they would never cuss like that, and certainly not at Cooper. Not even to stop him...

Mary shuddered. She didn't know what to think of what she had just seen her man do. She didn't know what to call it.

Not even to stop him from killing those guys?

But it wasn't Sheriff Andy. And she could see Deputy Dan, panicked and wiping coleslaw and gravy off his service revolver.

A third man had entered the tableau and was pointing a gun at Cooper's head. Ice water sluiced through Mary's stomach, and a strange numbness spread out from her fingers and toes. That gun looked as big as a cannon to her. The muzzle was inches from Cooper's head.

And then it wasn't.

Mary had not really understood what happened when Cooper intervened to stop the two men attacking Ross Powell. It had happened so quickly, and she hadn't been expecting it. It was all over before she could put the pieces together like a jigsaw puzzle. Nonetheless, later on, she could sort of reconstruct what happened.

With that gun, however, she never understood. Not even looking at the videos people took on their phones. And a lot of people took videos. Lizzie Margolis, who pretty much ran the high-school newspaper on her own, even had the presence of mind to use the slow-motion setting on her iPhone.

A lot of people watched that video later, including Sheriff Andy and Tom Margolis, Lizzie's dad, and the county prosecutor. None of them could say for sure what Cooper did or how.

You could only be sure of the result.

There was an indistinct smear of pixels on the video, and then the man with the gun was on the ground, and Cooper Fox was standing over him, pointing the gun at his face.

2

Sheriff Andy and Deputy Dan arrived on the scene a few moments later. Both men had their guns drawn, but Andy told Dan to holster his weapon when they saw Cooper standing over the last man, pointing the gun down at him.

"Put the gun down, Coop. That'll be enough, son," Andy Briscoe said.

Sheriff Briscoe was only a couple of years away from retirement. He had a farm a few miles out of town and was wont to ride into work on one of his two old horses. It had given him a bandy-legged gait, which seemed to be exaggerated by the small gut hanging over his utility belt. But he was a popular, even much-loved figure in town. Nobody had run against him for the Sheriff's office in twenty years, and he was a man much happier holstering his gun than aiming it at somebody.

For one chilling second, Mary Doyle was sure that Cooper was going to shoot him.

Then whatever cold, murderous thing had taken up residence behind his eyes disappeared, and he was just Cooper Fox again. In fact, his look of confusion and distress recalled the Cooper she had first met two years earlier when he'd wandered into town after his accident.

"I'm... I'm sorry," he stammered, dropping the gun on the grass, well away from the men who had attacked him.

The words seemed to affect the crowd like a magic spell. The frozen moment in which nobody had moved or dared to speak passed, and everyone unlocked.

"That's fine, son, just move away from those men," Sheriff Briscoe said. It was an order, no doubt about it, but gently delivered.

Cooper nodded his head and backed away slowly. Uncertainly. All the strange animal power and grace was gone. He almost tripped over his own shoes.

Andy and Dan advanced on the criminals, their hands on the butts of their service weapons.

"I think we're going to need Doc Schofield here," Dan Ferrucci said. His face was pale and sort of haunted as he looked at the human wreckage of the three attackers. The one with the broken leg was screaming. That leg of his was bent completely the wrong way around. The gunman looked like he might even be dead or well on the way there.

Mary did not care about their suffering. Those men had attacked her Cooper and got what they deserved for it. Even so, like Deputy Dan, she had a hard time looking at them or listening to the wails and the moaning.

The buzz of the crowd came back, nothing like the happy roar it had been, but enough that she had to raise her voice to call out to her kids. Matty and Jess had been in the little ones' mosh pit, dancing with Cooper, and she had no idea where they were now or whether they had witnessed the terrible thing that just happened.

"Matty! Jessie!" she cried out, adding her voice to those of dozens of other parents calling out for their children and hundreds of people asking each other what was going on or loudly declaring their version of events.

Mary was torn between wanting to run to Cooper, who looked absolutely lost and upset, and needing to lay hands on her children in the sudden chaos of a night gone terribly wrong."

"I've got them, Mary," an old, familiar voice called out.

Mary Doyle turned in the push and pull of the crowd and saw that Gabby Washington had already gathered up her two and had them wrapped protectively under her arms.

"I got them," she called out again. "You go, you look after Cooper. I'll take your guys back to my place, and they can sit with Sarah."

Relief and gratitude washed through her. At least, that was something she didn't have to worry about. Mary turned back to the...well, to the crime scene, she supposed. It was hard to see because so many people were crowding around, but it seemed that Deputy Dan was cuffing one of the men – the one without the broken arm – while Sheriff Andy administered some rough and basic first aid and called over Jamaal Brown, his other deputy, who had been manning the roadblock at the edge of town. Brown towered over both men. He had played offensive tackle for the Tigers the last time they had come close to the championship, ten years ago. He'd gone into the Army as a medic, and he took over from Andy, examining the gunman, pronouncing him unconscious but alive.

When Mary pushed her way through the throng, she found the three lawmen trying to decide how to restrain the two attackers with badly broken limbs and whether restraints were even necessary.

"That guy's not going anywhere," Jamaal said of the one with the shattered leg.

He was a giant, possibly bigger even than Jamaal Brown. But the deputy was right. He would be lucky if they didn't cut that leg off, it was so badly broken.

"Man, if he was a horse, we'd have to shoot him," Dan Ferrucci said.

The screams of the big man were enough to turn your stomach.

Mary felt cold and a little sick at the idea of Cooper being somehow responsible for this. But he *wasn't*, she told herself. Those assholes were. They'd brought it all on themselves, wrecking everybody's night.

"Ambulance will be here soon," Sheriff Andy said in his gruff but reassuring way. "How about we leave it to someone who knows what he's doing to decide on how to get them from here to wherever they're going? Hospital for two of them, I reckon. The cells for this fella with the gun."

He pointed down at the man Cooper had disarmed.

The man's face and neck were covered in crude tattoos. Mary was not one to judge people by appearances, but this fellow appeared to have spent most of his life in prison. She edged closer to Cooper, who was standing next to Sheriff Andy. He was staring at the ground as though he wanted it to swallow him up. It was such a terrible contrast with his pure joy of a little while ago that Mary had to clutch at her heart, which wanted to lurch up out of her mouth.

"Oh, Cooper," she said, mostly to herself.

She was close enough to Sheriff Andy that he heard.

"It's all right, darlin'," Briscoe said. "You come on over here. Coop didn't do nothing wrong. I saw it all. Dan saw it, too. Hell, most of the town saw what happened. He'll be fine. It's these fellas are gonna answer for what they did."

He glowered at the three men on the ground, but his dark expression shaded into a worried frown when he looked over at Cooper Fox.

Mary didn't care. She went to her man and threw her arms around him.

"Baby, are you okay?" She spoke quickly, the words rushing out of her. "I don't know how you did that. I don't know what you did. But I'm so, so glad that you're okay. You are okay, aren't you? Did they hurt you?"

She reached up for his head, and Cooper let her probe his scalp with the tips of her fingers. She could feel a bump under the waves of his thick black hair. It was big, alarmingly so. Like half an egg under his skin or something.

"What happened?" Cooper asked.

MARY KEPT HOLD OF HIM, but at a distance where she could quickly look him up and down. He wasn't bleeding. Nothing was broken. Not like those other guys. But he was terribly shaken up. She could see that. She knew her guy.

"You got hit in the head, Coop," she told him. "Do you remember that? When that guy hit you in the head with the soda can?" He put one shaking hand up to the side of his head, which was still wet and sticky with soda. Pepsi, she thought. Cooper seemed surprised.

"No," he said. "I remember I had to get a soda. That's all."

Mary's heart gave another lurch. She turned to Sheriff Andy.

"Andy, he says he can't remember anything. He got hit in the head. He might have brain damage," she said, regretting it instantly. That was something people used to say about Cooper. One of the kinder things. She had heard much crueller words over the years. Not from people in town, not once they got to know him. But she was always very careful about how she described his injuries from the car accident.

Sheriff Briscoe's frown grew deeper. He told Dan and Jamaal to keep an eye on the prisoners. That's what he called them: prisoners. And he turned his attention to Cooper.

"How many fingers am I holding up, son?"

"Two," Cooper answered correctly.

"And you think you could take a little walk for me? In a straight line, just over to the pharmacy over there and back."

"I think so," Cooper said.

"Mary, why don't you go with him?" Sheriff Andy suggested. "Just halfway there and back, make sure folks don't bump into him. But don't give him any help."

"But he's not drunk, Sheriff. He got hit in the head," she protested.

"I know," Sheriff Briscoe said patiently. "I want to see if his balance is off."

"Oh, right."

Mary took Cooper gently by the arm and led him onto the road.

"Make a hole," Briscoe called out. "Give them space."

Cooper moved slowly and a little awkwardly, but no more than you'd expect from somebody who'd just taken a headshot. And, to be honest, less unsteadily than she was expecting. They got about halfway to Osgood Little's pharmacy, turned around and came back. Cooper seemed to have recovered most of his balance by then.

His physical balance, anyway.

To Mary, he seemed all at once distant and drifting and upset and sort of...broken. When they got back to Sheriff Andy and the others, she was all at odds with herself, wanting to rush him straight home to bed, get him off to Doctor Schofield, and wishing that everything could just go back to the way it was earlier that night.

With the threat from the three hoodlums over, thanks to Cooper and Roscoe, too, it did seem as though the celebration might get rolling again. Deputy Dan was already shooing people away, telling them to go back and listen to the band and grab a burger. She could hear music, muted by distance, coming from inside of Clem's place. And lots of people had gone back to whatever they were doing before, mostly eating and drinking.

When the ambulance came, it did so quietly, without its flashing lights or the siren. That was probably Sheriff Andy's doing, she thought. He always preferred to handle things with as little fuss as possible. By then, Cooper was sitting on a park bench, drinking a bottle of water, and the band was playing again. But slow tunes this time, something to calm everyone down. The only ones still making a fuss were the hoodlums. The one with the busted leg was crying like a baby now, and the gunman was down on his hands and knees, dry retching onto the ground while Deputy Brown kept watch.

The two injured men went into the ambulance for a quick trip up the interstate to the hospital at Jacksondale. Sheriff Briscoe assured Mary that they would be kept under guard there.

"No need to worry about them," he said. "They got a secure ward at Jacksondale, and Sherriff Bannerman will chain those hoodlums good and safe."

The man with the barbed wire tattoo etched around his neck, the one Cooper had disarmed by some feat of magic, was going straight behind bars, Andy said. He had a black eye and a bruise on the side of his neck, but nothing that would constitute a get-out-of-jail-free card.

"I figure you'll want to be along with Cooper while I interview him," Andy said. "As a responsible adult, you know, given his condition. If you want, I can get Dan to walk you over, or you can ride along with me and this fella here."

He nodded at the disarmed man, who was now sitting handcuffed on the ground, shaking his head.

"I thought you said Cooper was going to be okay," Mary shot back. "Why do you need to interview him?"

Sheriff Andy patted her on the shoulder.

"Don't you worry none. He is not in trouble. I guarantee you. But I do need to take a statement."

ANDY BRISCOE LOOKED UNCOMFORTABLE, and Mary bristled. It was like being thrown back in time to when she first started going out with Cooper, just after he'd turned up in town. When people thought he was feeble.

"I'm not his guardian, Andy. And he's done nothing wrong," she said, annoyed.

"I know, I know," he said, patting the air between them. "But I have rules I have to follow, and if these fellas get even a half-decent public defender and he finds out I interviewed my main witness, who has an acquired brain injury and who is under treatment for it, if they find out he made his statement without a support person along, well, they could make all kinds of merry hell with that. Suggesting that I put words in his mouth and such."

"But I'm his partner, Andy. Won't they play hell with that?"

"I know you're not his guardian, Mary. But the law says he should have one in this situation. And you're the closest thing he has to kin, unless you want I should get the Coach or Doc Schofield?"

Mary took a deep breath. It was all so unfair. She hadn't had to deal with anything like this for a long time. Cooper was part of her life and part of the local community now. He was so much a part of it that it was possible most days to forget how difficult it had once been.

"Okay," she said, "I'm sorry. I'm just upset, is all."

"Understandable," Sheriff Andy said. "So, you want to ride along or have Dan walk you over?"

Mary shrugged. She stared for a moment at Cooper, who seemed almost blank.

That was almost as scary as watching him in the fight earlier.

Not that it was much of a fight.

"What about Coop?" She asked.

"I'm going to get Jamaal to bring him over once things settle down here."

"Okay then," Mary said. "I might go with them if that's all right. I want to keep an eye on him. I think he needs to see the doctor."

"Already taken care of," the sheriff assured her.

———

DOCTOR SCHOFIELD ARRIVED while Sheriff Briscoe was taking a statement from Cooper at his office over on Longfellow Street. He was a young man, which some folks in town still held against him; the sort of folks who preferred their country doctors silver-haired, a little stooped and full of folk wisdom. But Mike Schofield had been very good to Cooper, and Mary Doyle thought he was just about the best doctor she had ever known outside of a TV show.

"Whoa, now, what's going on here?" Schofield called out as he bustled in through the door. While the door was open, Mary could hear the band a ways off in the distance. She was sitting next to Cooper, across a cheap desk from Sheriff Briscoe. Sharon Ferrucci was sitting in, too, taking shorthand notes to back up the little mini recorder that lay between them, capturing all the questions and answers. When Schofield came in, Sharon stopped writing and paused the recording.

"Just taking a witness statement, Doc," Sheriff Briscoe explained.

"Maybe do that after I've examined my patient. Thanks, Andy,"

Doctor Schofield said. "I can't even tell you whether he's in a fit state of mind to talk with you."

"I'm okay, Doctor Mike," Cooper said. "Just a bit shook up, is all. They reckon the big fella got me a good one upside the head."

Schofield looked alarmed to hear that.

He hurried over, dropping his medical bag onto the table and pulling out all sorts of devices and doodads.

"I'm afraid nothing is going to happen until I give the all-clear," Schofield said. He sounded very serious. A little scary, to be honest. And it made Mary frightened for Cooper all over again. She had started to calm down some while Deputy Jamaal had walked them over to the jailhouse, as the old folks called it. Cooper had been fine. Not even a little wobbly by then. She'd even wondered if the party would still be going by the time they finished. Mary didn't feel like getting back to it, but she had volunteered to help serve the food, and she felt guilty about skipping out on the promise.

Sheriff Briscoe raised his hands as if in surrender.

"Fine by me, Doc. You do what you gotta do. I'm gonna make a fresh pot of coffee if you're man enough to join me. I got a long night of Sheriff stuff ahead of me. Turns out these hoodlums mugged a young fella for his computer over in Jacksondale, and that pickup they were driving came from out of state. It's been reported as stolen, of course. I'm gonna have the *federales* knocking on my door looking for them, I reckon. US Marshals or FBI. Be a coin toss who gets here first."

"I'll make the coffee, Andy," Sharon Ferrucci said. "I can't drink that radioactive mud you like to brew up."

"I won't be long," Mike Schofield promised. "But Cooper took a significant blunt force trauma to the head. I can't let that slide, given his history. And his statement won't be much good to you anyway, Andy, if his judgement and recall are impaired."

"Fair enough, Doc. I was just trying to get ahead of my chores, is all."

"Have your coffee. I'll have one, too, when I'm done. Cooper, I'm going to take some measurements, draw some blood, and ask you a few questions. That okay?"

"I'm good," he replied.

Slowly, Mary started to calm down again.

Doctor Schofield had arrived in town just a little before Cooper. Or maybe a little while after, but not too long. He'd worked as one of those fill-in doctors for old Doc Bratton, who really was old, white-haired, and stooped with it, too. Locals or locums or something they called them, Mary thought. Doctor Mike bought out Henry Bratton when the older medico had decided to retire. Paid him a big whack of cash for the practice, it was whispered. But he made house calls in emergencies, and he took on some patients without insurance. Treated them for free at a special clinic he ran on Saturdays.

Cooper wasn't one of them.

Cooper Fox had medical insurance because the court-appointed executor of his parent's estate insisted on it. Cooper was not feeble or simple. He had what Doctor Schofield called an 'acquired brain injury' from the car crash that had killed his family three years ago. And he had a very, very large settlement from the trucking company which had employed the amphetamine-addled driver who killed them. Money, at least, was not a problem for him. Not that Coop was allowed to spend it. The executors took care of all that.

While Andy Briscoe checked on his prisoner and Sharon Ferrucci made drinkable coffee, Doctor Schofield ran a whole bunch of tests on Mary Doyle's man. Some of them were simple, and she recognised them from previous visits to Mike's practice. He shined a pen light in Cooper's eyes, listened to his heartbeat through a stethoscope and gave him a tap on the knee with a little rubber hammer. Some others she hadn't seen before, and she didn't even recognise from TV. He had these white patches with wires coming out of them that he stuck on Cooper's temples. He had something that looked like a computer watch that he made Cooper wear on his wrist while Doctor Schofield studied the results on his iPhone. He asked Cooper questions. Lots of questions. In the end, he seemed satisfied with whatever Cooper and all the gadgets told him.

"And you are taking your medicine every night after dinner, right?" Mike Schofield finished.

"Sure thing, Doc," Cooper said. "Every night. Mary always reminds me."

"Does she have to remind you?" Schofield asked.

Cooper grinned, and Mary's heart lifted to see it.

"Nah. But I like it that she does," he said.

Schofield started to pack away his equipment as Sheriff Briscoe returned from the cells, and Sharon appeared with a tray full of hot drinks and cookies from the little kitchenette off the side of the main office.

"I made you and Cooper hot chocolate," she said to Mary. "It will help you sleep later."

"I like hot chocolate," Cooper said. "And cookies."

"Everybody does, son," Sheriff Briscoe said. "Doc, if Cooper is good to go, I'd like to finish up our interview so these folks can get home. Mary, your kids, who's looking after them?"

"They're at Gabby's place," she said, taking a mug of steaming hot cocoa from Sharon. It tasted so good she was almost giddy with drinking it.

"Cooper should be fine," Doc Schofield said. "But Mary, make sure he gets home right away and straight to bed. And call me if there's any problems. I mean, *any* problems, okay?"

"I will," she promised, a little anxious again. "Is he going to be all right?"

She squeezed Cooper's hand, and he squeezed back.

"If he takes his meds, yes," Doc Schofield assured them. "He'll be fine."

But Doc Schofield was wrong.

3

Cooper Fox woke early, as he always did. He had a headache and a lump on the side of his head, but he ignored both to get out of bed and make breakfast for Mary and the kids. He did this every morning. If he didn't, they'd end up eating peanut butter and jelly sandwiches or big bowls of sugary cereal. So, every day, even on his birthday, Cooper rose early to cut up fresh fruit and mix it in with the muesli he toasted himself. He poured fresh orange juice over tumblers full of ice cubes. The ice wasn't just to keep the juice cold. Mostly, it just took up space that would have been filled with juice. And sugar. People thought OJ was healthy, but it wasn't, not if you drank too much of it.

He wasn't sure how he knew that, but he did know it, and Doctor Mike told him he was one hundred and one per cent right, which sounded like a lot. Doctor Mike was interested in how Cooper knew about fruit juice and sugar. He was always interested when Cooper knew something about anything. Doctor Mike said OJ was something Cooper had learned about before the car crash and held onto afterwards. Mike often asked Cooper if he remembered any other stuff from before the car crash.

The truth of it was, though, he remembered almost nothing. They told him his mom and dad and his sister had died in that crash. That's why he had so much money in his trust account. That was cool. He liked the idea that there was an account you could put money *and* trust into.

But he didn't remember his family. He didn't remember anything from before his time here in Gainesville with Mary and her kids.

He loved Matty and Jess. And he loved Mary. He knew that, at least, and was sure he would never forget it. Mary had been his friend when he first got here, and he had no other friends. And now she was much more than that. So, he made her a nice breakfast. Every day.

When the table was set, and the juice was chilled, he got everybody out of bed. For Mary, this meant placing a mug full of hot coffee on the bedside table and kissing her on the ear. Sometimes, he would kiss her on the forehead or the neck, but this morning, it was the ear. Sometimes, she wouldn't let him go back to the kitchen or get the kids up until they had snuggled, but this morning, they both had work, so she didn't.

Cooper woke the kids by belting out the best bits from that book they both liked about the boy who would not get out of bed.

"The alarm can ring. The birds can peep," Cooper cried out. "Today's the day I'm going to sleep."

He couldn't read the book for real, but he'd heard Mary read it to them so many times that he remembered all about the birds peeping and the alarm ringing. It was funny because there was no way the kids could sleep with him marching around the bedroom, shouting out rhymes about sleeping all day.

This morning, however, his head hurt when he started to do the rhymes in his loudest wake-up voice, and he had to be a lot quieter. But Matty and Jess still got up and charged out into the little kitchen, where they all crowded around the table to have their muesli and juice.

Everyone except Cooper, who pulled on his running shoes while Mary and the children ate.

"Are you okay to run into school?" Mary asked. "After last night."

"My head hurts," he confessed. "But I run to school every day."

"But shouldn't you walk in today? Or even catch the bus with us?"

He shook his head, which hurt a little more. He never caught the bus. He never got into any cars or buses if he could help it. "No, Mary," he said. "I run into school every day. You know I run in, and I do my weights, and I have the sportsman's breakfast with Coach Buchner. That's what I do."

She didn't look happy, even though he'd cut up extra strawberries for her muesli, and she really liked strawberries. But she didn't stop him from running either.

He pulled on his Nike shoes, which were very good and quite new because the trust money lawyers bought him new ones when the old ones got too old to use any more. Cooper had never met the trust find lawyers, but he loved them because they did nice things for him.

Cooper also loved running to school every morning, even when it got cold. He didn't like it quite so much when it got cold *and* it rained. And he couldn't run if the snow got too thick in the middle of winter. But Gainesville was warm most of the time.

They lived in a small house a little way outside town. It didn't take Cooper long to run the two miles into Gainesville High. He usually did it in about fifteen minutes. He knew that because Coach Buchner told him. He told Cooper that if he always left Mary's place when the big hand on the clock was pointing straight up, then he, Coach Buchner, would be able to work out how quickly Cooper had run by looking at where the big hand was on the clock in the school gym when he arrived. It was a sort of magic.

Cooper didn't bother himself thinking about how quickly he was running, how many steps he was taking, how long those steps were or anything like that. He just liked to feel the fresh morning air on his face and to look at all the trees as he raced along the road. The little house the trust fund lawyers bought for him was in the forest, and there were lots of lovely trees to look at. Pines trees and cedars and hickory. Sometimes, when he got to town, he passed people he knew, and he waved to them, and they waved back. Sometimes, he had to wait for the traffic lights to change. Mary had been worried about that when he first started running to the school, but he told her that it was very simple.

"When the little green man in the traffic light is walking, then I can walk too. But when the red man is standing still, so do I."

He ran a little slower this morning.

His headache did start to ease off as he moved from running through the forest south of Gainesville to running along the footpath beside the little park at the edge of town. The more he breathed in the cool, fresh morning air, the better he felt. He could have run all the way, except the lights at the corner of Main Street and Browne made him stop. The little man in the lights was standing still and red, and Cooper knew what that meant.

It was time for him to stand still and wait, too.

He didn't think much about what happened the night before because he couldn't really remember it. It was almost as though that part of the night had somehow slipped from his memory back into the years before his big car crash. It was gone. Like his family.

Instead, he enjoyed watching his breath turn to steam, and he waved to everybody he saw. Mister MacGilvray was sitting on the front porch of Miss Stutchbury's boarding house, drinking milk straight from a carton. Mister Gooch was opening his hardware store and waved when he saw Cooper. Miss McKee, who made the best blueberry muffins at her little cafe, *The Baker's Spoon*, tried to wave him over to tempt him with a treat, which was a trick she did every morning. Sheriff Andy, who always sat at the table by the front window reading his paper, raised a big cup of Joe in greeting. Something he did every morning, too.

"Good morning, Mister Coffee," Cooper grinned.

Some kids from the high school drove by and yelled and waved at him from the back of their car, which Brady McGovern was driving.

Brady played defensive end for the Tigers. He could bench press three hundred and forty-two pounds, and Cooper knew, he just knew, that with a little longer to work on that, Brady could really do some damage to his PB. But Brady was graduating soon, and he would probably go away to college, and that would be that.

It was a shame. Because all he had to do was lower the bar to his chest, pause for a couple of seconds while he inflated his lungs, breathe in deep enough to raise the lower tummy - and then press. If he kept the reps low and controlled the weight completely, say five reps for three sets, Brady would totally set himself up for some big numbers in future.

This was the sort of thing Cooper did as the assistant to the assistant coach.

Nobody, least of all him, had any idea how he did it.

He just did.

"Maybe you were Arnold Schwarzenegger's assistant before the crash," Doctor Mike joked once.

But Cooper was pretty sure he hadn't been.

He just knew about stuff like how to be strong and not to trust orange juice.

He didn't know about much, but he did know about that.

THE TRAFFIC LIGHTS CHANGED, and the little man turned green and looked like he was walking, even though he wasn't really moving, and

Cooper started to jog again. He jogged across the road, careful to look both ways, and he was just about to speed up on the other side when he stopped. He stopped so quickly that he almost got tangled up in his own feet and tripped over. He stood just short of the curb, staring at a girl.

No, it was a picture of a girl stapled to a telephone pole.

The girl in the picture was young, and he knew her. It was Mrs Washington's daughter, Sarah. She was smiling in the photo, and her teeth were very white. But for some reason, her smile made Cooper feel sad. He felt so sad that he could barely take another step. He stared at the picture and felt his chest getting tight and his throat closing. There were words on the paper, too, but he didn't try to read them. That wasn't the sort of thing Cooper Fox was very good at after his car accident. He stood at the edge of the road, staring at Sarah Washington, trying to stop himself from crying, until somebody leaned on a car horn and made him jump with fright.

It broke whatever spell he had been under, and he shuffled on, feeling out of sorts and upset and not quite knowing why. It took him most of the rest of his run to the school to feel better, and he didn't recover completely until he had gone to the gym and done his strength training.

He did extra training that morning because it always made him feel better, which he needed. He was so upset, in fact, that he forgot to look at the clock in the gym to remember where the big hand was when he arrived.

Nothing was working the way it should. So, he did some more weights.

Because that always...

"Hey Cooper, you good, man?"

He dropped the dumbbell he had been lifting in a bent-over row, all seventy-five pounds of it, back to the rubber matting.

It was Coach Buchner.

Cooper shook his head, but not because he wasn't good. He had completely lost track of the time. He could see that from where the big hand and the little hand were on the gym clock. They were in the wrong place.

"I'm...good, coach," Cooper said.

"You been in here two hours now, kid, smashing out the big lifts. You sure you're okay? After last night, I mean. Things like that, they can sneak up on a guy afterwards, you know."

Coach Buchner was a little shorter than Cooper, but he was much bigger across than he was up and down. He was dressed as always in the school windcheater and a Chicago Cubs baseball cap.

"They can't sneak up on me, coach," Cooper said. "Sheriff Andy put them in jail."

Coach Buchner snorted.

"Yeah, I guess he did. Why don't you hit the showers, kid? You got a real sweat going there, and you won't have any takers in here today. You and me are probably the only ones in town without a hangover."

Cooper knew what a hangover was. He never got them because he didn't drink. Neither did Coach Buchner anymore.

"Oh," Cooper said, disappointed, "so I can't be the assistant to the assistant today?

Coach smiled, which made him feel better. Lots of the kids were frightened of Coach because he could be pretty frightening when he got angry about stuff, but he never got angry with Cooper Fox. Right now, for instance, he slapped Cooper on the shoulder and grinned. "Son, you're welcome here anytime. And after the big win this week, I think I'm a good chance of getting you on staff. For a real job."

"With a payday and benefits?"

Cooper knew what a payday was because Mary had hers at the beauty salon every second Thursday. He wasn't quite sure what benefits were, but everybody with jobs seemed to talk about them.

"Yeah," Coach Buchner said. "Pay and benefits, too. Although you got your insurance taken care of anyway. If you don't want to take the health cover they offer here, I reckon we can probably get you a bump in pay. More money," he added when Cooper frowned at the weird idea of a bump in his pay. A dollar bill with a big lump on it? Just like the one on his head? That was crazy.

"I meant we can probably get you more money," Coach explained.

Cooper, who had been feeling all out of sorts, was by now completely lifted out of his earlier mood. Mary would be so happy if he had a job. The car crash money paid for groceries and their little house and stuff, and if he asked nicely—which meant if Mary sent an email with all the pleases and thankyous—sometimes the lawyers at the trust account would even give him money for other stuff that he didn't really need, but that he wanted. That's how they paid for Disney+ on the television. If he had a job, and a payday and a bump like Coach Buchner said, he could get even more stuff for Mary and the kids.

His face lit up with a smile.

"There you go, Champ," Coach Buchner said, smiling right back at him. "Go hit the showers, clean yourself up, and we can talk about next season. The School Board are gonna get a taste for that pennant."

That was weird, Cooper thought, because you couldn't eat a pennant.

But he shrugged it off because he was getting a payday with a bump, and Mary was going to be happy. He wiped down the bench he'd been using, put away all the plates he'd loaded onto the bar, and took himself off to the showers.

He could feel the need for a long, hot shower deep in his muscles. He had overdone it with his training. But that was okay because he was the only one in the showers that morning. He could have as much hot water as he wanted.

In the locker room, he stripped off, stuffed his sweaty gym gear into a plastic bag, which Mary put in his backpack for just that reason, took out a fresh set of clothes, and took the shower nearest his locker. As he always did. The water took a few seconds to warm up because he was the first to use the showers that morning. As soon as it was hot enough, Cooper stepped all the way under, closing his eyes and letting the water stream down his body.

He imagined himself through the deadlifts that he had just completed. Imagined placing his feet just so under the bar, bending his knees and dropping his hips, taking a hook grip on the bar, settling his centre of gravity, controlling his breathing, and pushing up through the...

Cooper Fox cried out in horror.

He wasn't lifting a weighted bar. Behind his eyes, he was lifting a dead body. A young man, or what was left of him. It was raining and dark, and the young man was heavy and difficult to hold onto. He was slick with rain and blood, and full of holes, and missing pieces of himself.

Cooper tried to drop the body and get away, but he couldn't.

He tried to run, but a stranger was blocking his path.

A one-eyed man, who stared at him.

'You what, mate?' the man said.

Cooper screamed.

4

Ray Buchner heard the cry from his office on the second floor of the school sports centre. He was busy with a grant application for new bleachers, and it wasn't unusual for the grunts and snarls and even the occasional roar of one of the boys making a big lift, or screwing it up, to drift into his office. It was only when he heard the high, warbling scream so familiar to him from his two tours of Afghanistan that he remembered there was nobody down in the strength training zone, and he was alone in the centre with Fox.

That scream was the chiller. It made his balls crawl all the way up. He jumped up so fast that his chair flew back and tipped over, forcing him to step around the upturned legs. Once he was clear, he rushed out the door and down the hall. His joggers thumped on the metal stairs as he took them at speed, ignoring the sharp pain in his knee from the shrapnel he'd taken in the Korangal Valley six years ago.

He was not the only one responding to the cries. He saw Riley Martin, the head of English, running towards the showers as well. Martin was precisely the thin and tweedy sort you would expect to find heading up an English studies program, but Buchner knew that he was also a hardcore cycling nut. Like, insane about it. Martin rode hundreds of miles all over Virginia every weekend. He couldn't lift worth a damn, but there was nothing wrong with that guy's cardio.

They both ran into the changing rooms at the same time. The door to one shower stall was closed. The water was running, and steam poured out.

"Who is that?" Martin asked.

"Cooper, are you okay in there?" Buchner called out, ignoring his colleague.

Fox wasn't screaming anymore. He wasn't making any noise. The two men hurried over to the door, and Buchner pounded his fist against it.

"Cooper, can you open the door? If not, keep back out of the way, son. I'm gonna have to kick it in."

"Hold on a moment," Martin protested. "You might hurt him."

But Ray Buchner wasn't listening. He was lining up his shot at the door. He was about to kick it in, the way he'd been taught in the Corps, when he remembered that his knee probably wouldn't stand the shock. Instead, ignoring Martin's objections, he hunched over and charged forward, smashing all two hundred and forty pounds of his muscle and bone into the composite panel. The cheap lock exploded under the impact, and the door flew inwards, slamming against the side of the shower stall.

It missed Cooper Fox by a good two or three feet. He was foetal in the far corner, shivering and moaning quietly. There was no way he was shivering from the cold. Buchner could hardly see him through the steam. He got drenched turning off the taps and nearly slipped on the tiles as he got one hand under Cooper Fox's left armpit.

"Give me some help here, Marty," he said, and to his credit, the word nerd didn't hang back at all. He got in, he got wet, and together they pulled the young man out.

Cooper Fox was shaking like a dog in a thunderstorm. His eyes had The Stare.

He was a fucking long way from Gainesville. They got his towel wrapped around him, and Riley Martin hunted up a few more for good measure.

Fox stopped shivering and moaning after a minute. The close human contact seemed to pull him back from wherever he'd been. He blinked at Buchner as though he didn't recognise him.

"Cooper," the coach said. "It's Ray Buchner. Coach Buchner, from Gainesville High. You had some sort of seizure, kid. I'm gonna get Nurse Szetey, and if she says so, we're gonna get Doc Schofield."

He was pretty damn sure Schofield was gonna be making a call out for this one, but for now, Ray Buchner was just filling up the echoing space of the locker room with happy talk to calm the guy down. He'd done that plenty of times in the Valley. Had it done for him, too.

"Coach?" Cooper Fox said. He didn't sound all that sure.

"Yeah, it's me, kid," Buchner said. "Mister Martin, too."

"Hello, Cooper," Riley Martin said.

Fox stared at the English teacher with that strangely vacant intensity he sometimes got. Buchner couldn't help but wonder what was going on inside his damaged brain. How many millions of neurons were firing blind?

"Dead," Fox said. His breathing hitched, and he gulped, "Fucking dead."

Buchner blinked at that. Fox wasn't one for profanity. Matter of fact, Ray Buchner had never heard him swear, not once.

Fox tried to slither away from them, but Riley Martin had a grip on one arm, and he tightened it. At the same time, he leaned in and mouthed a lot of soothing bullshit that meant nothing but seemed to calm the kid down.

Not that Fox was a kid, of course. Nobody seemed to know his actual age, but he had to be late 20s or early 30s, making him only seven or eight years younger than Ray Buchner.

"Dead. He was dead," Fox muttered. "Dead, and I lifted him."

Martin frowned.

"You were doing deadlifts? Is that what you're trying to say, Cooper?"

"No," Ray Buchner," said. "I don't think so, Riley. I seen this before. I think the kid was having a flashback. Probably to his accident."

Cooper Fox turned his big, wet eyes on Ray Buchner. He shook his head, but it was a small gesture, and he was trembling so much that it got lost.

"No, he was dead. I lifted him, and I carried him. The dead man."

"Jesus Christ," Riley Martin breathed. "I think you're right, Ray. I think he's flashing back to the car accident. Did he... Did he carry someone...away?"

Buchner shrugged off the question.

"Dunno," he said. "Don't know much about it. Just that his family was killed. And, I'm not..."

He trailed off for a second before coming back.

"Look, I'm not a shrink," Buchner said. "But I dunno that we need to be making this worse for him. He took a bad hit upside the head last night. Maybe it's knocked a few memories loose."

Fox made an awkward move to stand up. He slipped on the tiles. They helped him to his feet and led him to a bench.

"I'm gonna sit with him here," Buchner said. "I think you should go get Kat Szetey. Right now."

Like most people caught in a crisis, Riley Martin was only too glad to be told what to do. He assured Cooper Fox that he would be back with help soon.

"You just sit tight, Cooper."

Cooper nodded.

The English teacher hurried away, and an echoing silence took over the change room. Buchner gave the young man another once over to make sure they hadn't missed some injury, but he found that he could not look into Cooper Fox's eyes. It was unsettling. Like there was some-body else trapped in there, but somebody who didn't know they were trapped.

"Looks like that guy really laid one on you last night, kid," he said.

"Dead," Cooper said quietly.

"He woulda been if I got my hands on him, son. But that's why they don't make guys like me sheriff."

They sat for a little while longer until Fox stopped shivering.

"Do you want to get dressed, Cooper?" Buchner asked. "You got your bag here. You bring a change of clothes like normal?"

Cooper nodded but said nothing more.

"Okay then, let's get you dried off properly and dressed before Nurse Szetey gets back."

Cooper Fox was a slow dresser. He had a fresh pair of track pants on but was still naked from the waist up when Riley Martin returned with the school nurse. She was hurrying and looking very worried.

A cursory once-over was enough to reassure her that he'd suffered no significant injuries on her watch. She asked him to look up into the light while she peered closely into his eyes. She seemed to have no trouble doing that. Unlike Ray. And it helped calm her down a bit.

She breathed out. "Oh boy, the way Riley told it, I thought we were going to need an ambulance."

"It did look quite serious," the English teacher said.

"It probably was," she conceded. "But I think it was an episode. Maybe even a little seizure after the head trauma last night. But he looks okay now. His pupils are reacting normally. Honey, can you count up to ten for me?" She asked.

Ray Buchner winced. "I don't know that he can..."

"One, two, three..." Cooper started. He spoke slowly and carefully, like a child reciting their numbers for a teacher in front of the class. "Four, five, six..."

The nurse smiled. Buchner stared at him as though he'd started busting out advanced math equations.

"Okay, I think that's enough," Nurse Szetey said. "Do you have a headache at all, Cooper? Do you feel nauseous, you know, sick in your tummy?"

Cooper Fox shook his head.

"No. I feel better. I just got confused, I think. Sometimes I get confused."

"Did you take your medicine last night, Cooper," Buchner asked. "When you got home. Did you remember to take your medicine?"

Cooper's face creased with the effort of remembering.

"I don't remember last night," he said. "No. That's not right. I remember we had the party because we won the big game. And some bad guys came and..."

He trailed off.

"But I don't remember after that."

"I'm sure that Mary looked after him," Nurse Szetey said. "But I can call her and find out. And we must have a record of his medication on file."

"Maybe not," Riley Martin said. "I mean, he's not actually on staff, is he?"

Ray Buchner shook his head.

"See, there's a thing. A helluva thing. Cooper is supposed to be joining the faculty now. I spoke to Principal McGee about it after the win. And he was on board for it. We'll need to raise some more money, but I don't think that'll be a problem after the pennant."

The nurse furrowed her brows.

"You're right, though, Riley," she said. "I'm so used to Cooper being around and helping out that I forget he's not actually part of the faculty. So no, we wouldn't have his records."

The subject of their conversation sat quietly while they discussed him.

Cooper Fox made no effort to speak on his behalf. He did not move from where he sat on the bench while three people stood over and around him, discussing his fate.

They were discussing whether they needed to call an ambulance or whether the coach should drive him to Doctor Schofield for a check-up when Cooper smiled.

He had seen something. Or somebody.

Ray Buchner turned around. Andy Briscoe was striding across the change room towards them.

Buchner grunted in surprise. Nurse Szetey performed a creditable doubletake. Sheriff Briscoe had his hat in one hand and an expression of deep distaste on his face.

"Morning all," he said. "They said I could find Cooper down here. Everything all right?"

"Think so," Buchner said before the nurse could answer. "Cooper was dizzy, is all. Maybe a flashback or something. It happens."

Briscoe took that in his stride.

"Yeah, sometimes. You good there, Cooper?"

Buchner was glad he didn't start in on a loop about dead guys.

"I think so," he said. "I fell over in the shower."

Briscoe looked to Nurse Szetey.

"I think he's okay, Sheriff. I'll have to examine him properly back in the sick room, but he looks okay for now. Is there a problem?"

Briscoe worked the brim of his hat through his fingers.

"Could be," he said. "Those fellas last night are talking about suing the school for damages."

All three of the staff of Gainesville High reacted with shock, but Ray Buchner's came out in the form of profanity.

"They fucking what?"

Sheriff Briscoe shook his head.

"Cooper put quite a hurtin' on two of those fellas. I spoke to the hospital, and the docs over there say they look like mummies; they're wrapped up in so many bandages. The big one, his leg, was shattered like kindling for the barbecue. The other guy is going to need to be spoon-fed for about five or six months. Until he comes out of plaster."

Buchner snorted.

"Seems like everything worked out for the best to me."

"I would not disagree with you, Ray," Andy Briscoe said. "But these hoodlums lawyered up, and they got some legal weasel from Jacksondale to take them on contingency. He's saying they were assaulted at a high school function by a staff member, and they are looking for a settlement. They're talking about pressing charges against Cooper."

Andy Briscoe nodded at the young man who was still sitting on the bench, looking up at all the grown-ups standing around him.

"That sounds like some kind of a scam," Riley Martin said, unable to keep the disgust out of his voice.

"A shakedown, yeah," Sheriff Briscoe replied. "The threat to get Cooper charged with assault don't mean much. It's just for leverage on the compensation claim. But they are going to want that leverage. I seen this sort of thing before — hoodlums using the law against the folks it was meant to protect."

"Yeah, we'll see about that," Coach Buchner declared. "These assclowns aren't the only ones who can lawyer up."

"What, you think Cooper should go to Dave Harrison? No offence to Dave, but this is a little above his pay grade."

"No, I don't mean Dave," Buchner said. "I know a guy. Got out of the Corps the same time as me. He was a real Marine. But he was a lawyer, too. And a pretty damn good one. Plus, he owes me a favour. I'll give him a call. As soon as this Jacksondale gut maggot gets a call from Reese Needham, he'll back off. Guaranteed."

Sheriff Briscoe looked troubled.

"Everything's gotta be above board, Ray," he warned. "This is Cooper's future we're talking about here. He's done nothing wrong. He just had the bad luck of running into some worse characters."

Ray Buchner clapped one meaty hand down on Cooper Fox's shoulder.

"Cooper did exactly the right thing, throwing those three degenerates a beating. I only wish I got to see it. Didn't know the kid had it in him. And by the time Reese is finished with those assholes, they'll be begging for another beat down to get away from him."

5

Mary got the call at work. Mondays were always quiet at the beauty salon, and Cooper's encounter with the out-of-town criminals had dislodged Gainesville's triumph in the Mid-States conference as the story of the day. Sharon Weiss, owner of *Sharon's Beauté Chalet,* was only too happy to let Mary leave to get Cooper, as long as she hurried back soonest with news of whatever the heck was happening now. It was a five-minute walk from Sharon's to the school, but Mary hurried, arriving short of breath and even a little clammy with sweat. She texted Sissy Traynor on the way, asking if Sis could pick up Matty and Jessica from school and kindergarten. Begging, really.

Sissy—manicure, pedicure, and a wax every month—said yes.

Lauren Dowell—deep cleansing facial and hair removal, twice a month—working at the front desk of the school, took her through to the nurse's station where Cooper was waiting quietly with Katrina Szetey— cut and colour, once a month - and Coach Buchner (no treatments - probably did his hair with the same bar of soap he washed his privates).

"Hi, Mary," Cooper said, standing up as she came into the nurse's station. "Coach says I had a flashback and fell over. I was in the shower."

Mary looked from Coach Buchner to Katrina. The nurse shrugged and nodded.

"Seems like," she said. "He's got a nasty bump on the head from getting hit last night, but I've seen worse after most football games. I think he's gonna be fine, but you should probably go see Doctor Schofield as a precaution."

Buchner, who had been sitting on the edge of Kat Szetey's desk, stood up when the nurse was done.

"Coop is fine. You take a big hit like he did, it can make you wobbly for a couple of days afterwards. Like Katrina says, take him to see Mike. I called ahead, and they're holding open a slot for you this afternoon. And as for this other business, don't you worry about that. I'll take care of it."

She hurried across the room and threw her arms around Cooper, who returned the hug with one of his own.

"I'm okay, I'm okay," he said.

"He's better than okay," Buchner put in. "Go on, Cooper, tell her the good news."

Everything was happening very quickly. Mary was having trouble keeping up.

"I got a job," Cooper said. "A real job, with a payday and a bump and everything."

That brought her up short and chased away all her other thoughts, at least for a moment.

"What do you mean?" Mary said.

Buchner stepped up, ruffled Cooper's hair, and answered for him.

"Means we're putting him on staff. Deputy assistant coach, responsible for strength and conditioning. No way we could've done what we did this season without Cooper's help. And the Board agrees. We've got some paperwork to fill out. Probably should wait until that big ol' goose egg on the side of his head goes down. But, yeah, he's gonna be faculty."

Cooper beamed. "I'm gonna be faculty."

"Oh my God," Mary said. This was not at all what she had been expecting. "This is great, Ray," she said, reaching out to Buchner and squeezing his arm. "Thank you so much for this."

Coach Buchner dismissed her gushing with a backhand wave.

"Pfft. Coop did all the work. I want him on my team. And this other thing with those gangsters, don't you worry about that."

Mary's smile faltered.

"But what about this morning? And what do you mean...this other thing?"

Coach Buchner put an arm around Cooper's shoulder and steered him past the other women towards the door of the nurse's station.

"I think this morning was just last night sneaking up on him, but

Doctor Schofield is gonna check him out anyway. The other thing..." He paused. "Those guys Cooper fixed up last night. They're just mouthing off. Complaining. They're talking about suing the school."

He rolled his eyes. Her mouth dropped open.

But he waved it off again.

"Don't worry about it, kid. I got a buddy from my days in the Corps. He works for some big-ass firm in New York these days. Owes me a favour, and I'm gonna collect it. For Cooper. Nothing for you to worry about. You ask this guy to make a problem go away, and it just disappears."

Her heart was racing, and her head was reeling again.

"But if they're talking about suing the school, couldn't it stop Cooper from getting his job? A real job."

"With a bump," Cooper beamed.

"No, it couldn't," Buchner said. He took her upper arms in both of his giant hands and looked into her eyes. "You got my promise on that, kid. I want Cooper Fox here for as long as I am coaching this team. And I'm not going anywhere for a long damn time."

They were out in the main reception area now. Lauren was on the phone. Nurse Szetey had returned to her station.

"Do I need to talk to your friend in New York?" Mary asked.

Buchner shook his head.

"Nope. Don't reckon so. Already called his office, and they promised he would get back to me. I'll take point on this, Mary. I shoulda been there for Cooper last night. I'm gonna be there for him now. You just get him to Mike Schofield, then home. And make sure he takes his meds. It's easy to lose track of things when you've been knocked off the rails like he was last night."

She thanked him, shook his hand, and looked around for Cooper. He'd wandered off while they'd been talking. Mary saw him over by the main entrance, staring at a noticeboard. It was full of flyers and leaflets, but he was staring at one intently. A photocopied picture of a smiling young black girl.

Sarah Washington. Gabby's daughter.

He was crying. Not bawling or ugly crying. But Mary could see tear tracks on his cheeks.

S<small>HE HURRIED OVER.</small>

"Hey, baby? You want to go to Sarah's fundraiser? Gabby would like that."

"She died," he said.

Mary's heart lurched in her chest.

"Baby, no. Sarah's fine. She's just sick, is all. And they need money for her medicine. Her treatments ain't paid for like yours, so they're raising money. We'll go. We should go. Come on."

She took him by the arm and led him gently towards the door. He did not resist. Mary looked back over her shoulder and waved to Coach Buchner. She was grateful for everything he'd done. And the real job, that was just awesome. Between her paycheck and his money from the accident, they could always make ends meet, but it would be nice to have a little extra. It would've been nicer still if everything hadn't been ruined by those assholes last night.

Maybe they would get a car.

Cooper couldn't drive. He always ran to and from the school unless it was snowing. Doctor Schofield said it wasn't unusual, given his car accident. PTSD, he said. Like soldiers got. Coop wouldn't even go on the Tigers' team bus to away games. So maybe no to the car. Wouldn't be right to spend his money on something he couldn't really use. But still. It'd be nice to have a little more.

Cooper wiped the tears from his eyes as they walked out into the bracing cold of late winter in Virginia. It looked almost automatic, like a man scratching an itch without even thinking about it.

"I got the day off," he said. "We should do something nice."

"We have to go see Doctor Schofield before we do anything," Mary said. "But sure, if you like. After we've done that, it might be nice."

She linked her arm through his. She was dressed in a heavy coat, but Cooper seemed perfectly comfortable in his track pants and hoodie.

"I got the rest of the day off, too," she said. "Sharon said to come back as soon as I could, but Mondays are always quiet at the salon. And the kids ain't home. Maybe we could hang out together until I get back."

"You mean snuggle?"

"Maybe," she smiled, blushing a little. "It's a bit special being able to snuggle in the afternoon."

"Yeah, but I like doing it with you anytime."

Doctor Schofield's practice was on Woodrow Street, which ran off Main just before the town square where everyone had gathered to celebrate their win over Jacksondale. If Cooper had attached any sense of trauma to the place where those guys attacked him, he didn't show it. They walked along the edge of the park in companionable silence. If either of them felt unsettled, it was Mary, recalling what she had seen him do the previous night.

He seemed to have no memory of it, and she certainly had no explanation for how he got the better of three armed criminals. Cooper was strong and fast and very fit. He had what Doctor Schofield called a savant's ability with fitness and stuff. It almost certainly came from whatever he had done in his life before his car accident changed everything. Before it changed him. But he was gentle, too. Not cruel, or aggressive or violent in any way. It was one of the things she loved most about him. And she'd known it the first time they met, too. Wasn't long after Coop fetched up in town, and he was at Doc Schofield's for one of his brain injury check-ups. He had a carer looking after him back then. A frosty-looking businesswoman who said she was from his insurance company.

Mary was there with Matty, who'd sprained his ankle real bad playing Spider-Man on the jungle gym. Her little boy was howling up such a storm that Mary was terrified he'd broken his leg or something. The insurance lady kept scowling at them like she was the one in pain, but Coop came over and asked what was up. He was so kind and so gentle with a screaming kid, he didn't even know that it took Mary a while to realise that...well, he wasn't all there.

That's what people said about him when he first settled in town. Cooper Fox was a few beers short of a six-pack, they said. And worse.

But Mary didn't care, especially not when Coop was able to calm Matty down and even helped carry him through to the examination room. She had been hugely grateful and relieved for the help.

Those few moments were so different from all the years she spent with Brian. And in the years that followed, never once did she regret setting her sights on the kindly young man with the simple soul who'd helped her out that day. It was a tough gig, being a single mom.

They arrived at Doctor Schofield's with a couple of minutes to spare and tried to sit quietly in the waiting area, but the other patients there all wanted to talk to Cooper about the game, and the party, and what had happened at the party. It was a relief to get into the examination room.

Mike Schofield smiled when they came in, but he looked tired. He asked Cooper lots of questions about what he remembered of the night before, which were easy to answer because the answer was...almost nothing.

He nodded as though that was very significant.

"And this morning," he said. "Can you tell me about that, Cooper?"

Cooper shook his head.

"I don't want to," he said.

Doc Schofield nodded again.

"Okay, that's fine. I don't want to upset you, Cooper. You've been through enough already. But if I let you go home with Mary now, would you promise me to take one of these every day for the next week?" He pushed a blister pack of tablets across the desk. "And to take your normal dose of medicine? I don't want to send you up to Jacksondale for scans. I don't think it's necessary. But you need to get some bed rest and keep up your treatment."

Cooper smiled.

"Mary and I are going to bed this afternoon," he said. "We're going to have an afternoon snuggle."

"Oh my God, Cooper!" Mary blurted out. "He doesn't need to know that!"

She blushed a bright, hot red, and Doctor Schofield grinned. He didn't blush at all.

"You know what, Cooper? They say that love is the best medicine of all."

Mary put her face in her hands, mortified. Both Cooper and Doctor Schofield laughed.

"You only need to take these for three days," he said, tapping the blister pack of tablets. "They'll help you sleep. But you do need to keep up your normal meds. Promise me you will do that, and I'll be happy."

"I promise he will," Mary said quickly before Cooper could get another word out.

She signed for the bill – the trust money would cover it, as always – and hurried him out the door, still blushing but bursting into laughter as soon as they were out on the street.

"Oh my God, Cooper Fox, the things you say."

She linked her arm through his again and pulled him along.

"I was just telling the truth," he said. "We are going home to snuggle in the afternoon. Aren't we?"

"Yes," she said. Blushing again. "Yes, we are."

They snuggled three times that afternoon, the last time just before the kids got home with Sissy Traynor. Mary had to dress quickly and hurry out to meet them. They tumbled out of Sissy's pickup, full of mad sugar energy.

"We stopped in at Clem's for sundaes," Sissy explained, not even a little apologetic.

"Thank you," Mary said, not even a little pissed off.

Not after doing it three times in one afternoon.

COOPER LOVED MARY, and Cooper loved snuggling with Mary, and Doctor Mike was right. He was so sleepy after snuggling through the afternoon that he didn't think he would need to take any pills to help him sleep through the night. He would need a shower, though. Mary was good at snuggling, and he was very sweaty and sticky. While she got the kids fed, he took himself off to the shower.

He didn't even think about it. Cooper didn't think about much, really. Not even the stuff he helped Coach Buchner with at school. There were just some things that he knew how to do. And then there was everything else in life that passed through him like a breeze. The thing that'd happened that morning in the shower at the school gymnasium? He'd mostly forgotten about that. The stuff that happened last night, or that they told him had happened last night, the fight with those three guys?

Nope. Not much there, either.

He lived every day as it came, and if the days came with Mary and the kids and the chance to run through the forest and lift his weights, Cooper Fox was happy.

He saw his medicine on the bedside table. Not the sleepy pills, the other ones. The little white ones he took for his brain. They looked like Tic Tacs. Cooper liked Tic Tacs, and it made them easier to take. He almost took one right then by force of habit. He had a white pill at the start of the day and another one at the end. But he was tired and sticky, and he needed a shower, and he promised himself he would remember to take it later because he always remembered that, at least.

He could hear Matty and Jess running around and music playing while Mary cooked them burgers in the kitchen. He could smell the burgers cooking and thought he might even be able to hear the sizzle of the meat in the frypan. He loved that sound, and he loved hamburgers.

He turned on the shower. He was in the shower without really remembering how he got there. Probably walked all the way from the bedroom, he thought. The water was hot, which was good because it was going to be a freezing night. He closed his eyes and put his face under the stream, and ran his fingers through his hair.

He thought about snuggling with Mary.

And he screamed.

Mary was dead. He could see she was dead. Pieces were missing. And there were holes in her. Terrible things were coming out of the holes, and he screamed and screamed and screamed.

A one-eyed man stared at him and Mary. The same man he had seen in the school gym.

'You what, mate?' the man said.

NEXT THING, Mary was alive again.

She was in the shower with him. She was wearing clothes, but she was alive. He was crying, and she was crying, too, as she tried to pull him out of the shower stall. It reminded him of something, but he wasn't sure what.

She pulled him out, wrapped a towel around him, and hugged him. The kids came running in, and they hugged him, too. They all sat like that for a very long time.

WHEN COOPER WAS FINALLY ASLEEP, Mary turned out the light and padded out of their bedroom. She was frightened. She thought about calling Coach Buchner, but it was very late. She did call Doctor Schofield, but all she got was the talking machine at his office. She didn't leave a message.

She sat for a long time by herself on the old couch in the living room. *Frasier* was on the TV, but the sound was turned down. She didn't know what to do. There was something wrong with Cooper; she was sure of it. And she was frightened. Everything that had gone well in her life since she had got away from Brian was good because of Cooper. His accident money trust had organised this house for him and said she could live here too. The money they sent him each week helped pay for everything. She had her job, of course. But the *Beauté Chalet* paid minimum wage, which in Virginia meant $7.25 an hour, before tax. And she couldn't always get the hours. If something happened to Cooper, they would be in big trouble.

But even worse, she would be alone again. And she didn't think she could face that. She had been alone when she got to Gainesville, and there weren't many fellas who were interested in taking on a single mom with two kids. Not unless they could figure out some way to push those kids all the way out of the picture.

Cooper, though, bless his simple soul; he just loved her for who she was. And he loved those kids, too. If she lost him, she would lose everything.

The tears flowed, hot and unstoppable, as she sat in the darkness, watching *Frasier* with the sound down. She was ugly-crying, so loud she had to stick her face in a cushion after a while in case the kids heard her. Or Cooper woke up. She'd had to hold him for an hour before he could get to sleep. He was shaking like she'd hauled him in from the cold outside.

"You got to get your shit together, girl," she said into the cushion. "Come on now. You can do this. He looked after you. You got to look after him. That's what people do."

Gradually, she got her feelings back under control. The tears stopped. She wiped her eyes.

Mary did not bother having a shower. She promised herself she would have one early in the morning. Instead, she crawled into bed next to her guy and lay there in the dark, listening to him breathe. Occasionally, he mumbled, and once, he groaned. Mary Doyle wrapped her arms around him and held him tight.

Eventually, she fell asleep.

She forgot to make him take his medicine.

6

Cooper slept in. He did not dream, and he did not wake all night. Not even to go to the bathroom. He might have slept forever, except little Matty came in and climbed up on the bed and asked whether Cooper was going to cook any breakfast for them.

"Oh gosh, no!" Mary cried out. "Look at the time."

There wasn't much point in Cooper doing that because he couldn't tell the time since his car accident, but Mary was so insistent that he looked anyway.

7.13 AM.

Huh, he thought. *It is thirteen minutes after seven o'clock in the morning.*

Knowing what that meant came as such a surprise that he almost cried out—*I can tell the time!* —but Mary was already out of bed and hurrying around, pulling open drawers and closets and trying to find clothes for both. Matty protested that he wanted his breakfast, and it had to be pancakes. Mary shouted at him that they didn't have time because she forgot the alarm, and Cooper decided it might be better to tell her his 7.13 AM news later. Sometimes, when things got busy in the mornings, Mary got grouchy.

It was now 7.14 AM on the little clock radio.

And he knew what that meant, too, which was cool.

Cooper Fox hopped out of bed with a big smile and hurried Matty out of the room.

"Better get dressed, little guy," he said. "Clock's-a-tickin'."

Even though it wasn't. Because clock radios don't tick.

He didn't have time to make breakfast, but he poured emergency cereal for everyone and shook out some dried cranberries on top. While the others ate, he got dressed.

He almost had an argument with Mary about that.

"You're not going anywhere, Cooper Fox, but right to the doctor. Not after last night."

"But I feel fine, Mary."

"And you felt fine getting into the shower last night. You felt fine right up until you didn't, and I had to pull you out."

He couldn't really remember what'd happened, just that he'd been very upset, and he promised he would see Doctor Mike this morning and do whatever Doctor Mike said. Mary tried to argue with him, but they were so late, and the kids were acting up, and in the end, it was easier for her to let him run in.

The bus line followed his jogging route anyway, he pointed out, and if anything happened, they would only be a few minutes behind.

Mary was surprised by that, like she hadn't been expecting it or hadn't realised or something. She gave a little shake of the head and went, "Oh!" Matty started up with his demands for a pancake breakfast again, and, anyway, long story short, Cooper Fox jogged into school on his own. The same as he always did.

The only difference this morning?

He stopped on Main Street outside the Volunteer Fire Department. He liked the big red fire truck, but this morning, he stopped to look at the clock on the little tower above the big door where the fire engine came and went. It wasn't like the clock radio at home. It was a circle, with a big hand and a little hand, just like the clock in the school gym.

Cooper stood and stared at it.

The time was 7.42.

In the morning.

You couldn't tell whether it was morning or night by just looking at that sort of clock, but you didn't have to because you were outside, and you could tell anyway.

Cooper Fox stared at the big hand for three whole minutes.

7.42.

7.43.

7.44.

"Wow," he said quietly. His breath steamed in front of him. "I know the time."

With a smile as bright as the dawn itself, he went on with his run to the school. He very much wanted to tell Coach Buchner about this.

———

COACH BUCHNER WAS NOT happy about it. But he had two visitors, and they were all frowny-faced, and Cooper figured that was probably why the Coach wasn't as excited as he should have been about Cooper's newfound time-telling powers.

"Cooper, this my friend Reese Needham," Coach said. He lifted a hand toward a man in a dark suit. "He's the lawyer I told you about yesterday. Do you remember that?"

Reese Needham looked so much like a lawyer on one of the TV shows that Mary liked about lawyers and stuff that Cooper did not doubt he was the real thing. He had a nice TV suit and a briefcase and everything.

"Hello, Cooper," Reese Needham smiled.

His teeth were very white.

"And this is Doctor Ludgrove," Coach said. "He came with my friend Reese."

Doctor Ludgrove didn't look so much like a TV doctor to Cooper. He was a bit short and fat to be on TV unless he was very funny or a bad guy.

"But I saw Doctor Mike yesterday," Cooper said. "And he gave me some bedtime pills. For sleeping with the bump on my head."

He recalled his promise to Mary.

"Oh, and I said I'd talk to Doctor Mike this morning anyway."

He didn't mention that he'd been upset in the shower last night. He reached up and gingerly touched the spot on the side of his skull where the lump had come up. It was sore, but it was also smaller than it had been.

"And Doctor Schofield asked me to examine you this morning, Cooper," Doctor Ludgrove said. "A good thing, too, it sounds like."

Doctor Ludgrove looked around the office. He nodded when he saw the clock over the door.

"Can you tell me the time on Coach Buchner's clock?" Ludgrove asked.

Cooper looked up.

He nodded.

"The big hand is at eleven, and the small hand is almost at eight," Cooper said. "So that means it's just five minutes before eight o'clock."

The three men exchanged a look.

"This isn't helpful," the TV lawyer said.

"But I can tell the time now," Cooper said, pointing at the clock on the wall above the door. "Look, when the big hand is at twelve, it will be eight o'clock. Time for the sportsman's breakfast, Coach."

Coach Buchner did not seem pleased by that either, which was strange. Coach loved the sportsman's breakfast, which was what he called the egg and bacon burrito from the school canteen.

"That's great, kid," Coach said before turning to his TV lawyer friend. "The fuck are we gonna do? You seen the video. You seen him fuck those guys three ways from Sunday."

Wow, Cooper thought. Coach wasn't supposed to swear.

Reese Needham grunted.

"We deal with the first thing first. These two douchebags out of Saginaw and..." He checked a notebook. "And the retard. Lubbers."

Cooper shifted uncomfortably. He felt a hot flush of embarrassment on his neck.

When he'd first arrived in Gainesville, folks had called him that word. Some of them, anyway.

The 'R' word, Mary called it.

It was a bad word, and it made him feel bad.

He didn't know why Coach Buchner's TV lawyer friend would even say such a thing. But Reese Needham was saying a lot of things, and Cooper struggled to keep up with them.

"Local law enforcement has them contained for now. Normally, the best they could hope for is some court-appointed cuck from Legal Aid. But they lucked into a connection with this pissant firm in Jacksondale, Sharkey and Bass. Bottom-feeders. Trawling the ER for business."

"Too lazy to actually chase an ambulance," Doctor Ludgrove said, and Reese Needham snorted.

"Yeah, pretty much so." He looked Cooper Fox up and down. "Doc, I'll be guided by you after you've checked our boy out, but I'm inclined to go hard on this. Normally, we'd bargain them down to a cheap payout, but given this development..."

Needham nodded at Cooper.

"...I think we should move aggressively. Shut this shit down, hard and fast."

"Agreed," Coach Buchner said.

Cooper had no idea what they were talking about.

His happiness at unexpectedly finding out that he knew how to tell time was gone. He didn't like Reese Needham, and he wasn't sure he was going to like Doctor Ludgrove any better. He smelled bad. Like the locker room after a game, but worse.

"Sit down, Cooper," Doctor Ludgrove said. He pointed at a chair in front of Coach Buchner's desk. It was like the plastic chairs the kids sat on in their classrooms. Cooper did as he was told, although he didn't like the way that Reese Needham and Doctor Ludgrove hovered above him. At least Coach was sitting down with him.

"I'm just going to do some simple tests, Cooper," the doctor said. "You would have done them with Doctor Schofield yesterday, but I need to do them again. Okay? And when I've done those, I have some other tests I need you to do for me. Is that going to be okay?"

Cooper shrugged.

He was used to doing tests with doctors. There'd been a lot of doctors since the car accident. Doctor Ludgrove's tests started the same as Doctor Schofield's, but they soon got different. He held up drawings on pieces of white cardboard and asked Cooper to tell him what he saw. That was easy. There were drawings of cats and dogs and stars and trees and stuff. But then Doctor Ludgrove started showing him one card after another until he was showing Cooper four, five cards or even six cards in a row before asking Cooper to recall them in order.

"Tree, tree, cat, star, dog and tree again," Cooper answered.

"Excellent, Cooper, very good," the doctor said.

"I can remember things," Cooper grinned at Coach.

"That's great, kid," Coach said. But he really didn't look like he thought so. The TV lawyer, Mr Needham, looked unhappy and maybe even angry. He muttered some swear words under his breath when Cooper got a whole bunch of the cards right. Ten in a row.

"Jesus Christ, I don't think I could do that many," Coach said.

The tests went on for nearly half an hour. Cooper knew it was half an hour because he could tell the time now. The more tests the doctor did, the angrier Coach and his friend became. Doctor Ludgrove didn't seem to care as much. He just wanted to keep giving tests.

"Cooper, I'm going to show you a list of words," Doctor Ludgrove said.

"Now, I know that you can't read, but I want you to just look at each word and then draw a picture in the space next to it for me. Can you do that? You don't need to tell me what you see. Just draw it."

"I can draw pictures for sure," Cooper Fox said. "I like to draw. Sometimes Jess and me draw for hours. She's better than me, though."

Doctor Ludgrove put a piece of paper on the table.

There were three letters on the paper.

Another surprise. Cooper knew how many letters were written down just by looking at the word. But even more surprising? He knew what they meant!

"C-A-T spells cat," he said, grinning widely.

Cooper pulled his chair closer to Coach Buchner's desk to draw a cat.

"I think we've seen enough," Mr Needham said. "There's definitely been a change."

"You've seen enough," the doctor said. "But I need to finish these assessments and compare them to the baseline."

The TV lawyer closed his eyes and breathed out sharply.

"Fine, whatever. But don't take all day. I need to move quickly on this."

Doctor Ludgrove gave Cooper five words to read, one after the other.

Cup, bowl, spoon, table, chair.

He understood them all, and he drew them all.

"Holy shit," Coach said.

"Remarkable," the doctor added. He started to put away all his bits and pieces but stopped suddenly.

"Cooper," Doctor Ludgrove said, looking directly at him. "Have you been taking your medication? Not the sleeping pills Doctor Schofield gave you. The little white ones. For your brain injury?"

Cooper nodded, his eyes wide.

"I always take my medicine," he said. "Doctor Mike and Mary say it's the only way I can get better."

Doctor Ludgrove seemed happy with that.

"Okay, make sure that you keep doing that. It's imperative."

He closed the big black doctor's bag on Coach's desk with a snap.

"I'll do the baseline compare," the doctor said to the other two men. "But we're going to need to take him in for a full work-up. Something's gone wrong. There may be a lesion, a clot, or some other complicating factor from the kinetic trauma. But he is definitely diverging from baseline, and we need to find out why."

"We need to get him back there," Reese Needham said. "If these assholes depose him, and we go to court with this loser trending off base, we're fucked."

"Then deal with it," Coach Buchner said, stabbing a finger at his friend, the TV lawyer. "That's your fucking job."

Cooper Fox watched the men arguing with each other. There was a bad feeling in the room. He did not think Coach and the television lawyer were very good friends. This was not how friends talked to each other.

But that wasn't the whole reason he felt bad.

Cooper had lied to Doctor Ludgrove.

He hadn't taken his medicine for two whole days. Not since the night the bad men came to Gainesville.

He wasn't sure why he had lied because lying was something Cooper Fox never did. But it seemed much more complicated to tell the truth now that he had.

7

Doctor Ludgrove and the angry lawyer, Mr Needham, stayed in Coach Buchner's office for twenty-three minutes after they finished talking to Cooper, and they spoke to Cooper for a long time. He knew that because he checked the time on the clock when he left and the time on the big clock down in the gym when he saw them going. Knowing what time it was turned out to be so much fun that Cooper thought he might spend the rest of the day simply looking for clocks or asking to see people's watches, which were like little clocks some people wore on their arm.

Mr Martin, the head of English, called his an 'Apple Watch', which was funny because it didn't look anything like an apple. But Cooper just figured that was one of those things he didn't understand. There were lots of them. He saw Mr Martin on the cardio floor, riding one of the bikes that didn't go anywhere, and he hurried over to tell him the exciting news.

"Mr Martin, I can tell the time now," Cooper said. "If you show me your watch, I can totally tell you what time it is."

Mr Martin, who had been so nice to him when he fell over in the shower, had been peddling very fast. He slowed down and smiled at Cooper.

His smile looked a bit funny, and he tilted his head to one side as though he didn't really understand what Cooper was saying.

"I'm sorry, Cooper," Mr Martin said. "I didn't catch that."

He took a pair of little white earbuds out of his ears. Cooper knew what they were. Lots of the kids had them. There was music inside them, and sometimes people read stories and stuff.

"I can tell the time, Mr Martin," Cooper said. "Show me your watch, and I'll tell you the time."

Mr Martin blinked and shook his head in confusion, but he lifted his hand and showed Cooper his watch.

Cooper blinked just like Mister Martin.

It was nothing like the clock in coach Buchner's office. Mr Martin's watch was weird. It was full of all sorts of colourful numbers, some of them changing quickly. And there was a small cartoon of a little green man on a bicycle, peddling fast. It was all too much.

Cooper shook his head.

"But I *could*," he protested. "I *could* tell the time."

Mr Martin smiled.

"Try this," he said. He did something to the watch, and it changed. It suddenly looked like a regular clock.

Cooper Fox beamed at him after leaning forward to peer at the watch.

"It is twenty-two minutes after twelve o'clock," he said.

Mr Martin, who had slowed right down, now stopped pedalling altogether.

"It is indeed, Cooper," he said. "I'm on my lunch break. But this... This is..."

He climbed off the bike that went nowhere and patted the sweat from his face with a small towel.

"This is very exciting, Cooper," Mr Martin said. "When did you remember how to tell time?"

"This morning," Cooper said. "Mary forgot to set the alarm. And we got up late. And she was upset, but I looked at our clock radio, which has the red numbers and the letters, and I knew it was 7:13 AM. That means thirteen minutes after seven o'clock in the morning."

Cooper waited for Mr Martin to say something. The English teacher kept towelling himself off.

"This is really something, isn't it, Cooper?" Mr Martin said after a while. "Have you told anybody else?"

Cooper frowned.

"I told Coach," he said. "And his friend Mr Needham, who is a lawyer, although I don't know that he's much of a friend."

"I don't think lawyers have friends," Mr Martin grinned, and Cooper knew that was a joke.

"That's a good joke," he said. "Oh, and Coach's other friend, Doctor Ludgrove, was there too. Although he is not very healthy for a doctor. He needs to pay attention to his macros and do some cardio, although he should definitely start slow."

Mr Martin snorted as though he found that much funnier than his joke about lawyers not having friends.

"Is the lawyer helping with those fellows who attacked you?" Mr Martin asked.

"His name is Reese Needham," Cooper nodded. "And he is going to shut this shit down, hard and fast... Oh!"

Cooper realised he had just said a swear word.

"Sorry," he said.

"Don't worry about it, Cooper," Mr Martin said. "I'm sure that's how Coach Buchner's lawyer talks all the time. You should probably tell your doctor about this, though. I imagine he'll be delighted to hear you remembered how to tell time."

"Oh, I can do a lot more than that," Cooper Fox said. "I can read whole words as well."

"Really?" Mr Martin said.

Cooper nodded.

"Doctor Ludgrove showed me some words, and I drew pictures of what they meant. It was easy."

Mr Martin looked at him. Long enough that Cooper started to feel uncomfortable.

"Just... Just wait there a second, would you, Cooper?" he said. "I want to get something out of my bag. Just hang on."

The English teacher trotted across to the lockers on the far side of the cardio room. His running shoes squeaked on the floor. He fetched a gym bag from the locker and hurried back.

Kneeling for a moment, Mr Martin opened the bag and searched inside for something.

He pulled out a book and showed Cooper the cover.

A train with a smiling face.

"We use this book to teach some of the older students to read," Mr Martin explained. "The kids who didn't learn so well how to read in elementary school. Would you like to try reading it for me, Cooper?"

Cooper Fox found his heart was racing but with excitement, not fear.

He already knew what the book was.

He'd read the words on the cover when Mr Martin showed him.

"That's the little engine that could," Cooper said.

Mr Martin nodded.

"Yes, it is, Cooper. Very good. Have you ever seen this book before? Do Mary's kids have it, perhaps?"

"No," Cooper said. "I read the words when you showed me. And I saw the picture too, of course. That's the little engine right there."

He pointed at the cartoon picture of a puffing train struggling up a big hill.

"My word, Cooper Fox. You are reading like a champion. Come here. Sit down with me."

They sat on the bleachers overlooking the central court of the gymnasium.

Mr Martin handed him the book, and Cooper opened it.

His heart was beating even faster in his chest, and his mouth felt dry.

He opened the book to the first page, a colourful drawing of a red steam train pulling four carriages full of animals over a hill.

"Chug, chug, chug," Cooper read. "Puff, puff, puff. Ding-dong, ding-dong. The little train rumbled over the tracks."

He looked up to Mr Martin nervously.

"Did I get it right?" Cooper asked

Mr Martin was smiling and...and he was also crying a little.

"Yes, Cooper," he said. "You got it exactly right. Go on. Read some more."

Cooper's hand was shaking, but he turned the page.

The same little red engine was pulling all the animals in their carriages over a bridge. He put his finger under the first word, but he found he could read all three lines without needing to trace the words like Matty and Jessica sometimes did.

After a couple of pages, Mr Martin laid a hand on his arm.

"Okay, that's very good, Cooper. Let's try this one now."

He reached into his gym bag and pulled out a newspaper. Cooper almost gasped.

"That's the *Gainesville Sentinel*," he said. "I can't read that. Even Mary can't read that."

"Just try," Mr Martin said. "Indulge me."

"Okay," Cooper said, but he wasn't at all sure he could pull this one off. It was like Mister Martin had asked him to suddenly double or even triple his one-rep max on the bench.

Cooper unfolded the newspaper and laid it out on his lap. Some of the words were bigger than the others, and he pointed at them.

"That's the headline, Cooper," Mr Martin said. "Can you read that?"

He furrowed his brow. He drew out the first letter of the first word, which wasn't a real word like the ones in *The Little Engine That Could*.

"N-n-n-eurogen to add new production line to Gainesville plant," Cooper said. He looked up at Mr Martin.

The head of English was staring at him, his mouth open.

"Cooper," he said. "We need to get you to Doc Schofield right away. Can Mary pick you up?"

Cooper shook his head. "I don't think so," he said. "She already took a day off yesterday."

Mr Martin blew out his cheeks.

"I'd take you myself, but I have to get back to work. Look, this is important, Cooper. Or I suspect it is. If you're recovering cognitive capacity, you might start getting your memories back, too. I'm not a doctor, but either way, it sounds like a significant neurological event to me. You should see your doctor as soon as you can."

Cooper shrugged.

"I could just walk there," he said.

Mr Martin thought it over.

"I guess you could," he shrugged. "Season's over for this year. You don't have to be on campus. Would you like me to call the practice? See if they can fit you in?"

Cooper shook his head.

"No. That's okay. Doctor Mike always finds time for me. And I like walking."

He promised Mr Martin he would walk straight there.

He promised Coach Buchner, too.

The coach called after him just as he was leaving the gym.

"Hey Cooper, wait up? Where are you going?"

Cooper thought he might be in trouble for leaving during school. He struggled to think of an excuse, and then he realised he didn't need a reason. He could tell the truth.

"I'm going to see Doctor Mike about reading words and telling the time," Cooper said.

Coach Buchner looked worried.

"Probably a good idea, son," he said. "I'll let him know you're coming. I'd drive you myself, but I gotta meet with Principal McGee and some of the school board guys about your job."

"I'll walk," Cooper said. "It's a nice day and I like to walk."

Coach stared at him for a long time.

"All right," he said at last. "But you go straight there, okay?"

"Okay," Cooper agreed.

It was his second lie that day.

8

A big dumb thug like Warren Lubbers wouldn't usually end up in a hospital bed after losing a fight. But as a prisoner of the Gainesville Sheriff's Office, payment for his medical bills came off of the public tick. That being the sort of story that could make for a week of outraged editorials in the *Gainesville Sentinel*, the hospital at Jacksondale had strict instructions from Sheriff Briscoe's office to provide the absolute minimum of care.

"Just keep him alive, is all," Sheriff Andy told the admitting nurse.

Turned out they couldn't even do that.

Briscoe did not have the manpower to place a guard over the accused, and it was not necessary anyway. Had Lubbers not been handcuffed to the bed rails on a secure ward, his ability to make any getaway would have been severely constrained by his broken leg. He had suffered a terrible, crippling injury. It might have been the sort of thing to get a fellow down, except that Thomas T. Sharkey Esq., senior partner of the esteemed legal firm of Sharkey and Bass, Attorneys at Law, assured Warren Lubbers, his newly acquired client, that his untimely maiming would be worth "a kingly ransom".

"It was a vicious attack, son," Sharkey assured him less than one short minute after appearing at his bedside. "A hell of a thing to happen to a harmless traveller just making his way through the world. And the taxpayers of Gainesville are on the hook for every cent of damages."

It was for sure a hell of a thing, the way that retard had thrown them all such a beat down. And he was a genuine goddamn retard, too, according to the lawyer Sharkey.

"This fella Fox was under treatment for brain damage," Sharkey said, leaning over Lubbers' iron bed rails as if to whisper a dark secret.

Sharkey was a fat man who looked like he might have been much fatter at some point, the way his glistening, mottled skin hung in folds from his face. He had appeared on the ward within a few minutes of the Gainesville Sherriff's deputy cuffing Lubbers to the bed frame. They checked he was securely fastened there and left.

"Seems obvious to me, as it will to any jury, that letting such a potentially violent mental patient run wild at a school event was a clear and present danger to the general public," Sharkey said. "The tragic events of the evening were entirely foreseeable and thus compensable," he went on. "And my firm intends to secure every dollar of recompense, should you allow us, Mister Lubbers. For an industry-standard forty-five per cent commission, of course."

Warren wasn't sure what forty-five per cent of a king's ransom might come to, but he could give less than one wet shit about that. For damn sure, it would leave a healthy chunk of change left over. He signed the papers that Thomas T. Sharkey gave him and lay back in his pillows to enjoy the novel sensation of having an actual lawyer.

A day later, while Cooper Fox and Riley Martin were reading *The Little Engine That Could*, Warren Lubbers still lay abed idly daydreaming about how he might spend all his money. A speedboat? A condo? Or maybe just a heap of hot bitches. For once in his shitty life, it seemed his luck had finally turned.

He was, of course, entirely wrong about that.

A nurse slipped into the four-patient room where Lubbers lay chained to his hospital bed. He tried to suck in his gut when he realised she was a hottie. It was hard to tell at first, the way she'd tied her hair back until it screamed. She wore a mask, too, and that nurse's uniform wasn't nothing like the sexy nurses' uniforms you saw in porno flicks sometimes.

But as she readied a syringe, Warren Lubbers copped a look at the way her breasts strained against the cheap cotton, and he imagined what those long legs of hers might look like if he was able to grab a handful of that hemline and yank it up over her ass.

He grinned when she caught him staring.

Bitches liked a man who knew what he wanted.

She smiled back and winked, and he was surprised he blushed. He also felt himself stirring beneath the sheets.

"Sweet dreams," she said, sliding the tip of the needle into a valve on the drip running into his arm. She pressed the plunger, and Warren Lubbers felt a soft wave of sweet warmth flowing into his veins.

Hot damn, he thought. *This is the shit.*

And indeed it was. A lethal dose of synthetic morphine that the nurse, who wasn't really a nurse, had acquired on the dark web from a supplier in Shenzhen, China.

DEPUTY FERRUCCI WAS MINDING the fort when the two federal agents arrived. US Marshals, they said, as they flashed their badges and dropped warrants for Joe Don Porter and Duray McClintock, federal warrants which overrode any charges arising from the minor local altercation two nights earlier.

Deputy US Marshal Smith and Deputy US Marshal Black were professional and courteous but insistent that Ferrucci render the prisoners into their custody without delay.

"Porter put a bullet into a Bureau agent in Florida," Smith said. "And McClintock is a militia captain for a bunch of whackjobs in Ohio who got jammed up in a plot to kidnap and murder the state attorney. You got a nice town here. You don't want these guys stinking it up."

Ferrucci tried to call Sheriff Briscoe, but Andy was over in the Hollows doing a welfare check on Monica Sanewski. Monica's ex had been threatening her and their kid, and the office had a report of raised voices and crashing noises from her address thirty minutes back. Radio and cell coverage was terrible out there.

Jamaal Brown, who had less time in the job than Dan but all that experience overseas, was out near the interstate, looking to write some speeding tickets.

Instead, Dan consulted with Sharon, his wife, who did all the typing and administrative work for the office. She chewed her lower lip with no more idea of what to do than he did.

"I don't know, hon," she said. "These warrants are pretty heavy, and they got this court order from Judge Osterman, and you know what he's like. You don't want to get crosswise with him."

"I know, honey," Dan said while the marshals watched on impassively. "But I don't wanna get crosswise with Andy neither. These guys attacked Cooper Fox and Roscoe Powell, and now they're suing the high school, and I think that Andy would flip if he got back here and they were gone, even if it was into federal custody."

Marshall Smith stepped into the exchange.

"Excuse me, did you say the prisoners are suing a school?"

Dan Ferrucci nodded.

"Yeah," he said. "The high school. There was a big celebration after we won the Mid-States and, look, it's complicated but..."

Smith held up one hand. Deputy Dan stopped talking.

"That'll be Mister Porter," he said. "He's done this before. I'm surprised it's the school he's suing. His usual side hustle is jamming up law enforcement with bullshit litigation."

His partner, Deputy US Marshal Black, rolled his eyes. "He'll get around to it. That asshole always does. Excuse my language, ma'am."

Sharon Ferrucci blushed but said it was no bother.

"Deputy Ferrucci," Smith said. "These guys are vermin. My advice – let us get rid of them, and quick as you can, you should fumigate their cell. Next thing you know, you'll have McClintock's militia buddies in town. They'll camp out on your front lawn."

"Exercising their constitutional rights to take a dump on your driveway," Black said. "You don't want that."

"You really don't," Smith agreed. "Turn them over to us. We're gonna drop these guys in a hole so deep and so dark nobody is ever gonna find them again. Including whatever douchebag lawyer they've got whispering sweet nothings at them."

They spoke the truth after a fashion, and Deputy Ferrucci took them at their word. He had some real misgivings about transferring the prisoners into their custody without being able to ask Sherriff Andy whether he should or not, but the marshals pressed their case hard. They had a domestic terrorist they had to pick up before the end of the day, they said.

"Antifa?" Sharon asked a little breathlessly.

"You know it," Smith said.

Dan Ferrucci signed the papers, and the marshals took their prisoners away.

The bodies of Joe Don Porter and Duray McClintock were never found. The old coal mine into which the two Deputy US Marshals, who were not Deputy US Marshals, dropped them was very deep and very dark.

As promised.

9

Cooper didn't want to go to the doctor. He wanted to walk around, reading things and telling the time. Gainesville was a small and tidy town, but it offered many opportunities to do both of these things. When you looked for them, Cooper realised words were everywhere. On the bus stop outside the school, in the windows of pretty much every shop, on street signs and billboards and even on the sides of cars and trucks. It wasn't quite so easy to find clocks to check that he still knew how to tell time, but there was the big clock on the tower at the volunteer fire department and another smaller clock over the door of the post office on Main Street.

The day remained chilly, but he enjoyed the feeling of the afternoon sun on his face as he wandered up and down Main and sometimes turned left or right into the smaller crosstown streets that ran out to the edge of the forest on one side of town, and into open fields on the other. He did walk past Doctor Mike's office. Old fashioned gold letters spelled Doctor Michael Schofield, M.D., on his window, and that meant Mike was a real doctor. There were lots of words to read in the posters that covered the rest of the window. Some of the words told people to get their flu jab early. Some were just days of the week and numbers, which Cooper, to his surprise, understood to be the times when the office would be open for sick people to come and visit.

He didn't understand everything. There were pictures of medicines that were full of words he could say out loud but which meant nothing to him. And even though he'd promised everyone he would see Doctor Mike, he really, *really* did not want to spend his afternoon answering more questions, especially not questions about whether he'd been taking his medicines. Cooper Fox put his head down and hurried on past.

Downtown was suddenly like Disneyland to him. A place of wonder and surprise. Cooper was pleased to stroll up and down Main Street, sometimes stopping to talk to people but mainly seeking out more words he could read. Most folks who stopped to chat wanted to know how he was feeling. Some offered their thoughts and prayers, and some of the men insisted that if only they had been there with him, they would have given those out-of-town criminals something to go on with. It was a funny thing to say, Cooper thought, because almost everybody in town *had* been there, so they could've easily given the criminals plenty to go on with. Still, he was so entranced with his newfound ability to understand written down words that he just smiled and thanked everyone for their concern and moved on as soon as he could, looking for more words.

He went into Clem's Bar and Grill and read the menu on the blackboard. He visited Mister Burbot's General Store and bought a small pack of his favourite candy to have a chance to read some of the words on the little magazine rack by the Slurpee machine. Mister Burbot, as always, counted out the change for him, but Cooper was thrilled to discover that he didn't need the help. He could do sums now, too! He didn't tell Mister Burbot, whose son had played for the Tigers before going to college and who had always been very kind, but the hairs on Cooper's arms stood up as he watched the dimes and quarters come across the counter, and he understood what was happening.

Cooper Fox was so deeply invested in exploring a world made new that even with his ability to know what time of day it was, the day still got away from him. The sun had fallen low in the sky and disappeared behind leaden grey clouds when he heard Mary calling out his name.

"Cooper! What are you doing? Where have you been? People are looking for you!"

Cooper was standing in front of Susie Wilkins' bookshop across from the town square, enjoying the brightly coloured covers on all the "New Releases". He knew the books were "New Releases" because Susie had written a sign and put it in the window. Cooper wasn't entirely sure how long he'd been standing there, grinning at the New Releases and wondering whether he dared go into the shop to see whether he could read an actual book – so many words, all smooshed in together – and he lost track of time. His smile faltered a little when he heard Mary's voice, or rather the tone of her voice, which was very angry and more than a little upset.

He did not like it when Mary wasn't happy.

Cooper turned towards her voice, and his heart gave an extra skip when he saw that Coach Buchner was with her. Oh no, his girl and his boss hurrying through the town square together. He was in big trouble. All of a sudden, he wished he could turn back the hands on the clock over the fire engines and go to Doctor Mike's office the way he had promised. Mary's expression was furious, and Coach looked as angry as he'd been that time Dante Wallace fumbled the ball on his way to a certain touchdown against the Springfield Lions.

"Cooper," Mary said again. "Where have you been?"

She had already asked him that, but he hadn't answered, so it was probably fair enough that she asked the same question again. Just angrier.

"I've been here all the time, Mary," he said. "I've been reading things. Did Coach tell you? I can read words now and tell time."

He looked around, searching for the nearest clock. The volunteer fire department was just down the street, and he could see the clock tower clearly.

"It is twenty-two minutes after four o'clock," he said, pointing at the tower. "In the afternoon," he added, just in case they weren't sure.

Coach Buchner, who had been there that morning when Doctor Ludgrove had given Cooper the tests, looked annoyed but also worried. Probably because he'd been looking for Cooper all day, too, as Mary explained. But Mary herself was staring at him as though he'd suddenly sprouted wings and flown up to the little tower over the volunteer fire department to get a closer look at the big hand and the little hand on the clock there.

"What do you mean?" she said. "Coach told me you had some sort of a stroke or something."

"This. This is what I was talking about," Coach Buchner insisted. "My guy Reese brought his specialist along this morning, and they reckon it's some sort of neurological event. Cooper really needed to get to the doctor today. But he didn't go."

It sounded like an accusation.

"We are going right now," Mary said, taking him by the elbow and pulling Cooper towards the corner of Woodrow Street. "I can't believe you would do this. Coach says you promised Mr Martin that you would go to see Doctor Schofield, and you didn't. You played hooky!"

Cooper could tell she was so upset that she was about to start crying, which was even worse than when she got angry. And he didn't want that. He allowed her to pull him a little way down the street. When Mary realised that he wasn't resisting, she loosened the grip on his elbow, threaded her arm through his, and dropped her head onto his shoulder.

"Please, Cooper, don't do that again," she begged. "It's good, I know, that you got your words back and stuff, but listen to the coach. You had a new, a nuro..." She struggled to remember the word.

"A neurological event," Coach Buchner supplied. He was striding along beside them. "It's like a thunderstorm in your brain, Cooper. It lights everything up, but it can be dangerous."

Cooper felt terrible. What had he done? All his friends were upset with him and worried about him. People on the street were starting to stare as they hurried toward the doctor's, and the little dog that Mister MacGilvray sometimes fed was barking up a storm across the road on the front porch of the boarding house. It was quite a scene. He did not like to be in scenes and was almost glad of the chance to get off the street. He'd probably get in trouble with Doctor Mike, too, but at least people wouldn't be staring.

The doctor himself opened the front door.

"Cooper, please, come in," he said. "I only just heard about what happened."

Cooper was expecting another telling-off and was very grateful when it didn't happen. Instead, they all went through to the examination rooms, and he hopped up on the same old table where he usually sat when he had to do all his tests. At least that hadn't changed, like everything else.

This time, however, Doctor Mike asked him to read something. It was a magazine called *TIME*. Mike passed him the old magazine – Cooper could tell it was old because the date on the cover was from four years ago.

Whoa. He knew about days and months and years now, too!

But he didn't really want to tell them about that. Nobody seemed to be happy about whatever was happening to him. Cooper opened the magazine and started to read. He said the words slowly and carefully at first but speeded up as they seemed to come right off the page and flow through him.

"In a...world of...conspiracy...theories...and Internet rumours, it's a wonder no one has ever called black holes a hoax. They're mysterious, they're powerful, but—oops! —they're entirely invisible. Trust us, though, they're there," he finished with a flourish.

"Okay, okay, that's enough," the doctor said, snatching the magazine back as though it had caught fire. He didn't throw it away, though. He stopped, looked at the words Cooper had just read, and then back up at him.

"Cooper," he said. "Do you know what a black hole is?"

Cooper Fox shook his head.

"I guess it's a hole in the ground or something," he said uncertainly. "And it's black."

He shrugged.

"But holes aren't really black, are they?" Cooper went on, mostly to himself. "They're just empty. That's what makes them holes."

Doctor Mike breathed out as though relieved.

"That's right, Cooper," he said. "They're just holes. They're empty."

Cooper saw Doctor Mike make a face at Coach Buchner. He didn't know what it meant, but he knew what Mary's expression meant. Her mouth had made a big 'O', and her head was moving a little from side to side like she didn't really believe what she was seeing.

"Oh my god," she breathed out quietly. "I just... He's never done that."

She turned around and grabbed Coach Buchner by the arm. Her fingers squeezed so tight that they turned white.

"Did you see that, Coach?" Mary gasped. "He just read that magazine like he was on the TV news or something."

When she turned back to Cooper, he could see that her eyes were filled with tears. But they were happy tears this time. He knew what Mary looked like when she was crying because she was happy. The first time they had ever snuggled, she had cried afterwards, and she'd looked a lot like this.

He smiled at Mary and reached his hand for her to take. She grabbed it and cried even harder. Coach Buchner put his arm around her and led her across the room to sit in one of the chairs against the wall where Doctor Mike kept his skeleton. He had to pull her a little to get her to let go of Cooper's hand.

That skeleton over there had always frightened Cooper, but he found himself looking at it as Mary sat next to it. It was sort of like he'd never seen it before. Or at least not like this. He kind of understood how all the bones went together and how all the muscles and nerves and other bits and pieces of the body fit inside them and around them. Sort of. He wasn't quite there yet, but he felt as though that skeleton had secrets, and he knew those secrets, but he had...not so much forgotten them as he'd forgotten how to remember them. Maybe when he had the car accident.

Doctor Mike put the magazine aside.

He looked very serious.

"Cooper," he said. "I'm going to ask you a question, and I need you to answer honestly. Okay?"

Cooper Fox nodded.

"Telling lies is wrong," he said.

"Yes, yes it is," Doctor Mike said. "Cooper, have you been taking your medicine?"

Cooper nodded.

"Yep," he said. "I take my white pill in the morning before I make breakfast for everyone so I don't forget. And I take another white pill at night before we have dinner."

"So, every morning and every night?" Doctor Mike said

"It says so on the little box," Cooper said.

"You can read the box, too?"

Cooper paused before answering. He hadn't lied to Doctor Mike before. He just hadn't told the truth that Doctor Mike was looking for. The doc wanted to know whether Cooper had taken his tablets today and yesterday. And Cooper had lied. Because he hadn't taken those tablets. He'd forgotten to take them after the fight at the football party, and then this morning, he had decided he didn't *want* to take them. He wasn't sure why. He had been taking his pills for as long as he could remember. His pills were important. But this morning, it had felt more important not to take them.

"I don't remember reading the box, no," he said at last. "But I've seen Mary read the words on the medicine that she gets for the kids and for herself and even for me. That's how you know what to do with the medicine," Cooper said. "It says so on the box."

He nodded as though acknowledging the immense rightness of this answer.

"I think he needs a top-up," Coach Buchner said.

Doctor Mike frowned.

"Ray, Cooper's medication isn't like a bottle of Adderall. I don't have it lying around. He's on a trial. You know that. It's why he has to come in for so many appointments. I need to monitor his progress."

He had started talking to Coach Buchner, but now he was talking to Mary, who was nodding as though hearing all of this for the first time.

"There has obviously been a profound moment of discontinuity," the doctor said, and Mary made a face like she didn't really understand what that meant. He tried again. "Cooper has suffered a serious kinetic trauma to the brain during his assault. I am very worried that, in layman's terms, something has come loose."

Mary bit her lip. Her hands, in her lap, gripped each other tightly as though she were praying as hard as she had ever done.

"But he can read again," she said. "And tell the time. And who knows what else? How can that be bad?"

Doctor Mike smiled kindly.

"None of that stuff is bad, Mary," he explained. "But the fact that it's happened so quickly after a damaging, physically traumatic event is very concerning. We had hoped that the medication Cooper was trialling would lead to a gradual reconnection of all the synapses that were damaged and destroyed in his car accident. What happened today is not gradual. It shouldn't have happened at all. And in medicine, things that shouldn't happen are generally really bad news."

Mary looked over at Cooper, and the fear on her face made his heart sink.

"Is he gonna be all right?" she asked. Her voice was tiny, but Cooper found that he could read her lips.

Doctor Mike waited a little too long to answer, but he did answer her in the end.

"I think he'll be okay," he said. "I'll give him a proper examination now, and if necessary, we might have to send him up to Richmond for scans..."

"Scans!"

"Routine scans, Mary. And only if he doesn't return to baseline soon."

"What do you mean 'baseline'?" she asked.

Doctor Mike opened his hands.

"His treatment was progressing exactly as it should before all of this,"

Doctor Mike said. "But Cooper is way off track now. You ever see that old movie with Robin Williams? *Awakenings*."

"I think so when I was a kid. It was on TV or something?"

"Maybe rent it tonight, if you can," Doctor Mike suggested. He smiled at Cooper. "Cooper could even read the online catalogues to find it. But do watch it. Robin Williams is a doctor whose patients all seem to make miraculous recoveries. But it's not a miracle, and it doesn't end well."

"That doesn't sound like a nice movie," Cooper put in. "I like fun movies. Like *Cars* and *Toy Story*."

"Solid choices there, kid," Coach Buchner said.

"My point is that slow and steady progress is best," Doctor Mike said. "Especially when dealing with challenges like Cooper faces. I'll examine him now, decide whether scans are needed, and then Coach, if you could drop them home and make sure he takes that medication, I'd be a lot happier."

"We all would, Doc," Coach said. "I'll run back to school and get my car."

Doctor Mike was a little over twenty minutes putting Cooper through a bunch of tests, although he didn't do any of the picture card stuff that Doctor Ludgrove had done in Coach's office. It was mostly prodding and poking and getting him to do little exercises. Mary stayed with them, and Coach returned just as Cooper was finishing the last test. Doctor Mike was dabbing a cotton swab doused with alcohol on Cooper's back and neck to see if he could feel the cold there.

"His physical responses are all within parameters. He's a very fit young man. Strong, too."

"He gave those gangsters a hell of an ass-kicking," Coach said. "That wasn't just strength, doc. That was...something else."

"Yeah, I know," Doctor Mike frowned. "I'm leaning toward scans. Maybe even a PET scan or a single photon imaging test."

Mary started up out of her chair by the skeleton.

"What the hell are they? What's up with him?"

Doctor Mike tried to calm her down.

"I'm not worried, Mary. I'm just concerned, if you get the difference."

He turned back to Cooper.

"Apart from the bump on your head, there's no physical manifestation of any neurological change. But there is change. We can all see it. We just need to understand it."

"Okay," Cooper said. "Can we go home now? I want to watch *Toy Story*."

"I'm on it," Coach Bucker said, twirling his car keys around one finger. "Let's roll."

COACH DROVE a big pickup and had them back home in just a few minutes. The kids were next door at Sissy Traynor's place, and once they were back, Mary asked Coach Buchner if he would like to stay for dinner, but all he wanted to do was make sure Cooper took his meds.

Cooper Fox took Coach through to the bedroom he shared with Mary. His pills were on the little table by his side of the bed. He popped one out of the blister pack and made a big show of putting it into his mouth and swallowing. He opened wide and moved his tongue for Coach to see that it was gone.

"Good work, son," Buchner said, slapping him on the back.

As soon as Coach turned and walked away, Cooper flicked the real pill under the bed. He'd hidden it in his palm. He followed Coach Buchner back out to the kitchen, his heart beating so fast it made him a little dizzy. If they found out he'd switched his meds for candy, he'd be in heaps of trouble.

It had been hard to swallow the Tic Tac he'd bought at Mister Burbot's general store that afternoon. It was furry and sticky from having sat in his pocket for a few hours, waiting for a moment like this. And it was a little bit bigger than his real brain medicine. They did look very similar, though, and he was glad that it was Coach he'd tricked. Not Mary. He hadn't been looking forward to doing that.

But he liked being able to read his words and tell time and do sums. It felt like all his thoughts were speeding up. Just like he did when he hit the downslope of the hill just outside the forest on his run into school every morning. But faster. Much faster.

And he wasn't going to give that up without a fight.

10

He had dreams, but they were only dreams. The nightmares did not return. Cooper woke, as he usually did, well before dawn. For the first time in days since the fight at the big party, his head felt clear. As soon as he realised he was awake, he blinked the sleep from his eyes and looked for the glowing red numerals and letters of the little clock radio on the bedside table.

5:40 AM

Cooper smiled like a small boy on Christmas morning. He still knew what '5:40 AM' meant.

Mary was asleep next to him. She was a heavy sleeper and needed the alarm clock most mornings. Her breathing was deep and regular, and with every couple of breaths, she snored lightly. Cooper lay on one side, gazing at her, at the curve of her cheek outlined by the glowing display of the time, at the rise of her hips under the blanket, and the soft mess of her shoulder-length hair on the pillow.

His heart felt like it was swelling inside his chest.

He loved her. He loved Mary Doyle so much that there wasn't enough space in his heart to contain all the feelings he had. He felt terrible about lying to her, and Doctor Mike, and to Coach. But he also felt that he had to. He was doing the right thing for himself and for Mary and her kids. He didn't just *feel* this, either. He *knew* it because he had *thought* about it.

Cooper Fox was not used to thinking deeply. Not in the way that other people did, people like Mr Martin, the English teacher. People like that had always been deeply mysterious to him. Cooper imagined they were always thinking about things, but he'd never been sure what that meant. Mostly, his thoughts were simple, and they ran directly into his feelings. But lying in bed next to Mary, he found his thoughts working the way that he imagined the thoughts of Riley Martin or Gabby Washington or even someone as smart as Doctor Mike would work.

Propped up on his elbow, happy to take a few moments to appreciate how lucky he'd been to find Mary, Cooper was able to follow a simple line of thought from start to finish.

He had been taking his pills for as long as he remembered. Basically, since the car accident, because that was as far back as he *could* remember. Doctor Mike told him, in fact, everyone told him, that besides losing his family, he'd hurt his brain in that accident, and taking his pills was the only way to get better. But he'd had another accident, sort of, when he ran into those guys at the party, and they'd hurt his head again. He didn't know whether getting hit in the side of the head with a can of soda was the sort of thing that helped you to read your words – but he doubted it. It wasn't like Mr Martin walked around his English class hitting the slow kids in the head with a can of Pepsi.

The other thing that had happened, and it was an accident at first until it wasn't, was that he'd missed taking his brain pills. A couple of days' worth. And now his brain seemed to work a lot better. That didn't make any sense at all, but he *knew* it to be true. He could feel it as a real thing while he stretched out in bed, fondly watching over his girl. And no way was he going back to being simple, happy, Cooper Fox, who didn't know how to tell the time or read even the simplest sentence.

He thought about this for a long time.

When next he checked the clock radio, it was after six o'clock. That was a *lot* of thinking. Cooper carefully climbed out of bed, slid his feet into a pair of slippers, and popped a pill out of the blister pack. He padded out of the room, quietly closing the door behind him. He took the medication to the little trash can in the kitchen, and he buried it under two handfuls of soggy rubbish. Nobody would find it there.

Then he did as he always did in the morning, preparing everybody's breakfast before they got up. This time, however, he read the label on the milk carton and all the ingredients on the box of granola to prove to himself that he could.

"Good to go," Cooper said, which was a strange thing to say when he thought about it, but it felt right. He really was good to go. He was good to serve the kids their breakfast, to get himself ready to run into school, and to start doing all the things he'd never been able to do before.

He might even go to the library today and tell Mrs Washington that he wanted a library card. He could borrow books from the library and read them to Matty and Jess. Only Mary had been able to do that before, and she often came home from work so tired that she had no energy to read stories. But Cooper, who loved to sit with the kids when Mary did read them a story, felt as though he'd be happy if he spent the rest of his life reading books, and milk cartons, and boxes of granola. So that was something he was going to do. The books. Not the milk cartons and granola boxes. He was going to get all the books from Mrs Washington at the library, and he was going to read them to Matty and Jess while Mary sat on the couch and watched the television.

There were all sorts of things he could do now. But before he was able to think of them, Cooper was all but flattened by a sudden and terrible sadness. He wasn't sure why at first, not until he thought about it. Then, he remembered that Mrs. Washington's daughter was very sick, and it made him sad. It made him so sad that Mary found him standing at the kitchen table over the breakfast he had prepared, staring out of the window and crying.

"Baby, what's up?"

She surprised him, and he jumped a little.

"What happened?" Mary asked.

"Mrs Washington," Cooper said. "Her little girl is sick, and she can't get the medicine she needs."

Mary hurried over to him, her arms thrown wide. She gathered Cooper into a hug and rocked him gently from side to side.

"I know, I know," she said. "It's very sad. But people are trying to help. We can help out, too. Remember? We're going to her fundraiser."

Cooper wiped the tears from his eyes with the back of his hand.

He felt better. Just the idea of having something to do made him feel so much better.

"Yes," he said. "We are."

"For sure we are," Mary promised. "And have you taken your pill this morning, like Doctor Schofield said?"

Cooper nodded solemnly.

"I did," he said.

"I know," Mary smiled. "I saw that it was gone from the pack by your side of the bed.

His mouth suddenly felt dry. She had checked. She had spied on him. He almost felt angry, which was something he never felt. But before the hot feeling inside his head could get any bigger or hotter, a thought occurred to him.

She had spied, but he had lied, and he had done that first.

Cooper Fox blushed with embarrassment. He had so many feelings, and they just kept coming at him. This was another thing that'd happened in the days since he had stopped taking the pills. It wasn't just that he was able to think about things now. He was unable to control his feelings about them.

Mary hugged him again.

"You're such a good man, Coop," she said. "I don't know what I'd do without you."

She pushed back a little, looked him in the eyes, which were still wet with tears for Gabby Washington's poor, sick little girl, and she leaned in and kissed him on the cheek.

"So, take your medicine," she said. "We don't want to lose you. We just want you to get better."

"I will," Cooper said, but his voice caught on the lump in his throat. "I'm going to run into school now," he said. "I want to get there early and talk to Coach about next year's team. Coach said he wants to start their conditioning even earlier."

Mary hugged him again.

"I'm so proud of you," she said before letting him go. "We had a rough week, but I reckon we're past that now."

Cooper left her to get the kids up while he got changed into his running gear and packed the little backpack he wore to carry his towel and some clothes to change into after a shower. He hurried out of the door, muttering a quick goodbye. He felt terrible about lying to her, and getting out of the door and away from their home was the only thing he could do to feel better. That, and running.

He felt better, much better, as his running shoes chewed up the miles between home and the high school. Cooper didn't stop to read anything or check on the time. He concentrated on matching his stride to his breathing. He found that when he did that when he thought about one particular thing, it helped get rid of any bad thoughts he had inside his head. In fact, he felt so much better by the time he had run the two miles into school that he continued for another mile before turning around and doubling back.

When he finally got to the gymnasium, he was slicked with sweat but feeling as strong and as clearheaded as he had ever been. The morning air was so cold that it almost hurt to breathe, but it was that delicious sort of hurt that you got from exercise. The kind he really liked.

Cooper finished his run and did a lap of the football field at a walking pace to cool down. He went straight to the weights room in the gymnasium and worked through a full-body routine.

He was heading for the showers when he passed the heavy punching bags hanging from thick chains at the edge of the space they kept clear for doing functional movement. Cooper stopped and stared at the bags. They were not part of his usual routine, but he knew that they could be an excellent cardio workout, especially having exhausted himself with the run and an hour's powerlifting. With no clear intent, no plan or even any real purpose, he found himself standing in front of the last of the three bags. He reached out and laid the tips of his fingers against a length of battered duct tape that had been wrapped around the bag just below eye level. It felt... Just right.

Cooper slipped off his backpack and tossed it a few feet away. He took up a stance in front of the bag, his feet just slightly more than shoulder-width apart, the left foot just slightly ahead of the right. His hands floated up in front of him as though some invisible puppeteer had drawn them there. He took a deep breath and...

"Hey! Cooper!"

Five punches exploded out of him before he could stop them. They were too fast to count. They hit the bag with a rippling roar that sounded like a string of massive firecrackers going off together. But he knew he had hit that bag five times. And he knew how he had hit it. The exact sequence of strikes.

Left jab. Right hook. Left elbow. Double-handed palm strike. Inner knife hand strike.

"Whoa, dude, is that how you took out those douchebags at the kegger?"

Cooper turned around, his mouth hanging open a little. He had surprised himself just as much as he had his visitor. Roscoe Powell. The Tigers' wide receiver. Rosco looked like he'd played a hard game without armour. He was a mass of bruises and bandaging, and one eye was swollen shut. But he was smiling.

"That was awesome, man," Roscoe said. "I didn't know you could do that. Or I guess maybe I did after the other night. I just got out of the hospital late yesterday. My dad told me you saved me from those assholes, which is kinda embarrassing, 'cos I was trying to save you."

Cooper didn't know what to say, so he said nothing.

That didn't seem to bother Roscoe, who came up like a happy, grinning Labrador puppy and punched Cooper on the shoulder.

"Anyway, I knew I'd find you here, man," Roscoe said. "Been wanting to catch up with you after that whole mess. "

Roscoe put out his hand to shake. Cooper took it.

"I really wanted to say thank you, Mr Fox. Sheriff Briscoe told me one of those guys had a gun, and you took it off him like it was nothing. I've seen it on Facebook. Watched it about fifty times, man. And I still don't know how you did it. But I guess you've been holding out on us," he grinned, nodding at the punching bag. "How come you never taught us how to do that?"

"You don't need to do that to play football," Cooper said.

He wasn't sure why he said that. The answer just came to him, and it was the truth which helped.

"Guess not," Roscoe admitted. "It'd be hella cool, though. Anyway, I had to say thanks."

Cooper shrugged.

"Thank you, Ross," he said. "For trying to save me."

Roscoe Powell threw his head back and bellowed with laughter. Then he said, "Ouch", and his head came forward again, but he was still chuckling.

"Ah, man, that hurts. Don't rub it in. But you got me, you got me good, Mr Fox. Thank you. And my mom says if you and Mary want to come by the bakery, you can have your pick. I'd get the chocolate sour cream if I were you," Roscoe said. "That's her best one."

"Thank you," Cooper said again. "I like your mom's cakes. Mary does, too."

Roscoe said goodbye and reminded Cooper to make sure he got his free cake. Cooper picked up his towel and his backpack. The moment with the punching bag had passed. He had felt something within him, but maybe it had escaped in that flurry of blows. He had no more idea where they had come from than Roscoe did, but it was not a part of himself he wanted to go looking into.

He showered and changed and was heading for the cafeteria for a sportsman's breakfast when he heard Coach Buchner calling to him. Cooper was on the lawn between the admin officers and the senior class-rooms. When he turned towards Buchner's voice, he was surprised to see Doctor Mike standing next to the coach. They waved him over.

"I was going to breakfast," Cooper told them.

"Yeah, I saw you down on the strength training floor a little earlier," Coach Buchner said. "Looks like a solid workout, kid."

Cooper wondered if Coach had seen him with the punching bag and Roscoe Powell, and just wondering about it made him feel anxious. But Coach said nothing about that.

"Could you get your breakfast burrito to go, Cooper?" Doctor Mike asked.

"Sure," Cooper said. "Why?"

"You gotta go for your tests, kid," Coach Buchner said.

Cooper frowned, confused.

"But Doctor Mike did my tests yesterday. You were there, Coach. You saw them."

"Not those tests, Cooper," Doctor Mike explained. "I really need you to go for some scans. I'm sorry. I've been thinking about it overnight. I spoke with Doctor Ludgrove, who you saw yesterday. Do you remember seeing him, Cooper?"

He nodded. It was only yesterday, after all.

"Yeah, well, Doctor Ludgrove is a specialist in neurological trauma. All that means, Cooper, is that he is much better at this stuff than I am, and he wants you to get those scans today. I've spoken to Coach Buchner, and he's cool with you taking the day off and driving up to Richmond."

Buchner folded his arms and nodded as if the question was settled.

"But I don't like cars, and I only go to your tests, Doc," Cooper said.

The doctor tried to reassure him with a smile. "It's okay, Cooper. Your insurance has arranged everything. In fact, you've got a ride coming in about ten minutes. That's why I asked if you could get your breakfast to go."

"In a car?"

Cooper was aware of a strange numbness at the tips of his fingers and could feel an unpleasant prickly sensation spreading under his skin everywhere else.

"There's no need to be frightened, Cooper," Doctor Mike said. "It's a very big car. An SUV. More like a tank. And the drivers are professionals. You'll be safe."

"I...I don't know," Cooper started.

"He might need a couple of downers, Doc," Coach Buchner suggested. "He never comes on the bus when we play away. He freaked out the first couple of times we tried."

"I'd really prefer to keep his system clean," Doctor Mike said. "For the scans."

He turned back to Cooper.

"Cooper, do you remember the exercises we used to do when you would sometimes have trouble breathing."

"Uhuh," Cooper said. He was having a little trouble breathing right now.

"Could you do those with me now? Breathe in for seven seconds, hold, breathe out for eight."

They did the exercise together, and for once, Cooper didn't need Doctor Mike to do the counting.

He did let him, though. He was worried that if Coach or the Doc caught him counting to seven or eight, they might start asking about his meds again, and he would get in trouble.

After a minute or so of breathing in and out, he found that he did feel much better.

"So, are you going to be okay with going in the really big, safe car?" Doctor Mike asked. He produced a small bottle of pills from his pocket. "Because I have some Valium if you need it. But it'd be much better if you didn't. You might have to stay overnight if you took the Valium. So they could do the scans tomorrow."

"I think I'll be okay," Cooper said, and he believed it too. The breathing really helped.

"That's good, Cooper. Because the insurance says you have to do this, and the trustees agree."

He had never met anyone from the trust fund which paid his medical insurance, but he knew they were a huge and vital part of his life. They had paid for the little house in which he lived with Mary and the kids. They put money into his savings account every week. They paid Doctor Mike to look after him. Cooper had never really understood why they did any of this, but he supposed that's why they were called trustees. You just had to trust them.

"If they say so, I guess," Cooper said.

"They do say so," Doctor Mike said. "They insist on it, Cooper. They say you must get the scans done to meet the conditions of your insurance. What that means is if you don't get the scans, I can't be your doctor anymore. Maybe nobody could be your doctor anymore."

Cooper felt a small moment of panic at that. It was enough of a worry that he had to do the breathing trick all over again. Doctor Mike, like the trustees and Coach Buchner, was as much a part of his life as running into school every day and helping with the team and playing with Matty and Jess and being with Mary. He couldn't bear to think of losing any of those things.

"All right," Cooper said. "I will get my sportsman's breakfast to go, and I will ride in the big car to get the scans."

Coach called ahead to the cafeteria on his cell phone. They had Cooper's burrito all made up and wrapped in shiny foil when he arrived. They had even put some extra chicken in the bacon and eggs. For the protein, Coach said.

Cooper had eaten most of it by the time he walked back to the little car park in front of the school's administrative building. As promised, his ride was waiting. It was a big black car. Really big. The driver, a man in a suit standing by the front door, waved Cooper over to him. Doctor Mike was talking to another person, a woman who was also wearing a suit. They didn't look like doctors, but in their dark suits and white shirts, Cooper supposed they did look like limousine drivers you saw on TV.

Doctor Mike gave the woman a big envelope. She nodded, shook his hand, and told the driver to get in behind the wheel. She looked like a boss, Cooper thought.

The woman was wearing dark sunglasses so that he couldn't see her eyes. She opened the back door and gestured for him to get in.

"Howdy, Coop," she said, and it was almost as though he could hear a smile in her voice, even though there was no trace of one on her face. She sounded like she worked on a ranch, like a cowboy or something.

"Hello," Cooper said.

"These guys will get you to Doctor Ludgrove and back," Doctor Mike said, pushing him gently toward the door. "You'll be gone most of the day, but I'll tell Mary what's happening so she doesn't worry."

"Can I come back to the gym?" Cooper asked.

Doctor Mike nodded.

"Sure, if there's time."

Cooper climbed into the back of the big black SUV and buckled up his seatbelt. The woman closed the door behind him and got in next to the driver up front. She strapped herself in and closed her door, and all the locks on all four doors clicked down into place.

"Are you the trustees?" Cooper asked.

"As if," the woman said in her lilting drawl. "We're just the hired help, y'all."

Again, he heard the smile in her voice.

The driver turned on the navigation system, and a lady's voice told him to make his way to the exit and turn right.

Cooper didn't think he would be getting back to the gym and Coach Buchner today.

He was right about that. Sort of.

He never set foot on the school campus again.

11

They drove him north out of town, across the old, covered bridge over Horsefall Creek, past the big pharma plant where lots of folks from town worked, and out onto the state route heading for Richmond. Doctor Ludgrove's offices were outside of Richmond, they told him, about an hour and a half's drive.

At first, Cooper was very nervous. Coach was right. He had never ridden in the school bus, let alone a car. Or at least he hadn't since the accident. For the whole of his life that he could remember, he had avoided getting into any vehicle. Now that he was sitting in the back seat of this one, and it was very comfortable, and they were even playing music that he liked, Cooper wondered why he had been such a Nervous Nelly. This car was very nice, and the driver was good. Cooper wasn't sure why he would think such a thing, but he did. There was just something about the way the man held the wheel and worked all the controls with no fuss or bother that made him feel better about being in the back.

On the other hand, the lady in the front passenger seat did not make him feel good at all. She kept looking at him in the rear-view mirror. She was still wearing her sunglasses, but Cooper could tell. She would stare at him from behind the dark lenses, almost as though she knew him but couldn't quite remember his name.

But she had said, "Howdy, Coop," so that couldn't be right.

He closed his eyes so that he didn't have to see her looking at him. He practised the breathing exercise he had learned with Doctor Mike. It had made him feel better about getting into the car, so maybe it would help with feeling anxious about being in the car with the staring lady.

Breathe in slowly for seven seconds.

Hold for three.

Breathe out for eight.

Just counting the seconds was fun, and breathing was relaxing. It worked to calm his nerves,

It worked so well that Cooper fell asleep. The long run, the heavy-weights, the excitement and confusion of the last couple of days, they all piled up and rolled over him. The car sped along the state highway, and Cooper watched the forests rush past in a green blur, breathing in and breathing out, and the next thing he knew, the lady with the sunglasses was poking him awake. Like, actually poking him with a rolled-up magazine.

That was strange, he thought, as he woke up all groggy and disoriented.

"Giddy up, Sleeping Beauty," she said. "Get your soul back and your ass out of the bunk."

Cooper blinked and rubbed the crust from his eyes. He had been deeply asleep. The woman was standing back. She was still holding the rolled-up magazine. Her friend, the driver, was standing a few feet away from her, holding his keys as though he wanted to jab somebody with them.

These people were strange, Cooper thought.

But they were from the trustees or the insurance or something, so he had to do what they said. He climbed out of the SUV and looked around. He was in an underground car park. He was surrounded by grey concrete and the flat, sort of off-white light you got from fluorescent tubes. There were other cars parked there. They weren't the sort you saw in Gainesville. They looked very shiny and expensive.

Cooper stretched the kinks out of his back and neck. He rolled his shoulders. The drivers backed away a step.

The driver asked, "Gotta problem there, chief?"

Cooper just looked at him.

"I fell asleep," he said.

The woman smiled. For real, this time. Her lips curled up, and her teeth showed through.

"Yes, yes you did, little man," she said. "Let's go see the doctor, shall we?"

She pointed the way with her rolled-up magazine, indicating to Cooper that he should walk over to an elevator on the far side of the car park.

He started in that direction, and the man and woman fell in behind him after closing the car doors and locking them with a beep and click.

Each stood at opposite corners of the elevator behind Cooper as they rode up the three floors to Doctor Ludgrove's offices. Cooper knew that's where they were going because there was a small plaque that said so next to the number 3 button.

The plaque read: DR FRANCIS LUDGROVE. M.D. M.S. A.P.A. CONSULTING PHYSICIAN (NEUROPSYCHOLOGY).

There were other plaques, too, with the names of other doctors and even some professors. Cooper read them all. He liked reading.

There was a Doctor Scuderi and a Doctor Margolis and a Professor Schneider and...

The elevator stopped with a chime, and the doors whispered open. Doctor Ludgrove's surgery was nothing like Doctor Mike's place. It didn't even look like a doctor's office to Cooper. There were no posters advertising flu shots or pills for people who got sad. No children with runny noses or old people on little scooters. The windows ran from the floor to the ceiling and looked out over a forest and a lake. The forest leaves were all golden and red, and the autumn sun sparkled off the blue waters of the lake. It was very pretty out there, Cooper thought, but almost as nice inside. Doctor Ludgrove had lots of paintings on the wall. They weren't paintings of cows or trees or anything you would recognise. They were more blobs of colour, but they looked nice to Cooper. Staring at them made him feel good. Instead of rows of cheap plastic seats in Doctor Mike's office, there were only two black leather armchairs and one coffee table. And they all looked very expensive. Mary would've had a fit if she'd had to bring the kids here because, for sure, Matty would have tried to use one of those chairs as a trampoline. They were so big, and they looked...bouncy.

Cooper hesitated at the threshold, but he jumped forward when the woman patted him on his butt.

"The last mile is always the hardest," she said, which was a strange thing to say because as big as Doctor Ludgrove's rooms were, they were nowhere near as big as a whole mile.

But Cooper didn't want her touching his butt again, so he hurried forward.

A very pretty young woman sitting behind a desk stood up and smiled.

There were some words on the front of the desk, but Cooper didn't understand them.

TRIPLE HELIX, they said, in bright metal letters.

"Mr Fox," the young woman said. "Doctor Ludgrove and the technicians are waiting for you if you'll come through this way."

"We're supposed to keep an eye on him," the driver said.

The very pretty desk lady did not look pleased to hear that.

"Only medical staff in the diagnostic suites," she said.

"We got our orders," the driver said.

His friend, the lady in the sunglasses, stepped toward Cooper. He thought she was about to grab his private parts again, and he stepped away, blushing. She grinned.

"I don't think he's gonna be any trouble, Ted," she said. "The poor bastard. And I gotta drop Luntz and Merrill to the airport. We burned a couple of good legends, putting them on the sheriff. They're hauling ass to LA for six months. The lucky fucks."

Ted, the driver, frowned at that.

"What, so I'm stuck here wiping his ass?"

He pointed at Cooper.

What was it with these people and other people's bottoms? Cooper thought.

"If you don't like the money, y'all can always go back to pounding sand for government pay."

"Whatever, Kristin," Ted grumbled.

"Just get it done and get him back to Schofield," the woman said.

Her name is Kristin, Cooper thought.

"I'll take a ride from the pool downstairs," she said.

She lifted her sunglasses and stared directly into Cooper Fox's eyes. She was pretty too, like the desk lady, but scary looking. Cooper felt a shiver run down his back. It was like she could see things inside him that he didn't even know were there. And she thought it was funny.

"Damn shame," she said in her cowboy drawl. "Still..." She looked him up and down and stared rudely and openly at his groin. Cooper blushed even redder and turned away. "I guess they left all the best bits," she said.

The sunglasses came down, and she turned around and disappeared back into the elevator. Cooper caught the eye of the pretty girl from behind the desk, who looked almost as uncomfortable as he felt.

"I'm sorry," she said quietly. "Please, come with me, Mr Fox. The doctor will see you now."

Cooper followed her, and Ted, the driver, followed him.

"I said nobody but..." the girl started to say.

"Yeah, I know what you said," Ted replied, cutting her off. "And there's not a crapper anywhere big enough to hold all the shits I do not give."

Cooper decided he did not like Ted the driver.

He also decided, very quickly, that he did not like the "diagnostic suites": a white room full of strange machines and bright lights and hard lines. It was cold and smelled of chemicals. Cooper almost tripped over his own feet as he stumbled to a halt. He felt a heavy hand fall between his shoulder blades. It pushed him forward. Had to be Ted. The push was hard, and the pretty girl from behind the desk was walking in front of him.

He recognised Doctor Ludgrove's voice.

"Cooper, come here, come through my boy," Ludgrove said.

He was standing next to a big machine that made Cooper nervous just to look at it. It reminded him of a giant doughnut. There was a little bed on rubber wheels that looked as though it would roll right into the doughnut hole and a pillow where you would lay your head if you decided to take that ride.

It was not a ride he was interested in taking.

Doctor Ludgrove was dressed like a doctor today. He had a white coat, and he wore a stethoscope around his neck. There were two other men in the room, and they were dressed in blue smocks like nurses. They didn't look much like nurses, though. To Cooper, they looked a lot like Ted, the driver. They were big men and very strong. He could tell from the way the muscles bunched under all the tattoos on their arms.

Doctor Ludgrove was flicking through a file, reading each sheaf of paper carefully and making notes as he went.

"I've been reviewing your reports from Doctor Schofield," he said. "I'm just a bit worried, Cooper, that there might be some kind of lesion or blockage or even a growth somewhere in the deeper, older structures of your brain, and I need to have a look inside to reassure myself that this isn't the case."

Cooper stared at the gigantic doughnut machine. He was pretty sure that's what Ludgrove was going to use to look inside his brain. For one mad second, he imagined the machine unscrewing the top of his head, like taking the cap off a medicine bottle. The doctor must have seen the expression on his face.

"Oh, don't worry, Cooper," Ludgrove said. "It doesn't hurt. Nothing ever actually touches you or your head. It's like a flashlight that we shine into a dark place, that's all. I'm sure a big, strong fellow like you will have no trouble at all."

"You'll be okay, sweetie," the pretty girl said. She even squeezed his arm before saying she had to get back to her desk, leaving him with Doctor Ludgrove, Ted the driver and the two big-muscled nurses.

"Just a few questions first, Cooper," the doctor said. "Have you eaten this morning?"

"Yes, sir, I have," he answered honestly. "Doctor Mike... I mean, Doctor Schofield said I could if I got my burrito to go."

For some reason, Ludgrove found that amusing. He chuckled.

"And he's not wrong. It's not a colonoscopy, after all. But if you find yourself feeling sick inside the machine, call out to us, give us a wave, or whatever you need to do to let us know. We'll pull you out straight away. You're my only patient today, Cooper. You're very important to us."

Cooper Fox wanted to know who Doctor Ludgrove meant by 'us'. He didn't think that Ted the driver, or the two scary-looking nurses cared about him at all. Maybe the pretty girl from the front desk?

"Second, and this is very important, Cooper," Ludgrove went on, "have you been taking your medication? You have to answer truthfully."

Cooper was glad they didn't have him in the giant doughnut brain flashlight already. He was pretty sure it would be able to tell when his heart sped up and his mouth went dry. But he kept his face blank, and he nodded and lied just like he had a couple of hours earlier. Cooper found that he cared a lot more about that, about lying to Mary, and he felt a lot worse about it than he did about not telling Doctor Ludgrove the truth.

"I missed taking one pill after the fight with the men," he said. "But you can ask Coach Buchner. He came home with us last night to make sure I took my meds. He watched me while I put one in my mouth and swallowed it. And Mary checked this morning to make sure that I didn't forget. You ask her. You probably don't even need to put me in the big doughnut. Because I am full of medicine."

Ted the driver sniggered. One of the tattooed nurses grinned in a nasty way. Cooper had seen that kind of smile before. People always wore it when they whispered things about him, thinking that he couldn't hear or not even caring because they thought he didn't understand.

Doctor Ludgrove, however, nodded and made a note in his file.

"I will do that, Cooper," he said. "Not because I don't trust you, but because I do, and it will be nice to tell them that you have been doing the right thing, won't it?"

Cooper nodded carefully. He had a feeling that Doctor Ludgrove was being almost as sneaky as Cooper himself. After all, Cooper wasn't telling him a complete lie. Coach Buchner *had* followed him home and watched him take a tablet. It's just that the Coach didn't realise it was a Tic Tac. And Mary *had* checked on his packet of pills this morning. But she didn't know he'd already hidden the pill in the trash.

Doctor Ludgrove kept scribbling away in his file.

"Finally, Cooper," he said, "are you wearing any jewellery? Any watches or earrings or rings on your fingers. Any kind of metal at all?"

"I don't think so," Cooper answered. He looked himself over as if he might suddenly find a forgotten, magical ring on his finger or something.

Doctor Ludgrove chewed his lip and nodded at something in his file.

"You do have a pin in your right ankle and a titanium rod in your left shin. But we can work around that," he said reassuringly. "I will need you to change into a paper gown. You can do that over there."

Ludgrove pointed at a tall cloth screen with the pen he had been using.

"Okay," Cooper said. He was used to getting in and out of hospital gowns. He'd been in hospitals a lot after the car accident, and even now, a couple of years later, Doctor Mike often ran tests on him in the small hospital at Jacksondale that required him to change into one of those funny gowns you tied up at the back.

He was suddenly glad that Kristin had left to drive her friends Luntz and Merrill to the airport. He wouldn't want her getting a peek at his butt. She was handsy.

He disappeared behind the screen and stripped off all his clothes, making a neat pile of them on a small, wheeled table back there. He rolled up his socks and put them inside his shoes, even though he knew he wasn't supposed to do that. That's how things got stinky. But he didn't imagine he would be here long enough for that to happen.

He was nervous when he re-emerged in his light blue hospital gown.

He worried that he hadn't done the ties up correctly at the back. But he didn't want to ask anybody for help.

"How are you feeling, Cooper?" Ludgrove asked.

"I am worried about the big doughnut," Cooper said.

Doctor Ludgrove made a face like he didn't understand, but only for a moment, before throwing back his head and laughing out loud.

"Oh, you'll be fine, son," the doctor said. "It is very loud. I should warn you about that. Some people who don't like loud noises do find it a little bit unsettling when the machine starts, but if you prepare yourself for that, you will be okay. Can you do that, Cooper? Can you imagine a very loud noise and then imagine not caring about it?"

Cooper shrugged.

"I can try," he said.

That seemed to satisfy Doctor Ludgrove.

"That's all any of us can do," he said. "Now, you'll need to set yourself up on this gurney. One of the technicians will help you. You lie down, put your head on the pillow, close your eyes, and lay very, very still. Even when you hear the loud noise."

Cooper nodded warily. He held together the flaps of his gown so that they didn't come open when he climbed up onto the funny little bed on wheels.

"I'm going to do my breathing exercise now," he said. "It helps me stay calm."

"That's an excellent idea, Cooper," Doctor Ludgrove said. "We're going to gently roll you inside now. I will give you a minute to breathe and settle down so that you are very, very still. We will all leave this room and stand in the little room over there behind the window. That's where we control the doughnut from. You will hear a ping. And then the loud noise and the...doughnut...will start to move around you like a big wheel. That's the flashlight, Cooper. You can't see it, but when it's making the noise and rolling around, the flashlight is shining inside your head, looking for things we can't see from out here."

None of it sounded good, but Cooper was here now, and it was apparent they weren't going to let him leave without doing their scans.

He settled down with his head on the pillow. Closed his eyes. Breathed in and breathed out. He kept his eyes closed tight shut when they rolled him inside the big doughnut. There was something about being in such a small space that he did not like at all. But if he kept his eyes closed, he would not have to see how he was trapped in there.

He heard the ping.
The loud noise started.
It was very loud.

12

Cooper Fox had feared all sorts of things for a long time. Some of his fears were simple. Bears, for instance. Bears coming out of the woods when he wasn't around to chase them away. Other fears were more abstract. He was frightened that he would lose Mary. Or that something bad would happen to her and the kids. He was frightened of shadows and of the dark at night. That's why they had the clock radio with the big cherry red numbers and letters on the bedside table at home. It filled their room with a soft crimson glow at night, which he found very soothing. He had been scared about getting into cars and buses, but that seemed to have passed. He hadn't thought of himself as being particularly scared of loud noises, no more so than anybody. A sudden loud noise could frighten the bravest man. Even Coach Buchner would jump if you snuck up behind him and clapped your hands right next to his ear.

Cooper had been very worried about the noise the big doughnut would make and even more worried that it would be so loud and so scary that he would try to escape the long, narrow doughnut hole. He would bang his head and he would panic, and everything would go wrong. It was all he could do to concentrate on breathing in and breathing out to control his fear. And when the roaring, grinding noise of the giant mechanical doughnut crashed in all around him, he did jump, just a little. Anybody would have. But he was surprised and even a little pleased by how quickly he settled down.

Bears might be a problem, but loud noises he could handle.

The terrible uproar went on for a minute and a half. He counted out the seconds. In a way, it helped. There were sixty seconds in a minute: that was something he knew now. And he counted ninety-three seconds while Doctor Ludgrove's machine roared all around him.

And then it stopped. He heard a door open and footsteps on the hard floor. Two pairs of hands took hold of his legs, just above his ankles and pulled him out. They weren't gentle. It was the tattoo nurses, or technicians, or whatever they were.

"You can get dressed now," one of them said, pointing at the screen he had used earlier.

Cooper said nothing. He padded across the cold floor in his bare feet and pulled the screen over behind him. He dressed as quickly as he could. When he had his jeans, T-shirt, and hoodie back on, he pulled on his socks and his boots. They were nice boots. The accident money people had bought them for him, the same way they bought everything. That's why he'd come here today. He didn't like Doctor Ludgrove and didn't really trust him. Not like Doctor Mike. And he really didn't like Ted the driver, or the tattooed nurse men. But even though he'd never met them, the accident money trustees had always been good to him, and they wanted him to get the scans.

Mary was always telling him how lucky he was that he had the money from his accident and the trustees to spend it properly. It was a terrible thing, what happened to his family and to him in that car accident, she said. Cooper didn't even have a grave he could visit. His old man was a Navy guy, they told him, the lawyers who looked after everything. So, they dropped his family's ashes into the sea off Norfolk. All of them. Because of the Navy or something. Coop told Mary he was okay about that because he didn't even really remember much about them. He had pictures of his mom and dad and his sister, but they were just pictures. They could have been anybody. Mary would think about that, and it would make her cry, too. Life was confusing and often cruel, Cooper thought as he did up his belt. He was glad he had the accident money people looking after him, but if he'd never had his accident, he would not have *needed* looking after. But then he would never have met Mary... And...

He gave up trying to think about it. He was much better at thinking about stuff than he had been when he was taking his pills, but some things were just too hard to think about.

His pills.

Oh boy.

He could hear Doctor Ludgrove's voice somewhere in the room. He was muttering like he was angry about something. Cooper felt a little queasy in his stomach. They had shined the flashlight in his head to look for things. He hoped they hadn't found the place where his brain medicine was supposed to be, but wasn't. Because he'd stopped taking it.

Oh boy.

Cooper took a moment to calm himself. Doctor Ludgrove told him they were looking for lesions or growths or something. And if he had any of that stuff in his head, it would be way better to find it. That's why Mrs Washington's daughter was so sick. She didn't have accident money or trustees. And they couldn't afford to find all the growths inside Sarah. That's what Mary said.

"Cooper, can you come out here, please?"

It was Ludgrove.

Oh boy.

Cooper came out from behind the screen. The four men on the other side of the room all stood facing him in a line.

The technicians, Doctor Ludgrove, and Ted the driver.

Ludgrove was holding an iPad, like the one Coach used for all his plays on game day. But Cooper's focus dialled in on the technicians.

They stared at him with flat hatred in their eyes. Even the bad men he'd fought at the party had not looked at him like that. One of the technicians was holding complicated loops of plastic.

Zip ties, Cooper thought. They're called zip ties.

His friend, the other technician, held a strange-looking kind of gun. It was yellow and black.

A taser, Cooper thought. He's holding a taser.

The doctor frowned at the iPad. Ted the driver was shifting ever so slightly from one foot to the other. He looked even less happy than Ludgrove.

Doctor Ludgrove looked up from his iPad, shaking his head.

"You haven't been taking your meds, Cooper."

"Yes, I have," Cooper lied, but this time it felt like nobody believed him. Not the way they were all looking at him.

Ludgrove held up his iPad.

"No, Cooper, you have not," the doctor said. "I can see from the scans here that there are barely even trace amounts of medication left in your cortex. And none at all in your hindbrain. I'm curious, Cooper. Do you know what a cortex is?"

Cooper thought about it, and as he considered the question, he realised that, yes, he did know.

"Yeah," he said, nodding slowly. It was as much a surprise to him as to anybody else in that cold, bright room. "It's not the brain. People think it is, but it's not."

Cooper took a small step to his left.

Ted and the two male nurses moved left and right. Ludgrove shuffled back half a step.

"It's not an organ," Cooper explained. "It's the outermost layer of an organ like the kidneys or ovaries. Or the brain, where it's called the cerebral cortex, or the neo-cortex."

"Holy shit," one of the nurses said. The one with the zip tie. "The fuck is going on here, Doc? This guy is supposed to be a retard."

"Your language is not appropriate," Doctor Ludgrove said.

"No, it's not," Cooper added. "That's a bad word, the R-word."

The technician didn't seem to care. He sounded angry and scared.

"Fucking tase him, dude," he said to his friend.

Cooper surmised that if they hadn't tased him already, there was probably a good reason why. Probably something to do with those scans on Ludgrove's iPad. He took another step to his left, one step closer to a trolley filled with pill bottles, packets of syringes and other bits and pieces of medical equipment. The technician with the Taser aimed it at his chest.

"Stay right there, asshole," he said through gritted teeth.

"Everybody needs to calm down," Doctor Ludgrove said. "Nobody needs to get hurt. Cooper just forgot to take his medication, that's all."

The doctor reached into the breast pocket of his lab coat and removed a syringe. It wasn't in a plastic packet like the ones on the trolley. But it did have a bright orange cap on the needle.

"He's not feeling well because he didn't get his medicine. He just forgot to take it, isn't that right, Cooper?"

Ludgrove's voice was shaking almost as much as his hand.

Cooper Fox decided it was time for the truth.

"No," he said. "I decided not to take it. And then I decided to lie about not taking it."

Ted reached into his jacket and pulled out a gun. A real gun, too, not just a Taser. Cooper flicked his eyes over the weapon. Another surprise.

He recognised it. A Glock 47. His focus moved up from the gun to Ted's eyes. Ted did not look like a Customs or border patrol agent. Cooper doubted that he worked for the Secret Service, either. He wondered where Ted got the gun, and he wondered why he knew that only serving members of those agencies carried that particular weapon.

He pushed the thought out of his mind.

He could do that now. With every minute that passed, he felt increasingly in control of his thoughts and feelings. His actions, too. Thoughts, which had once seemed impossible heavy things, now flitted through his head like butterflies.

He knew, without measuring the distance, that the man aiming the Taser at him was eleven-and-a-half feet away. Cooper knew he could close that distance much quicker than anyone could imagine, but not before the Taser Guy could pull the trigger, and that if he did pull the trigger, the Taser would send two small metallic darts and a crippling electrical charge into his chest.

He slowly raised his hands as if in surrender.

"What do we do now?" Cooper asked.

Doctor Ludgrove breathed out, relieved.

"Now, Cooper," he said. "You are going to take your medicine. In fact, I'm going to give you a booster shot. You have missed a significant dosage, and it has had serious effects on your cognitive capacity."

Cooper said nothing. His cognitive capacity was improving by the moment. He had no idea who these people were or what they had done to him. Not really. He didn't understand their motivations. But he did know that there was no way he was letting Ludgrove stick that needle in him.

Doctor Ludgrove, M.D., M.S., consulting neuropsychologist, was not the immediate problem, however. Cooper's main problem was... it was... He searched for the word and found it.

Tactical. Cooper Fox's problem was tactical.

Four threat vectors opened in front of him. In descending order of danger, they were Ted the driver with his mysterious government-issue pistol, the tattooed nurse with the military-grade Taser, the second tech with the plastic handcuffs, and Doctor Ludgrove with his loaded syringe. In a way, the syringe was the greatest danger of all because once the needle slid into a vein, Cooper Fox knew that he would never have another chance to get free of whatever the hell this was. But it was a delayed threat. Ted's gun was pointed at him at him right now.

You could survive a bullet. He understood in some distant way that he'd already done that. The scars on his body were not from a car crash. They were from bullets and bombs and knives. But there would be no surviving Ludgrove's injection. One tiny little pin prick would destroy him as completely as a bullet to the brain.

"Put your hands behind your head, lace your fingers together and get down on your knees," the driver said.

Cooper Fox nodded. Not because he intended to do as he was told but because Ted had just confirmed himself as the most immediate threat in the room.

Cooper's hands were already raised. He started to move them slowly behind his head, stepping forward but bending his knees and dropping his hips as though to comply with Ted's order. It carried him a little bit closer to the man with the Taser.

"You! Cuff him," Ted barked.

Mister Zip Ties took one faltering step forward. His friend Taser Guy also shuffled forward a little to keep his weapon trained on Cooper.

"Get out of my way, you fucking moron," Ted growled.

He sounded nearly as angry and scared as Mister Zip Ties.

Cooper was down on one knee now. But he did not drop his second knee to the floor, instead remaining in a crouch that recalled the easy posture of a sprinter positioning himself on the blocks.

"Get the fuck down, both knees," Ted ordered, gesturing with the gun. The slight movement of the muzzle away from Cooper's centre mass was the only opportunity he was going to get. As the technician moved on him with the plastic cuffs, passing almost but not fully between Ted and Cooper, Cooper suddenly yelled out in his loudest voice.

He didn't shout any specific word. It was more a single, fierce, barking roar. A war shout. A *kiai*, part of him knew, as the energy of the shout and the sudden detonation of trillions of synaptic sparks carried him forward with inhuman speed. The same rippling mirage that had overwhelmed Joe Don Porter and his accomplices exploded at the four men in front of him.

Their only reaction was to...sort of...flinch. And hesitate.

Cooper drove out of his sprinter's crouch, straight past Mister Zip Ties and down low, driving his shoulder into the knees of Taser Guy. He heard a scream and the terrible, rending crunch and crack of separating bones as he crashed into the man's lower legs, destroying the knee joints.

Everything was fast but slow.

A gunshot cracked out, but not with the sharp, flat report of a supersonic projectile. In his hyper-accelerated state, Cooper heard the roar of Ted's gun as a low, rolling peel of thunder that seemed to go on forever. Glass shattered but in slow motion, the jagged sound drawn out into an atonal screeching. Men swore and cursed but without meaning as Cooper navigated strange and sudden channels of amplified velocity.

Somewhere, a trolley full of small glass bottles and medical equipment toppled over and crashed to the floor of the imaging suite.

Cooper kept moving, even as Taser Guy toppled backwards, hitting his head on the solid, immovable edge of the scanner bed. His skull plates came apart with a terrible crunching noise.

Another gunshot. A strangled scream.

But Cooper was where he needed to be. By some feat of magic, he was behind Taser Guy now, on the floor, using him as a human shield, one arm clamped around his throat, the sudden lack of a carotid pulse beating against the blade of his forearm confirmation of the man's death. Cooper gripped the dead man's wrist, his hand, the weapon he'd been carrying.

Cooper wrenched the dead man and the Taser around in a short arc, lined up on Ted and forced his finger inside the trigger guard.

Two silver prongs shot out across the room, trailing short loops of thin copper wire. Cooper could see the arc of their flight traced out in lines of possibility long before the darts bit into flesh. He seemed to exist in a cloud of potential actions and outcomes, which he perceived all at once until something happened to transform the world of probabilities into reality. Something like the Taser he now held delivering its full charge into the centre mass of Ted the driver, who went down in a shuddering, frothing spasm of neuromuscular collapse. His gun fell to the floor, but Cooper did not scramble for it. He spun around to deal with Mister Zip Ties, the next pressing tactical problem he had to solve.

But Ted had already solved it for him.

Mister Zip Ties was curled around a gut shot, bleeding out next to the giant doughnut scanner.

Good work, Ted.

That uncanny, simultaneous compression and stretching of time suddenly passed as if by the tripping of a switch in his brain.

Cooper turned a quarter circle to put Doctor Ludgrove inside his fighting arc.

Ludgrove was in shock.

His eyes were wide, his pupils small, his mouth gaping like a goldfish suddenly pulled from its tank. He held the syringe in front of him like a talisman.

Cooper's left foot shot up in a blur, the tightly executed crescent kick striking Ludgrove's forearm, breaking the long bones and sending the syringe flying across the room. The doctor fell to his knees with a cry of pain, clasping at his shattered forearm.

Only then did Cooper Fox retrieve Ted's Glock 47.

He quickly examined the handgun. It was free of any identifying marks. The sidearms issued to U.S. Customs and Border Protection were engraved with the letters "DHS CBP". The Secret Service stamped their agents' weapons with "USSS".

Where had Ted been to get his weapon, Cooper wondered? The 47s, he somehow understood, were not available to the public, but Ted's gun was not government issue either.

He couldn't very well ask the man himself. He had passed out in a puddle of urine. The techs, he judged, were both dead.

Cooper turned the gun on Ludgrove.

"Just a few questions, Doctor," he said. "And this is very important. You must answer truthfully. Who am I? And why do I know that this model of pistol is manufactured exclusively for a small number of US government agencies?"

13

Ludgrove's breath came in great, laboured draughts sucked through white lips skinned back over yellowed teeth.

"Don't...please don't shoot me," he begged.

Ludgrove cringed away from Cooper and the gun.

Moving around the room, keeping his aim on the doctor, Cooper's eyes darted over to the door through which the pretty girl had left. If she had called security guards or the police, that's where they would come from. He could hear alarms outside the room and a recorded voice warning staff that lockdown protocols were active.

He put the bulk of the giant doughnut scanner between himself and the door but kept Francis Ludgrove under the sights of the Glock the whole time.

That's a magnetic resonance imaging scanner, a voice, his own but somehow unfamiliar, told him.

Cooper ignored it.

"I'm not going to shoot you, Doctor," he said. "Unless I have to. But you need to answer my questions. What am I doing here? And what the hell are *you* doing here? Who am I? We both know I'm not Cooper Fox. But..."

He faltered.

It felt as though his mind was running at warp speed – the first time it had moved any faster than a snail's pace for years.

"But I..."

"But you don't remember, do you?" Ludgrove said.

Cooper struggled to put into words exactly what he meant. The situation wasn't just surreal; it was grotesque, the scene of Ludgrove's clinic or laboratory, something painted by Goya in the grip of some dark, psychotic break. Two bodies: one folded up around a single gunshot wound, the other man stretched out as though ready to sleep a lazy day away, were it not for the massive structural damage done to his skull and neck. And Ted, of course, still twitching in a slowly spreading pool of his own bodily fluids. Alarms blared, muted by distance.

He had done all of this.

Poor, sweet, simple Cooper?

"I don't know," he faltered. "I just...I don't..."

It was so frustrating that Cooper almost dropped the weapon, but when Ludgrove moved, he snapped the Glock back into place, aimed at the centre of the doctor's chest.

His centre mass, the unfamiliar voice in his head reminded him.

"I know stuff," he tried to explain. "I understand things that I...I couldn't even put a name to before..."

He trailed off.

Ludgrove finished for him.

"Before the kinetic trauma to your temporal lobe and subsequent failure to maintain your scheduled treatment regime," the doctor suggested.

Cooper stared at him.

"Yeah. My temporal lobe that's...the one...near the ear, right? It...it processes visual memories and language recognition and..."

IT WAS THERE. He knew it was all there, but he didn't know why, and he wasn't sure exactly where in the haunted mansion of his memories to look for it.

Ludgrove nodded, almost enthusiastically, despite his injured arm.

"You are not Cooper Fox, no," he said. "You are Subject Fox from Cohort Seven. And your...recovery of function is remarkable. Absolutely remarkable. Do you mind?"

Ludgrove gestured with his good hand that he would like to stand up. It was as though none of the last few minutes had happened. As if he'd stumbled and fallen somehow. He cradled his broken forearm close to his chest.

Cooper nodded.

"What do you mean by Subject Fox?" Cooper asked.

"There were a number of subjects in your cohort. Nine of them plus you in your sample group," Ludgrove said as if that explained everything. He climbed awkwardly to his feet. "Each subject was coded for differential development. You, Subject Fox, were coded for infiltration and kinetic solutions. Subjects Wolf, Owl, Raven, Crow and so on had different coding. Different abilities, if you will. But you were all my responsibility. The Agency had other cohorts, but you were mine."

Ludgrove was nodding, grinning as if he expected Cooper to remember everything and to approve of it all.

"I can show you. I can show you," he repeated, growing in self-assurance and possibly even excitement about explaining himself. "It is ground-breaking work," Ludgrove enthused. "Nobel winning, if we could publish, which of course we can't. Not then or now. I'm sure you understand."

Cooper didn't understand at all. And Francis Ludgrove seemed not to care that his lab was full of dead men. He was quickly recovering his confidence.

"That tablet, does that have any information?" Cooper asked. "About your ground-breaking work, or whatever this is. Something weird happened to me. Before, when I was... when they were threatening me, everything...slowed down."

"Like you had hours to make split-second decisions?" Ludgrove asked keenly, ignoring Cooper's question for one of his own.

"Yeah. I guess," Cooper said. Ludgrove seemed to understand what happened better than he did himself. Haltingly, Cooper went on. "It was like I could, I dunno... like I could...*see* all of my own decisions before I took them. And what would happen if I did, or something? And when I did move, everything happened so, so fast. It was...Jeez, I don't fucking know," he cursed at last, frustrated.

But Ludgrove wasn't upset. He was almost levitating with excitement.

"Preconscious omniscience," he said, almost hungrily. "We were testing for this when the field program had to be wound up and the data transferred out. Remarkable, just remarkable. I told them they were making a mistake shutting us down, putting you into containment. I warned them. The professor, too. Or at least he tried to."

The alarms outside the diagnostic suites fell silent, but the recorded warning to shelter in place still played on a loop. Cooper knew that he needed to get away from here, but he needed to know what was happening, too.

"Your iPad," Cooper said, interrupting the man's enthusiasm. "Is your research on that?"

Ludgrove seemed surprised by the question.

"No, of course not," he said. "That's just your scans from this morning."

"Okay, then you're going to get me the data," Cooper said.

Ludgrove laughed, a flat barking sound like a trained seal begging a fish.

"Ha. No, Michael, you would be..."

A soft, stuttering chatter of automatic weapon's fire set Doctor Francis Ludgrove to dancing a short, ungainly jig. His white coat sprouted bright red flowers as the pretty girl from the front desk emptied half a clip of ammunition into him.

Cooper ducked for cover, dropping out of sight behind the MRI scanner.

He could see the pretty girl reflected in the window of the control room where the others had retreated during his scan.

Her face was blank, and she moved with almost robotic precision, holding a sound-suppressed machine gun close to her body, sweeping the room, looking for him.

In a very real sense, Cooper did not mean to do it. He still had Ted's gun, but he did not *want* to kill her. No conscious thought went into his decision. No decision chain led him to act as he did. But as she passed in front of the long doughnut hole of the MRI scanner, he shot her three times in less than a second.

The young woman cried out as she fell to the floor. Her weapon clattered on the hard tiles and fired a short burst. The stray rounds caromed off the base of the long, moving platform where they had laid Cooper down for his scan not ten minutes earlier. The pretty girl fell silent and lay still. She was not quite so pretty anymore. A slow-moving pool of blood crept away from her body toward the dark, sticky puddle spreading out from the gut-shot technician.

Cooper emerged from cover with Ted's gun held in a shooter's grip. He swept the room.

Ted was breathing but unconscious.

Everybody else was dead.

Cooper picked up the submachine gun. He recognised it. A Brugger & Thomet MP9.

Again, he had no idea how he knew that, but he took the gun anyway, wiping it clean of her blood with a moist towelette from a wall-mounted dispenser.

He kneeled next to Ted, pointing the fat, black tube of the suppressor at his head while he searched for Ted's wallet and car keys.

He found both, put them in his pocket and stood up.

He almost killed Ted then. Another automatic response, like a sneeze or blinking in a sudden bright light. Cooper lowered the iron sights of the MP to aim at the back of his skull, ready to put a bullet in his brain.

In his mind's eye, he saw himself as though from across the room.

A killer, standing over his victim.

"Whoa!" he muttered.

He backed off, shocked at the casual, almost involuntary way in which he was about to take a man's life. To murder him.

"Nuh," he went, shaking his head. "No way."

He backed off.

Doctor Ludgrove's iPad was dead. The screen shattered. Cooper left it behind, heading for the door. He went through with the gun up, ready to fire, but the waiting room was empty. The recorded warning was louder out here.

"Active shooter on site. Shelter in place. Active shooter on site..."

He searched the front desk and came up with two magazines for the MP9.

He took them, expecting to hear sirens at any moment.

The road through the forest leading to the building was clear.

Cooper Fox left.

TURNED out Cooper Fox was just fine with cars. He took a fire escape down to the underground car park and found the black SUV in which they had driven here. Cooper unlocked the vehicle, a Volvo XC 90, and climbed in behind the wheel. He took a few seconds to familiarise himself with the controls. But this was something he did not even have to think about. He knew how to drive a car, and after a quick check of the dashboard and a minor readjustment of the mirrors and his seat position, he was good to go.

Cooper started the motor and reversed out of the parking bay. He expected to hear shouts or even gunfire at any moment. But nobody followed him. The active shooter warning looped endlessly back on itself. Nobody attempted to stop him from leaving. He drove up two levels and out through an automatic gate. From the outside, he could see that the building in which Doctor Ludgrove had worked was a blue glass cube, at least four storeys high. There should have been a couple of hundred people working there. He had seen nearly a dozen vehicles parked underneath. But Kristin, the lady in the sunglasses, had talked about taking a car from the pool. So maybe those cars didn't have drivers. Perhaps Doctor Ludgrove had the building to himself?

If Cooper hadn't been so confused and upset by the strange events and the violence of the morning, he might have stayed to investigate. But everything was all messed up. It was so different from the clarity of those few moments when he had been fighting for his life. Now, he couldn't get his thoughts in a straight line. And they kept coming at him from all directions. Who was he, really? Ludgrove said he wasn't Cooper Fox. He was Subject Fox of Cohort Seven. And there were other patients and other cohorts who were just like him but different. Were they really like him? People without memories? He pulled out onto the road through the forest and accelerated away from the mystery.

Ten minutes of driving through dense stands of old-growth woodland, thick with red oak and maple, yellow poplar, and beech trees, took him to a four-lane blacktop. He paused at the intersection, uncertain of which way to turn. Part of him, the unknown, unnamed mystery of who he had once been and all the things he had done before the accident, urged him to pick a direction, any direction, and drive as fast as he could away from here.

Cooper Fox, who loved Mary Doyle and who had helped the Gainesville Tigers to their first pennant in thirty-six years, just wanted to go home. He desperately, *urgently* needed to get back to Mary and the kids and to the school and everything that had made his life good.

He turned left, heading south. Or at least he was pretty sure it was south from the position of the sun in the sky.

Again, he didn't understand how he came to know such a thing. But he did know.

He drove south toward Mary and home.

It felt good to drive, to be in control of something. He had three-quarters of a tank of gas and no need to stop. But he did pull into a Texaco half an hour down the highway. He took Ted's wallet into the roadhouse and paid cash for a cheap cell phone, some protein bars, and a bottle of water. His skin crawled the whole time. He was aware of every lens of every CCTV unit in the place, but he wasn't quite sure why he should care. Nothing made any sense to him. None of it. He found that he held vast, almost unknowable troves of information within himself, but he did not know the meaning of that information.

The security cameras at the Texaco, for instance, were made in China and commonly subject to sun-induced image burnout, infrared glare, and interference from faulty cabling.

Without conscious thought, he moved into the field of a camera he could tell would be washed out by the afternoon sun.

But what did it mean that he knew to do so?

Poor, confused Cooper Fox of Gainesville, Virginia, had less than no idea.

Back out on the highway, he turned on the radio and flicked through the channels, anxiously imagining he would hear news of a shooting in a doctor's office. But there was nothing, just the usual politics and sports and celebrity gossip.

Even so, Cooper could feel his head clearing with every mile. It was as though he'd been driving through heavy fog banks, crawling through them, really, because he had no idea where he was going. And now, the sun had burned off the fog, and the whole world lay before him, bright and clear and hard as diamonds. Even twenty-four hours had made a huge difference. He felt as though he was himself again. Even though he had no idea who that was.

His cognitive capacity. Doctor Ludgrove had talked about cognitive capacity and how skipping a couple of days of his medication had severely affected it. But Cooper felt as though his intelligence, his wits, and the speed with which he could process complex thoughts and ideas had all significantly increased within the last day. He remembered yesterday what a miracle it had been to be able to tell the time or read a few words. He could look back and see now that his "cognitive capacity" had still been severely constrained. But he could look back even further and see that for as long as he could remember, ever since the accident, he had been functioning at an almost moronic level.

He hated that word. There had been people who had sneered at him and called him a moron. But he conceded that they had not been wrong. They'd been cruel, unchristian, whatever you wanted to call it. But they had not been wrong on the facts to call Cooper Fox a moron.

His vision blurred, and hot flushes rolled over him in waves.

He pulled into the breakdown lane. His hands were shaking, and he had trouble breathing. It was a panic attack. He understood what that meant: the somatic equivalent of the hallucinations or flashbacks or whatever they'd been, which he had experienced in the shower when he saw the terrifying one-eyed man and Mary, all in pieces. He was responding to trauma. Cooper understood that, but it did not help to ease the sudden rush of freefalling terror.

Something had happened to him. Something vast and mysterious. It had been happening to him for at least three years, and it was happening right now in the driver's seat of the car he had stolen.

He fumbled the cap off the bottle of water and took a couple of long, messy swallows. Water spilled down his chin and onto his hoodie. But it helped just a little. His heart slowed down, his pulse stopped racing, and the dark flowers that had been blooming at the edge of his vision started to fade away.

He sat like that at the side of the road for a long time. He practised his breathing exercises.

When he felt that it was safe for him to drive again, he pulled out and resumed his journey home.

Home.

He had no better idea about what he would do when he got there, but he knew that he had to see Mary.

14

Mary sat on the edge of the little two-seater couch where they watched television together most nights. The kids were in bed. Cooper had used some of the money from Ted's wallet to pick up burgers and fries from Clem's Bar-N-Grill. A rare and unexpected treat. They were very unhealthy.

Mary had been so happy to see him back after hearing from the school that he had been taken away for tests. But confusion cut through her delight when Cooper pulled up in the big black Volvo, as though he drove home from work in an expensive Swedish SUV every day. Confusion became disquiet as Cooper fed the kids, got them bathed, and hustled them off to bed with a story for each.

That disquiet was now runaway fear, and he hadn't even told her about Ted or the technicians or the pretty girl he had shot three times in the heart. A clean kill, part of him whispered, even though there had been nothing clean about how she died.

Just talking about the pickup at the school and the drive to Ludgrove's office was enough to unsettle Mary, who sat on the very edge of the couch, her face blotchy with high colour in some spots and a sick, almost green tinge in others. Cooper's voice, his demeanour, his choice of words, and the way he arranged them in long, complicated sentences all worked to unsettle her. And he hadn't even told her the worst of it yet.

"I don't understand," Mary kept saying. "You took your meds. You should be better. But you're not. You're counting numbers and reading words and talking like a damn stranger. What happened, Cooper? What happened at that doctor's office?"

For his part, Cooper, or Subject Fox, or whoever the hell he was, struggled with his own sense of dislocation and alarm. All his feelings for Mary remained, but his understanding of their relationship, his appreciation for who she was and what she had done for him, had undergone a profound transformation.

For all the time they had been together, he had looked to her as... what? Their leader?

No, that wasn't right. Relationships didn't have leaders and bosses and stuff like that. But it was undeniable that Mary had been the one who took the lead and made things happen. She was the driver, if you like. How could it be otherwise? Until yesterday, Cooper Fox could not read the time on a clock or even the simplest sentence in a children's book. Until he'd stopped taking his medication, he'd been incapable of anything beyond the simplest intellectual challenges.

Except, of course, for his work at the school with Coach. And he had been more of a...what was the word? More of an idiot savant at that. He'd even heard some of the teachers describing him that way. They didn't say the word idiot, but he had once or twice heard them whisper that he was some 'savant' or 'adept'. It meant nothing to him at the time. Now he understood.

Mary barely touched her food. She leaned forward and worried at the paper napkin that came with the take-out. As Cooper recalled his day for her, she tore the small red square of paper into smaller and smaller strips. At times, he caught her looking at him as though he was an intruder who had broken into her home. Even though it was his house. The accident money trustees had paid for it.

And the trustees had sent Ted and Kristin for him.

"I don't know what was supposed to happen at Ludgrove's," Cooper said. "But that's not how it worked out."

"They told me you were going for scans, Coop," Mary said. "The school called me, and I spoke to Doctor Schofield, and they both said that the specialist wanted to do scans. They said it was routine, but it was important, too."

Outside, the sun had gone down, and a cold night was closing in. There would be hard frost on the ground tomorrow, perhaps even a dusting of snow. Cooper wasn't sure how to tell Mary what happened next without completely freaking her out. There probably was no way.

He reached out and took hold of her hands. They were shaking.

"The people who took me there, Mary," he said. "They had guns. Or at least one of them did. The driver. His name was Ted. And the nurses in the doctor's rooms where they were going to do the scan, they didn't look like the nurse at Doctor Schofield's office or any of the nurses up in Jacksondale at the hospital there. There were two of them, big guys with lots of tattoos. One of them had a Taser, and the other one had zip ties."

"Whaaat?" Mary breathed. She tried to take her hands away, but Cooper held on.

"They didn't like what they saw on the scans," he said. "And the guns came out."

She stared at him.

"What happened then?"

Cooper looked back at her.

"I'm here. I got away."

She didn't understand. She couldn't put the pieces together. For as much as he had looked to Mary to lead him through each day, Cooper Fox understood now that she was, as he had been, a simple soul. Nuance and layers of meaning were not for her. Mary Doyle was no fool. But she had left school to work in the salon as soon as it was legal. Apart from Facebook, she read only those children's books that Matty and Jess had received as gifts over the years. She was not...

Cooper felt profoundly uncomfortable and somehow unworthy of her in saying this, even if it was only to himself, but Mary was not an intelligent woman.

He found, to his surprise, that he did not care. He loved her. He had always loved her, and nothing that had changed about him in the last few days would ever change that.

"They were going to hurt me, Mary," he said, squeezing her hands a little. "Ludgrove was going to inject me with whatever drug they've been testing, and if I didn't let him, they were going to use their weapons. I couldn't let them do that."

"No, no, you couldn't," she said quietly. They were sitting in the semi-dark, with only one light in the kitchen turned on. "What happened, Cooper? What did you do?"

He was quiet for a few seconds.

"It was like when those three guys attacked Roscoe," he said at last. "That's how it went down."

"Are they..." She hesitated. "Did you...hurt them?"

Cooper looked at her.

"It happened very quickly," he said. "I tackled one of the techs. He fell and hit his head. Hard. The driver, the one with the gun, tried to shoot me. He hit the other tech. The one with the zip ties. I got the Taser, and I used it on Ted. He was alive, but the other two..." He shook his head. "That was all the guys with the guns. I was talking to Ludgrove. I wanted to know what was going on. His receptionist came in, except I don't think she was really there to answer the phones or do the typing. She had a machine gun. She killed him. I shot her. Then I drove home to you."

Mary did not move. She was like a small animal caught in the headlights of a speeding truck. She stared at him for a full second before blurting out, "Oh my God, Cooper, we have to call Sheriff Andy. And Coach. and Doctor Schofield."

He shook his head.

"Not Sheriff Briscoe, no. Or at least not yet. He's already looked out for me with those three guys. I don't want to make it any worse for..."

He stopped, noticing the expression on her face.

"What's up?" Cooper asked.

"Oh my God," Mary said, putting one hand up to her mouth. "You don't know. I forgot to tell you because of – because of all this. One of those guys who attacked you, the one who hit you with the soda can, he died. He died in hospital. Deputy Jamaal called me today. He said he didn't think it would mean any trouble for you, but..."

Cooper cut her off.

"What do you mean he died?"

His voice had a harsher edge to it than he intended, and Mary pulled back a little.

"I mean, he's dead, Cooper. Like the guys you killed at the doctor's office today."

As soon as she said it, Mary stopped and apologised.

"I'm sorry, I'm sorry," she said hurriedly. "I didn't mean that, Coop. I just...it's just so much to take in. And you, honey, you're so different. You're not even you anymore."

He put his hands on her shoulders.

"I am who I've always been," he said quietly. "I'm your guy, Mary.

Yours. I love you. I always will. We will figure this out, and we will get through it, but only if you trust me when I say I haven't changed."

She leaned forward, laying her head on his shoulder, and he put his arms around her, kissing the top of her head.

"I'm sorry," he said. "I've got you into something bad. And I don't even know what it is."

He eased her back a little. Her face in the half-light was streaked with tears.

"You said one of those guys died. What did Deputy Jamaal tell you?"

Mary rubbed her eyes and then her nose. She sniffled a little.

"He said the guy had, like, a heart attack or something. But he said you shouldn't worry. There was no way you were responsible for it. And..."

She looked up at him, her eyes a little wider.

"And he said that the other two guys were gone."

"What do you mean gone?" Cooper asked, keeping his voice level even as his stomach clenched with worry.

"He said that the feds grabbed them up. They were his exact words. 'Two deputy US marshals came in and grabbed them up, Mary.' That's what he said."

A strengthening wind gusted through the trees in the forest outside, setting the chime on their front porch to tinkling. Cooper couldn't help himself. He scanned the tree line through the window, looking for threats. Danger seemed to be everywhere.

"Do you think it's the government?" Mary said. "Like that deep state they been talking about or something like that?"

Cooper shook his head.

"I don't know what any of this is about," he said. "But I don't think it's the government, no."

"Why?" Mary asked.

He had no answer for her. Ludgrove had talked about an "agency". But he seemed to work for a company called Triple Helix. It seemed that maybe his research started at the agency but moved to the company. Cooper let go of her and moved over to the window, positioning himself to one side so he could see out without being seen. There was nothing out there. The Volvo sat parked in front of the house. The trees creaked and swayed in the freshening breeze. It was dark, with low clouds blocking out any starlight.

Mary came up behind him, and he gently tugged on her elbow to move her away from the window.

"I think we need to get out of here," Cooper said.

"What do you mean?" Mary asked, her voice full of concern. "The house? Do you think someone is coming to the house?"

"No," Cooper said. "I mean Gainesville. Probably Virginia. Maybe even out of the country."

It was so quiet he hardly heard the little gasping sound she made.

"But where and why and...I just..."

Cooper took her back into his arms before the fear could get hold of her.

"Something terrible is happening," he said. "It's already happened to me, Mary. I don't want it happening to you guys. And I don't even know what it is. That's why we need to get away. When I know you're safe, I'll be able to work it out."

"But where would we go, Cooper? How would we even live? This is our home. Can you even get your accident money if you're not here? Can the trustees find you?"

He laughed, a sound without joy.

"Mary, the trustees sent me to Doctor Ludgrove. The trustees have been paying for my treatment."

He puts sarcastic air quotes around that last word.

"I think the less the trustees know about where we are and what I'm doing, the better. Matter of fact, I'm starting to wonder if there even are any trustees."

"What do you mean?" Mary breathed.

They had never met the trustees. They got letters sometimes, and they had an email they could write to with requests for stuff like running shoes or extra money for the power bill in winter. Requests that were always met with a prompt and positive response.

"I don't know what I mean, not really," Cooper said quietly. "None of this makes any sense."

Mary snorted. A soft sort of giggle.

"What?" Cooper asked.

She looked up into his eyes. She looked so beautiful to him but sad.

"Honey, until yesterday," she said, "the words on the Cap'n Crunch box didn't make any kinda sense to you."

She hugged him to show that she meant no offence, but Cooper already knew that. She was just speaking the hard truth of it.

Neither of them said anything for the next few moments. They stood holding each other in the dark. It was Mary who finally pushed away.

"Do you think Doctor Mike is involved?"

Her voice was a whisper.

"I figure as much," Cooper said. "I don't see how it could be otherwise. I was part of an experimental program, Mary. They were testing some drug on me. And the only medicine I've been taking regularly is the pills that Schofield prescribed. And that the trustees pay for."

He found that it helped to talk it through with her. As he and Mary spoke, his thoughts came into sharper focus. Schofield had to be part of the program. But who else? If it was the government, they might have enlisted the help of Sheriff Briscoe, but Cooper didn't want to believe that. And he could talk himself out of it. Small-town sheriffs were notoriously difficult individuals, mindful of their autonomy and heeding of the oath they swore to protect and serve their own, not some faceless authority hundreds of miles away in Washington. Cooper knew that. Somehow. Even so, it wouldn't be wise to involve Briscoe just yet. After all, Cooper had put three bullets into a woman just a few hours ago. Her body might be growing cold and stiff on the floor of the scanner room, or it might have disappeared along with Ludgrove and Ted and Mr Zip Ties and Taser Guy.

"Mary," he said. "Go pack a bag for you and the kids. I'm going to get you out of town. I'll put you somewhere safe for a couple of days. And I'm gonna sort this shit out."

She stared at him, a look of wonder and fear in her eyes.

"Who are you?" Mary asked.

"I don't know," Cooper said. "But we're going to find out."

15

The kids were full of burgers and close to sleep when Cooper started putting together a go-bag for them. Three days should do it, he figured.

There was no reasoning behind that decision. None. Something inside of him had just settled on it. Some long-buried part of him that he did not yet understand. Cooper grabbed clothes and a couple of soft toys to stuff into a Gainesville Tigers gym bag. He could hear Mary emptying the kitchen cupboards of road food. Stuff they could heat up in a motel room if they had to.

Matty watched him through drooping eyelids. Jess tried to stay awake. She even asked where they were going, but the long school day and all the treat food caught up with her, and she dozed off.

"What's happening?" Matty asked when Cooper fetched one of his joggers out from under the bed.

"We're going on an adventure."

The boy yawned.

"Where?" he asked.

"If I knew that, it wouldn't be an adventure," Cooper said. "You never really know where they'll take you."

"Guess not," Matthew conceded but with obvious doubts. He sat up in bed. "Are you okay, Cooper? Mom says you got your medicines wrong."

Cooper stopped looking for the second jogger. He smiled at the elder of Mary's two children.

"Some might say that the medicines got me wrong, Matty."

"What?" Matty said, shaking his head and trying to come fully awake. "What d'you mean?"

Cooper had to remind himself that these children would be used to dealing with a much simpler version of Subject Fox. They would have to get used to a new model, but they were also about to experience a lot of disruption and chaos and possibly real danger, and it wouldn't help matters much if they also had to deal with a sudden, drastic change in his personality.

"Yeah. I got my medicines wrong," he said, slowing his voice down. "But it's okay, Matty. I can stop taking them now."

"Oh, all right," Matty said. He lay back down.

"Hey. Don't fall asleep," Cooper said. "We have to go soon."

"But...the bus isn't until tomorrow," Matty said, already dozing off.

Cooper was debating whether to wake them both or finish the packing and bundle a couple of sleeping kids into the stolen Volvo, when he heard a vehicle pull up outside.

He dropped the gym bag and hurried over to the window, edging aside the curtain.

He recognised Coach Buchner's pickup immediately.

Coach killed the engine and climbed out of the driver's door.

Doctor Mike got out on the other side.

Cooper squeezed his eyes shut for a moment and shook his head to clear it of all the thoughts and feelings colliding in there. That wasn't Doctor Mike, his friendly physician. That was Doctor Schofield, who had worked with Ludgrove, who was running some experiment for God only knew who. They were literally messing with people's heads. The two men spoke briefly before pushing through the little wooden gate at the end of the path out to the street. Cooper's first thought was "weapons". His second thought was to remember that he had left Ted's handgun and the receptionist's MP9 under the seat of the Volvo. He hadn't wanted to scare Mary when he got home, and he really didn't want either of the kids picking up a loaded firearm.

Schofield and Buchner walked up the short path and knocked on the front door. Cooper thought about climbing out of a window around the side of the house and retrieving the weapons from the SUV, but the vehicle was locked, and the keys were sitting on the bench in the kitchen.

He had no time. Mary was already at the door. He heard the latch and the murmur of the men's voices. He heard the uncertainty and unmistakable edge of fear in Mary's voice.

Matty started to sit up in bed, yawning and looking around.

"Who's that? Visitors?"

"Maybe. Stay here," Cooper said.

For a wonder, the boy did as he was told.

"Hey, Coop! Cooper Fox, are you here?" Coach Buchner called out.

He heard Mary try to argue with them, but he couldn't make out what she was saying, just a growing panic in her voice.

He couldn't stay in the kids' room, and he couldn't get to the weapons. He was sure that Schofield had to be wrapped up in Ludgrove's scheme, whatever the hell it was, but he wasn't sure about Coach. He could see no way through other than straight ahead. He took a breath, centred himself, and relaxed his face into a non-threatening, almost vacant grin. He shuffled out of the room.

Doctor Schofield and Coach Buchner were standing just inside the front door, with Mary trying to block their way. They all turned toward him when he emerged from the short corridor that led down to the bedrooms at the back of the house. Mary had turned on the main light in the lounge room and the fluorescent tube in the kitchen. She had the TV on and tuned into one of those Real Housewives shows she loved so much. She had been listening to it with the volume right down while she gathered supplies for the road trip.

"There he is," Coach Buchner grinned. "There's our boy. How you feeling, Coop?"

"I went in a car today," he said. "And I saw your friend who is a doctor."

He saw confusion writ large on the faces of both men. And wariness.

Doctor Schofield was staring at Cooper, grinning nervously. Coach Buchner's expression was harder. More sceptical. His grin was fixed in place. There was no joy behind it.

"Cooper, I tried to call Doctor Ludgrove to see how your appointment had gone," Schofield said. "But I couldn't get through. And I couldn't reach the drivers who took you there."

"Their car is here though, isn't it, Cooper," Coach Buchner said. "Did they bring you home? Are they here now?"

Cooper kept his empty, happy face in place as he nodded.

"Ted is in our bathroom," he said. He chuckled. "He drank a whole bucket of Coca-Cola, and he had to do a whizz."

Schofield shook his head bewilderment.

"Huh?"

"Ted's here?" Coach Buchner said.

"Doing a big whizz," Cooper whispered as though it was the most outrageous secret he had ever heard.

Buchner started to move deeper into the lounge room, pushing past Mary as though she wasn't even there. He called out, "You there, Ted?"

"Coach, please," Mary pleaded. "You'll wake the kids. They've had a tough week, and I just got them down to sleep."

Cooper felt a warm swell of pride deep inside his chest. Mary was playing along, pretending everything was normal. He could see it was unbalancing Schofield, who kept looking at Buchner with a lot of unspoken questions in his eyes. Unfortunately, Coach Buchner was not so easily put off.

"Hey Ted," he called out again, louder this time.

Nobody answered, of course. Buchner looked at Cooper, raising one eyebrow.

"Game over, pal," he said.

Buchner reached behind his back and produced a pistol. It wasn't a big, heavy-calibre weapon, but it was big enough. It must have been tucked into the waistband of his track pants, Cooper thought.

"Time to take your medicine, Cooper," he said.

"Coach, no!" Mary gasped. She stepped toward him, raising her hands as if to stop the much bigger, stronger man from going any further. Buchner casually whipped her in the face with the pistol. Mary cried out in pain and fell to the floor with a heavy thud. Doctor Schofield swore loudly.

"The fuck did you do that for, Ray?"

It happened so quickly, so unexpectedly, but to Cooper it seemed to take forever: he was suddenly back into that weird, liminal space between real-time and the impossibly accelerated speed of his thoughts.

Cooper Fox's gentle smile disappeared.

An almost wolfish grin emerged on Buchner's face in response.

"There he is," Buchner said. "There's my boy. Doc, give him the shot. I'll cover you."

Coach Buchner raised the gun, which that distant, foreign part of Cooper Fox recognised as a Ruger LCP. Polymer stock. Six-round mag. .380 rimless cartridges.

"Why did you do that?" Cooper asked plaintively. "Why did you hit Mary, Coach?"

It required very little play-acting to let the anguish in his voice come through. Mary was conscious. Buchner hadn't knocked her out. But she was curled up in a ball, crying and clutching at her face.

Cooper kept his face blank except for the thin spectres of confusion and distress he allowed to run free. It was as though he could not just imagine Mary's shock and violation but feel it in his nerve endings.

"You sit your ass down now, Cooper," Coach Buchner said, "and let the Doc give you the shot. Either he gives you the shot, or she *gets* shot."

He turned the gun on Mary.

Icy water filled Cooper Fox's stomach and all the channels running through his body. In the chill of this eerie detachment, he perceived the real as being hyperreal and all the potential pathways branching out from this moment as other competing realities that he could bring into being by a simple act of choice.

In most of those realities, Mary died.

But not all.

Doctor Schofield shuffled forward, hesitated, took a step back, and came to a stop.

"I don't know about this, Ray," he said. "I don't know if we got good information here. He looks like he's been dosed, and if I give him this..."

He held up a syringe with an orange tip. Just like the one Cooper had kicked out of Ludgrove's hand. Cooper dialled in on the hypodermic needle. His vision was so sharp he could see a tiny air bubble clinging to the side of the thin plastic tube, between the black millilitre markings.

"...he could overdose or something," Schofield trailed off.

Coach Buchner shrugged.

"So what? He'd be an even bigger dummy this time around? I guess we might have to give up next year's pennant if he can't help out at the gym, but I can live with that, Doc. I'm still getting paid. Give him the shot."

Doctor Schofield didn't move.

"This isn't your research, Ray," he said. He was almost whining. "You're just security and overwatch."

Coach Buchner snorted.

"Yeah, and I'm not the one who fucked up, am I? That was you brainiacs. Give him the goddamn shot. He's dangerous."

"But if we've got this wrong, we'll be trashing hundreds of millions of dollars worth of research. And it's me they'll blame, Ray."

Coach Buchner kept the gun trained on Cooper but turned his eyes toward the doctor.

"Schofield, either you put a shot into him, or I do. And he's not getting any better if it's me. Just do it."

Doctor Schofield shuffled forward.

"Cooper, what happened today?" he said. He sounded genuinely upset.

Coach Buchner shifted position just a little bit to keep them both within his firing arc.

Cooper was acutely aware of everything, as though the filters he usually wore on all five senses had been stripped away, letting the world pour in like water from a firehose. And yet, at the same time, he was able to separate the critical details that might make a difference.

The way Coach Buchner's left knee creaked and the jogger on his foot shifted ever so slightly to take pressure off an old wound.

The runaway pulse in Doctor Schofield's neck, beating a mad tattoo at 147 times a minute, causing his hand to shake, as blood rushed away from his extremities and deep into his large muscle bundles, preparing for flight or fight.

The way Mary's occasional moans and cries would draw Coach Buchner's attention involuntarily.

"I just went in a car, that's all," Cooper told Doctor Schofield, letting the sick turmoil he felt at endangering Mary strain his voice. "And Ted had the big Coke."

Schofield uncapped the syringe but looked imploringly to Buchner. The other man sneered and shook his head.

"Just get it done, Snowflake."

"But I don't like needles," Cooper whined. "They hurt. They always hurt."

He backed away a step.

Coach Buchner pointed the gun at Mary.

"I know what you're doing, pal," he said. "Knock it off and take your fucking medicine or so help me God, I will put a bullet in this dumb bitch and her little brats before I put one into your brain. I don't care how much fucking money those Helix assholes spent on it."

Still playing his role, Cooper wailed, "No, Coach. *Noooo...*"

"It's okay, Cooper. You're not going to remember any of this," Doctor

Schofield said. He glared at Coach Buchner. "And are you suggesting we put Miss Doyle on the treatment, too? Because she's a witness to this now."

"Like I fucking care," Coach Buchner said like coldly. "It's not like anyone's gonna notice that dumb bitch getting any dumber."

Cooper shuffled a few steps towards Mary, forcing Doctor Schofield to turn slightly and follow him.

Coach Buchner recognised the danger, but it was too late.

"Hey, Doc," he said. "Watch out that..."

Cooper exploded into movement.

He drove a front kick into Doctor Schofield's midriff, expelling all the air from the man's lungs and forcing him backwards into Coach Buchner. The coach of the Gainesville Tigers got one shot off, but it went high and wide, harmlessly digging a hole into the ceiling of the lounge room. Both men went down in a tangle of arms and legs, but Buchner took the brunt of the impact, with Schofield dropping onto his chest and cracking his rib cage. Cooper distinctly heard the wet snap of three ribs as he closed the gap between himself and the Coach with animal swiftness. He was a liquid blur of dark colour, flashing across the room and stomping down on Coach Buchner's gun hand. More breaking bones and a warbling cry of pain from the older man. Cooper kicked the firearm away.

There was no science or art in the short, brutal assault that followed. He put five kicks into Doctor Schofield's torso. He wasn't targeting particular organs for specific effects. He just delivered as much kinetic trauma into the body as quickly as he could. Schofield screamed, cried, grunted, moaned, and went limp.

Beneath him, Coach Buchner wasn't moving.

Cooper pulled Doctor Schofield off him and saw why.

The syringe was hanging out of Coach Buchner's thigh. It looked like he got the whole dose. Whether it was the drug or the impact of his head on the floor that finished him, it didn't matter. He wasn't a threat to anybody.

Cooper's heart was beating slowly, and his whole body sang with a pleasing, harmonic tone. The strange, almost transcendental moment of experiencing everything with icy clarity was fading.

It was an intimately familiar feeling but not something of recent experience. The fight with the three cons had been nothing like this, and he felt like he was still processing everything that had happened at

Doctor Ludgrove's offices. But as he stood over the bodies of the two men he had just bested, Cooper Fox understood that he had been here before. Many times.

"Cooper? Mom?"

It was Jessica. The little girl stood at the corner of the island bench, separating the small kitchen from the living area. Her brother stood beside her, holding a baseball bat. They both looked terrified, possibly of Cooper.

"Is Mom okay?" Jessica asked in a tiny voice.

Cooper nodded and hurried back to Mary.

"She's hurt," he said. "But I think she'll be okay."

Mary was still curled up in a ball. She was shaking and crying. In shock, he imagined. He tried to turn her over gently, but she flinched away from him. It was only when her children ran to her that she unclenched.

Cooper Fox stood back. Feeling soiled and useless.

What did he have to offer this family but more chaos and violence? He needed to get away from them for their own good. But he couldn't just leave them. Coach Buchner had straight up threatened to kill Mary and the kids. And Cooper did not doubt that whoever he worked for, whoever both worked for, would think nothing of doing the same.

He stood where he could keep an eye on Schofield and Buchner, but most of his attention stayed with Mary and her children. Both kids were distraught. Mary was sobbing and holding her face but trying to comfort them at the same time.

Her eye socket was swollen, and a bruise darkened the flesh where Buchner had pistol-whipped her. Cooper felt cold fury seeping through him at the sight of it. Feeling worthless and guilty, he retrieved Buchner's pistol from where he had kicked it under the couch.

Cooper turned the weapon over in his hands, careful to keep part of his attention focused on the two men who had forced their way into the house. The gun was a Ruger subcompact, just as he had thought. But also, not.

There was something unfamiliar about it. He knew this gun, but not quite like this.

Was it a newer model?

When had he ever held another one, perhaps an earlier version?

Before, he thought.

Before the accident. Before Mary. Before Gainesville. Before everything. He made the weapon safe and slid it into a back pocket.

Mary was sitting up, one child under each arm. She was still sobbing, but the deep body tremors had eased off.

"Cooper," she said quietly, beckoning him to her.

He moved over and kneeled, kissing her on the top of her head, wrapping one arm around her shoulder, and pulling all three of them into a light embrace. The whole time, he kept a close watch on Schofield and Buchner.

"What's happening?" Mary said. "What's got into everyone?"

"I don't know, honey," Cooper said. "But we can't stay here. I don't know why Coach did that. I don't know what Doctor Schofield was doing either, but I do know we have to get out of here right now. No more talk. Finish packing. I'll take care of these guys."

Mary suddenly grabbed onto him and hugged him fiercely.

"Cooper, no. You can't kill them."

He was about to deny he intended any such thing, and then he realised with something like horror that Mary had read his intentions perfectly. He was going to do precisely that after extracting whatever information he could from them.

He felt nauseous.

What the hell *was* he?

It was not a question he could answer yet. Possibly, he would never be able to. But he did know that he could at least protect his family.

"Finish packing," he said. "Like you're going away for a couple of days. No more. I'll tie these guys up. I need to ask them some questions. But I won't be long. Pack your bags and wait for me in the car. Do not touch the weapons under the seat."

"Okay, all right," Mary said warily. "But you hurry up, Cooper. And… and don't you hurt them. I know they did something wrong. But it's still Doctor Mike and…Coach."

"I promise," Cooper said. He gave her another hug. "Go on now."

They stood up on shaky legs. Jess clung tightly to her mother's side. Matty grabbed his baseball bat from the floor. He looked as though he wanted to hit somebody with it. Instead, he followed Mary into the kitchen.

Cooper grabbed Doctor Schofield by his collar and pulled him away from Ray Buchner. He dumped the physician up against the edge of the couch, fetched a glass of cold water and threw it in his face. The doctor coughed and spluttered back to life.

Cooper pointed the little Ruger at him.

"Tell me what you know," he said.

Doctor Schofield winced. He shook his head. The movement caused him some obvious pain.

"I can't," he croaked. "I signed contracts. NDAs. The research... It's radical, but it has to be secret. I can't..."

"Mike," Cooper said. "I think we have moved beyond your nondisclosure agreements here. Tell me what you know."

Doctor Schofield raised his head from the abject misery into which he had sunk. He stared at Cooper.

"It happened, didn't it? Remission. Recovery of function."

"I don't know what you mean by that," he said quietly. "Explain it."

"You recovered from the therapy."

Cooper looked at him, trying to understand. He could hear the others behind him in the kitchen.

"As far as I know, Mike, you don't recover *from* therapy. Therapy is supposed to help you recover from something else. What was I recovering from? How did I end up on your trial or experiment or whatever it was?"

They spoke in low voices. Mary moved slowly around the kitchen. She still had both children with her.

"I can't tell you," Doctor Schofield said.

"There was no car accident, was there?" Cooper said.

"I...I don't know, Cooper. I just ran the tests."

Cooper had been expecting him to say something like that, and yet the world still tilted slightly on its axis.

"And my family? They weren't killed in any car accident, were they? Did I even have a family?"

Doctor Schofield shrugged weakly.

"I suppose you had one somewhere," he said. He seemed to be talking to himself.

"Jesus fucking Christ," Cooper spat.

That got Doctor Schofield's attention back. He chuckled, but it sounded more like he was trying to cough something up.

"You really have gone cold turkey, haven't you? I didn't know you before the experiment. Didn't know anything about you. I've only ever known you as Cooper Fox. A nice guy with an acquired brain injury. But I can see you're not that guy anymore."

"I never had an acquired brain injury, did I?" Cooper said, pressing the point.

Schofield sighed. "No. Even a first-year med student could have looked at your CAT scans and told you that."

Cooper leaned forward, whispering urgently.

"What did I have? What were those pills you had me on?"

Doctor Schofield smiled.

"You won't believe me, but I don't know. Honestly."

Silence.

Glass jars rattled against each other in the kitchen.

"You're damn right I don't believe you."

Doctor Schofield shrugged.

"I had tests to run. That's all. I managed the meds, and I ran the tests. I sent the results through to Ludgrove. I mean, I understand the results. The cognitive impairment. But I don't know what the drug is, Cooper. I swear. It's like nothing I've ever seen or even heard of."

He looked up, suddenly worried.

"What happened to Ludgrove? Did you...kill him?"

Cooper shook his head.

"No."

Doctor Schofield relaxed a little. But Cooper wouldn't let him enjoy the reprise.

"He's dead. His receptionist shot him. Then I shot her. She's dead, too. And a couple of technicians, and maybe one of the drivers. The other one got lucky. She wasn't there."

Doctor Schofield stared at him.

"Holy shit," he said.

"Who did Ludgrove work for? Who did he report to?"

"I don't know," Doctor Schofield said quietly. "Just the biotech company. Triple Helix."

"You don't know much, do you, Mike?" Cooper spat back at him, losing patience. "How the hell did this work? Did you answer a job ad online somewhere? Sketchy Doctor needed to run off-the-books medical experiments?"

Doctor Schofield laughed. This time, it was a genuine laugh. Small and sad, but real.

"Something like that, yeah," he said. "I, ah, I got into my own stash, you know. Self-medicating. Happens all the time. The medical board was going to pull my licence. This lawyer reached out..."

"Buchner's friend? That Needham guy?"

Doctor Schofield stared at him for a second.

"You know, a week ago, there's no way you would have remembered that guy's name. Not after just one meeting."

"Yeah, turns out I'm a frustrated Jeopardy champion. Was it Reese Needham who reached out to you?"

Doctor Schofield nodded.

"He said he could sort out my problem with the Board. Organised rehab for me, too. All I had to do was move here and take over some guy's practice. I could run it as a legitimate business. He gave me a float and put me in contact with Ray. Said if I had any trouble, Ray would take care of it. I just had to stay off the Oxy and monitor your progress."

"My progress?" Cooper said flatly.

"Okay, yeah, you got me. Your lack of progress."

"And you didn't ask any questions? You just did what Reese told you?"

"No, I did what Ludgrove told me. I knew you didn't have any cerebral trauma. But there was something wrong with you. I thought at first that Ludgrove was trying out some insane nootropic therapy."

"*What* sort of therapy?"

"Nootropics. Smart pills, literally. Meds that make you smarter. I thought you were maybe some basket case they picked up somewhere. A state ward. A homeless guy. Profoundly handicapped. Who knows? I didn't care. I ran the tests. I sent Ludgrove the results. I got paid."

"I've got a whole packet of those pills in my bedroom," Cooper said. "I should jam them down your throat. See how you like it."

Doctor Schofield blanched. His eyes went wide.

"Please," he said, choking on sudden fear. "I was just a junkie. That's all. You don't know what it's like. You'll do anything, fucking anything."

Cooper said nothing.

Both men fell silent again. Mary had taken the children to the bedroom, and Cooper could hear them packing.

"What about him?" he said after a while, pointing the pistol at Coach Buchner.

"What about him?" Doctor Schofield lobbed back. "He got a hotshot. The dose that was meant for you. If he wakes up, he's not going to be good for much besides sitting in the locker room looking at his own drool."

Cooper Fox stood up. He kept the gun on Doctor Schofield.

Mary and the children reappeared. They were carrying three gym bags between them. Jessica held her favourite doll close. Matty was still holding the baseball bat.

Mary had washed her face and changed. Her black eye was swelling closed.

"We're ready," she said quietly. She couldn't bring herself to look at Doctor Schofield.

"Go on out to the car," Cooper said gently. "I won't be too much longer."

"C'mon man, I was just doing my job. That's all," Doctor Schofield whined.

"Shut up," Cooper said. He turned back to the others. "Go on," he said gently. They all filed out with the bags, swerving around Schofield and Buchner.

"Get down on the floor. Face down," Cooper said.

"What are you going to do to me?" Doctor Schofield asked. His voice was shaking.

"Don't piss your pants, Mike," Cooper said. "I'm going to tie you up. Then I'm leaving. We're going away, and we're not coming back. You're not going to find us. Nobody is going to find us. And if they try, I'll kill them. You tell them that. That's your job now, Mike. You tell Reese Needham, you tell anybody who was involved in this, that we are done. It's over. And if they come after us, I'll kill them all. Not just the operators but the people who sent them. I will go all the way to the top. You think you can do that?"

"No problem, Cooper. I can do that, for sure. Good luck, okay? You can count on me."

He was babbling by then, but he did as he was told, getting all the way down on the floor and even putting his hands behind his back so that he could be properly restrained.

Cooper took a roll of duct tape from the kitchen and bound up Doctor Schofield's ankles and wrists. He thought about rendering the man unconscious. A light blow with the butt of the pistol to a spot just behind his ear would do it. But it might also kill him, and he really did want Doctor Schofield to deliver his message.

He didn't imagine for a second that it would make any difference.

But it was worth doing.

If they thought he was running, they might not see him coming for them before it was too late.

16

"Not that car," Cooper said as Matthew raced away to claim the shotgun seat up front in the Volvo. Matthew skidded to a halt, half turned around. He was dressed against the chill, bundled up in a hoodie and a puffer jacket, and his little white face was a picture of surprise.

"We're taking Coach's pickup," Cooper explained.

"But I want to go in the cool car," the boy said.

Mary had pulled up short of the Volvo as well. She was giving Cooper her *"What gives?"* look.

"Trackers," he said quietly. "I didn't think of it earlier. I'm sorry. I'm still not a hundred per cent. But there's a reason they knew to come here. Maybe somebody called them. Most likely, that's a fleet vehicle, and there's a GPS tracker somewhere inside it."

Mary's eyes went wide, but whether in surprise at his being able to follow through a line of reasoning or in fear at the idea of their being traced, Cooper couldn't say. Probably a little of both.

"How do you know?" she asked.

"It's procedure," he said, trying not to sound as though he was patronising her. He hadn't even thought of this stuff until a few minutes ago. It frightened him to wonder what else he was missing. He felt as if his mind was like a map at the start of a video game. He could see a few illuminated areas, but most of it was still dark.

"I'm sorry," Cooper said. "I'm sorry about everything, but I'm gonna have to ask you to trust me about stuff like this. Even if I can't always explain it."

"It's okay," Mary said. She sounded exhausted and scared. "I don't know what's happening either. I don't know why Coach had a gun. I don't know why Doctor Schofield was..."

She struggled to find the words and started to cry in small, jerking gasps.

"I don't know why he was hurting you," she sobbed as if every word caused her pain. She stared at him with her one good eye for a long time, and he could feel just how much she was suffering. "And I don't know who to trust anymore."

Cooper took her into his arms and held her close. The children piled in for the group hug.

"I love you," he said, his voice muffled in Mary's hair. "Always will. Trust that."

She returned his hug with sudden fierce strength.

"Now come on," Cooper said. "Let's go."

He had Coach Buchner's keys and wallet. He stripped out the paper money, seventy-six dollars in cash, and threw the rest away. They had another two hundred and twenty from Doctor Schofield and whatever was left in Ted's wallet. Cooper knew they couldn't use any of the credit cards. He knew they would need a lot more money, even if it was only for a couple of days. The choices he had to make all rumbled downhill towards him. An avalanche of consequences.

It was almost enough to undo him, but the kids climbed into the back seat, and Mary got in upfront, and that decision was at least made for him. He fetched the guns from the Volvo and took the driver's seat in Coach Buchner's pickup.

Cooper checked over the weapons again, making sure they were safe, before stowing them in the hard pocket of the driver-side door. The MP9 did not sit comfortably in the space, but he could not leave it anywhere within reach of the children.

"What's going to happen to them?" Mary asked as he turned over the engine and put the big Ford into gear. "Should we call Sheriff Andy or someone?"

Cooper shook his head.

"No. I don't think Andy has any part in this, and it would be wrong to drag him into it now."

Cooper pulled out onto the road and turned away from Gainesville. Twin cones of white light from the powerful quartz halogen headlights blazed into the darkness ahead of them. There were only a handful of properties scattered along the road back into town, and most folks would be buttoned up for the night by now, having their dinner and watching TV.

"But Coop, you can't just leave people and bodies and stuff lying around. The police won't like that at all. You could get in big trouble."

"Somebody will come for them," Cooper said. "When they don't report in."

"What will happen then?" Mary asked.

"I can't tell you," he said. "The people who took me to Ludgrove this morning, they weren't like scientists or anything. They were operators."

"Like *Mission Impossible*?" Matthew said from the back, excitement in his voice.

"Like the bad guys from *Mission Impossible*," Cooper said, his eyes flicking up to the rear-view mirror. Both children were wide awake back there and listening to everything.

"Are you one of those guys," Matthew asked.

"I don't know," Cooper said honestly. "Once upon a time, maybe. I guess it would explain a few things."

"Like how you fought those guys at the cookout," Mary said. "And how you know about things like trackers and *Mission Impossible* guys."

"Yes," he said, reluctant to even entertain the possibility. "There's so much I don't know about myself, about any of this. And even though some stuff is changing – like knowing how to read again..."

"And getting smarter," she said. It almost sounded like an accusation. One which hurt her to make.

"Yes," he conceded. "And getting smarter. Even though all that stuff *is* happening, and it's maybe even speeding up, I can feel it... Even with everything, I still don't know like what the hell's going on. It doesn't feel like my real memory is ever coming back."

They drove on in silence for a while, putting miles between themselves and Gainesville. Just before they reached the turn-off for the state highway, Mary reached over and squeezed his arm.

She didn't say anything, but it made him feel better.

COOPER DROVE for three hours and put nearly a hundred and fifty miles on the clock before pulling into a Howard Johnson's just outside of Radford. The children had fallen asleep a little after Lynchburg, and Mary soon joined them. It gave Cooper time to think. He would stay with them tonight, make sure they were safe and that they hadn't been followed. His mind swirled with images of satellites being re-tasked and drones stalking them along the highway. He knew he would have to change vehicles again. But that wouldn't be a problem. He would steal another car if he had to. He was unsurprised to learn that when he thought about it, he knew how to do that. Most of the cash they had, he would leave with Mary. He had Ted's driver's licence, and from that, he knew the man's address. A condo in Washington. He would start his search there.

Mary woke up as he pulled into the parking lot of the motel.

"Where are we?" she asked groggily. She was full of painkillers. Her face was badly swollen.

"Safe, for now," Cooper said. "I'll go check in. You get the kids up."

"You want I should come with you?"

He shook his head and brushed one finger against her cheek.

"Buchner gave you a black eye and a nasty bruise on your face. You walk in there like that, any decent sort of person is gonna put a call into the cops or child welfare. Best you keep a low profile. I'll find some more food and some cream for the bruising."

Mary put her fingertips to the swollen cheekbone.

"It hurts," she said. "I didn't want to make a fuss."

Cooper frowned.

"How much? Does it hurt to talk? Is it constant? That sonofabitch might have broken something."

His voice was growing dense with anger.

Mary reached over and touched his unmarked face.

"I'm okay. I just... I worry, is all."

"We can find a doctor."

She smiled.

"No. I'm okay. The black eye will fade. It's not my first. I just worry that you won't like me anymore."

Cooper blinked.

"Jesus, no. Mary, I love you," he said. "That will never change. I might not remember much before I got to Gainesville, but I remember you. Your kindness. How you looked out for me. I'll never forget that."

Mary turned to look at her two children in the back.

They were silent but wide-eyed.

"But you're changing, Coop. You'll be another man soon. Smarter than me, for sure. Y'already are. You'll be different and..."

He cut her off with an emphatic shake of the head.

"No, Mary. I'll be who I always was," he said. "One thing that drug did was it simplified me. Cut everything away. All the stupid, complicated thoughts and memories that people have and the way they have to construct all these different versions of themselves to deal with everybody else's stupid constructs and expectations. You got the real me. You'll always have the real me. Always."

She favoured him with another sad smile.

"My Cooper would never have said something like that," she said.

He took her hands in his.

"I am your Cooper, and I'm telling you that my Mary..." He turned around to the kids, who were staring at him with gape-mouthed wonder now. "...and my Matthew and my Jessica are the only things that matter to me. And I will always look out for you. Ahead of myself. Ahead of everything else. Now, I'm gonna get us a room."

"I'm not sharing with Jessica!" Matthew declared.

IT WAS LATE, but a handwritten sign stuck to the front door promised lodgings 24 Hours A Day.

Just ring the bell, it said.

Cooper did, but nothing happened. He gave it another ring and another minute and was about to try again when a man appeared through a door behind the reception desk. He wore a dressing gown over flannelette pyjamas, and his thin hair was everywhere except where he most needed it, over the bald patch on top of his head.

He smiled when he saw he had a customer, however, and he released the door lock by pressing a button somewhere on the desk.

"Hi, we're looking for a room," Cooper said as he pushed open the door. A small bell tingled overhead.

"Well then, sir, you are in luck," the motel owner said, "for as it happens, I am in the business of renting rooms."

The man was so genuine in his hail-fellow-well-met routine that

Cooper could not help but smile. Perhaps the world wasn't full of evil men and dark conspiracies, he thought.

The world would soon enough give him reason to question his naïveté.

17

The habits of an unremembered lifetime stayed with him. Cooper Fox woke early. He kissed Mary without waking her and rolled out of bed, dressing in the gloom before dawn. He left a note by the bed.

"Gone for supplies. Back soon."

Ten minutes along the state route, he found a truck stop and pulled in. It was busy with long-haul rigs and a smattering of road-trippers filling up on grease and sugar for breakfast. He parked as far away from the roadhouse as he could next to a battered, rust-stained Camaro with Nevada plates.

A brisk walk through the pre-dawn chill took him into the warmth and light of the restaurant, where he ordered four breakfast sandwiches, two black coffees, and two fruit juices to go. While the kitchen prepared his meal, Cooper spent some of their small pool of funds on another burner phone, a small packet of disposable rubber gloves, and a cheap tool kit. On the way to the checkout, he passed a small section of shelving given over to medicines and healthcare products. He saw a tube of sports gel with arnica and aloe vera. It would help Mary's bruising and swelling, so he bought that, too.

Back at the food counter, he collected the sandwiches. Twelve minutes later, back at the motel, he slipped quietly in through the door. Everybody was still asleep.

He woke Mary by shaking her gently, and they ate a quiet breakfast together in the darkness, perched on the edge of the bed.

"What happens now?" she asked in a low voice.

"You stay here until I come back for you. If I'm not back in three days, you take the kids, and you drive away."

He gave her the keys to Coach Buchner's pickup and all but twenty dollars of their remaining stash. All her concern was focused on him.

"What about you, Coop? You're not gonna do anything stupid, are you?"

He sipped the coffee and shook his head.

"Don't worry about me," he said. "I'm going to find out who these people are and what they want. If I can negotiate with them, I'll do that. If not, I'll either come back for you, and we'll go, or if I don't think they'll let us go...I'll deal with that."

"What do you mean, deal with that?" Mary asked, her voice carrying a brittle edge.

"There'll be evidence," he said. "At Doctor Schofield's office. At Ludgrove's. Maybe at Coach Buchner's place. Unless it's all the government, there'll be a company involved. Ludgrove worked for something called Triple Helix, and I think Coach Buchner mentioned them, too. They'll have offices and corporate details on a register somewhere. And there's me. I'm evidence. There was no car crash. My family didn't die. But I must have had a family somewhere. Parents? Siblings, maybe. A history. Give me three days, Mary. You'll be safe here."

He gave her the phone with the number of his burner programmed into the memory.

"Don't call me unless you think you're in danger," he said. "I will find some way of getting more money to you. I'll send you a text every day just to let you know I'm okay. I know it'll be hard. Two little kids in a motel. But you have to go dark. Do not let them find you."

She was scared. Cooper could see that, but he could also tell that she had gathered up whatever it took for her to trust the stranger her man had become. She lifted her chin and pushed back her shoulders. Strong. Determined to do whatever it took.

"Okay," Mary said. "I will. But you be careful, Cooper Fox. You do whatever you have to, and then you get yourself back here to us."

She punched him in the arm to emphasise that she meant business.

"That's a promise," he said, and they sealed it with a long kiss.

His movement plan was simple. He packed just a little food, a bottle of water, and all the guns in one of the gym bags. He hitched a ride back the way they had come, grabbing a lift from a trucker hauling cheese to Richmond about twenty minutes after he'd walked away from the Howard Johnson's. They parted ways in Staunton, where he was stranded for two hours by the side of Route 250 until a history adjunct from Mary Baldwin University picked him up and gave him a lift to Charlottesville. In this way, Cooper Fox made his way across the Commonwealth of Virginia, over the border with Maryland, and into the DC Metro area over the course of nine and a half hours. When he arrived in Washington, he still had the better part of fifteen dollars left, having purchased just one cup of coffee and an egg McMuffin. He had his last ride with Calvin, an Amtrak porter who spoke for more than an hour about how the President, "The actual President, Cooper," had called up when his daughter got sick and asked if there was anything he could do. And all because ten years ago, Calvin, the Amtrak porter, had clipped his ticket and helped him on and off the carriage to Delaware when the President, "The actual President, Cooper," had been doing the daily commute.

Cooper Fox thanked him for the ride and the conversation. Maybe he should have asked Calvin to give the President a call on his behalf. Maybe the President might be of a mind to lend a hand to another fella who found himself in a tough spot.

Or maybe Cooper Fox was an escapee from some black budget Pentagon program, and any such call would result in the speedy dispatch of a wet work team to erase all trace of his existence.

He thanked Calvin again and waved goodbye to him.

It was late in the afternoon, with the threat of cold rain and sleet in a lowering grey sky. Cooper took a wallet from his back pocket and opened it to examine the driver's licence behind the clear plastic window.

Ted stared out at him.

Ted Sorensen, age 42, of Suite Five, Hampshire Mews, Woodley Park.

It sounded expensive. Not the sort of place somebody on government pay could afford.

Cooper googled the address on his phone and got walking directions. It was an hour away. It would be dark and getting dangerously cold when he arrived.

THE LAST HE had seen of Ted Sorensen, the man had been unconscious, lying face down in Francis Ludgrove's office with a couple of Taser darts dug into his chest.

Cooper had been a heartbeat away from putting two bullets into his head on general principles. But he hadn't pulled the trigger. There was no mystery about why. It would have been wrong, is all. Sorenson had nothing "planned" for Cooper. Sorenson was not a guy who made plans. He executed them for other people. He followed orders. For sure, he would have delivered Cooper back into the hell of a pharmaceutical lobotomy, but whichever way Cooper turned the puzzle piece of what he should have done as he fled that room full of the dead and dying, he could find no justification for killing Sorenson beyond mere convenience.

And that would have been wrong.

As he bustled along the footpath of a busy, brightly lit shopping strip, threading his way through the crowds at the end of their day, he struggled to reconcile this simple sense of what was right and wrong with the bloody chaos and madness of the last few days. But he couldn't. Perhaps he remained, in many ways, the childlike simpleton he had been these last three years. Three years that accounted for the entirety of his life as he recalled it.

The wind picked up, and he huddled deeper inside his hoodie. It was fleece-lined and warm enough to get through most of autumn, but it would not protect him when the temperature really plummeted. It was just another task on his to-do list. Find a weatherproof jacket or overcoat.

He passed through a café and restaurant strip, and saliva jetted into his mouth as he smelled the cooking odours coming from a Turkish pizza restaurant. He was famished, and his stomach rumbled, but he ignored it and pressed on.

Ted Sorensen had an apartment in a gated townhouse development halfway around a cul-de-sac lined with lovely old maple and oak trees. The leaves had turned and started to drop. They rustled and crunched underfoot as Cooper approached the front gate. There was no guardhouse, for which he was thankful, but he could already see there was a keypad entry.

He checked the wallet again. Besides the driver's licence and the usual collection of credit cards and scrap paper, there was a plain white swipe card, but it didn't work when he waved it over the keypad.

Cooper stood back and scoped out the defences. The wall around the complex was at least seven feet high and topped with broken glass. He looked up and down the street, searching for a tree that might offer him a way in over the wall, but all the trees lining the front of the property had been pruned of any branches reaching from the street into the gated sanctuary.

It was dark, and he knew that he would soon draw suspicion simply by hanging around. He walked on for another minute until he judged it safe to prop himself against a tree and watch the front gate.

Commuters returning from work drove into the cul-de-sac every couple of minutes, but it was at least a quarter of an hour before any vehicles turned into Hampshire Mews.

Cooper Fox studied the sequence.

The driver pulled up at the entrance, waited, and finally rolled through when the wrought iron gate rumbled open. Cooper counted fifteen seconds before it closed again. Plenty of time.

Not wanting to delay or arouse the suspicion of any neighbourhood watch types, he followed the next vehicle through the breach. An Audi sedan. Cooper started moving up the street as the driver indicated they were turning into the gated compound. Cooper increased his pace to a jog as the Audi disappeared inside. The driver turned right. Cooper went left, concealing himself in the shadows behind a bush. He used the camera on his phone to snap a couple of photos of the front doors of the nearest suites. He was too far away, and it was too dark to be able to read the numbers on the doors, but the camera was good enough for him to zoom in and work out the numbering scheme. Suite Five would be somewhere to the right, where the Audi had gone before. Maybe it was even Sorenson.

He hoped not. Cooper would much prefer to find the man's apartment unoccupied. He stopped for a moment.

What if Ted was married and his partner was home? What if he shared the apartment with a roommate?

Cooper Fox stood in the freezing dark, entirely at a loss for what to do under those circumstances.

There was nothing else for it. He had to press on.

Hampshire Mews was an exclusive, expensive community, a mix of townhouses, apartment blocks and freestanding homes. The grounds were well cared for, and the pathways well lit. He saw at least three CCTV cameras and knew his movements were being observed. But probably not by a guard who would surely hurry to investigate a random, hooded stranger wandering through the Mews. Had that been the case, the responders would have been there already. Perhaps he was being recorded, and some bored police officer would examine the video a day or two from now, seeking clues to the identity of the man who had broken into Mister Sorensen's place.

Cooper pulled the hood of his fleecy top a little further forward and dipped his head down to hide his face. If a security guard came, he would have to deal with them. But that might prove to be as simple as handing over Ted's wallet and telling them he came to return it. A thin story, but better than hurting somebody who was just doing their job.

He found Suite Five, and his breath plumed white as he blew out his cheeks with relief. There was no car in the parking space out front and no lights on inside. He walked straight up to the door, holding Ted's wallet. He could see a small red light under the door handle. He waved the wallet over the sensor.

Nothing.

He tried it again.

Nothing.

His heart was starting to beat faster. He opened the wallet, removed the swipe card, and waved it over the panel. The electronic lock disengaged, and the red light turned blue.

Cooper Fox slipped inside the apartment.

He pulled on the pair of cheap rubber gloves he'd bought at the truck stop, fumbled for a light switch just inside the door, and found it. LED strip lighting blazed into life, and Cooper found himself standing on the verge of a large open-plan living space. In some ways, it was very similar to the little house he lived in with Mary. A lounge room running back through a dining area into the kitchen.

But Ted Sorensen's apartment was much more luxurious than their modest little home. No children's toys lay scattered on the floor. No clothes waiting to be ironed, draped across the back of chairs, or piled up on the dining room table. Ted had nice black and white photographs hanging on the wall. They looked like nude ladies, Cooper thought. But it was hard to tell. They were mostly just light and shadow. A very expensive TV seemed to float a few inches out from the wall. A single leather and stainless-steel recliner sat directly in front of it. Four chairs surrounded the small table where Cooper imagined Ted took his meals, but there was no sign of anyone ever having cooked as much as a pop-tart in the kitchen. It was spotlessly clean. No stale bread slices spilling out of bags somebody had forgotten to do up. No bowls of fruit with the bananas going black. No unwashed coffee mugs in the sink.

With no obvious point of interest in this area of the apartment, Cooper moved through the kitchen and into a corridor that led to a series of rooms in the rear. He flicked on the lights as he went. He wasn't concerned about Ted coming home and finding him here. In fact, he very much wanted to talk with Ted Sorenson.

The first room on the left was a small laundry. A bathroom stood open on the other side.

The next room was obviously the main bedroom.

There was more evidence of human occupation here than he had seen anywhere else. The bed was made, but not to the military-grade standards of neatness out front. A cupboard door stood open. He could see a couple of suit jackets hanging inside. He searched the small bedside unit, finding and pocketing a couple of hundred dollars in cash, but there was nothing else of use or interest.

Cooper turned away from the bedroom to start his search in the room on the other side of the hallway. You might have expected it to be used as a child's bedroom, but Ted had turned it into an office. An iMac and a laser printer sat in the middle of a glass-topped desk.

The computer looked just like the one behind the pretty girl's desk at Ludgrove's office.

He pressed the space bar on the keyboard, and the screen came to life, but only to ask for a password. He didn't bother with the computer any further. There was no point. A filing cabinet offered a better chance of success. It was locked, but people were lazy, and they often fell into the habit of hiding the keys to such things nearby, usually somewhere convenient.

Cooper scanned the room. There was no stupidly obvious place to look, like a desk tray. But there were less obvious places that drew his eye. He pulled the filing cabinet out from the wall.

No keys stuck to the back.

He turned over the expensive office chair and examined all the hidden surfaces, especially under the lip of the seat where a man's hands would naturally fall.

Nothing.

Undeterred, he ran his hands over the legs of the glass-topped desk. He up-ended the empty wastebasket, inspected every inch of every book-shelf and admonished himself for not thinking of it earlier when he woke up the computer, the underside of the keyboard.

Still nothing.

He was looking at the room as an outsider, an intruder. He needed to see it from a different angle. He got down on his hands and knees and then lay on his back. He did not hurry. He allowed his eyes to roam over every surface that had been newly revealed to him by the change in perspective, methodically quartering the room and quartering it again.

After two minutes of silently scanning the makeshift office inch-by-inch, Cooper saw a glint of metal under the windowsill, a small silver key stuck into a knob of Blu-tac, hidden well out of sight. He stood up and retrieved the key. After a quick clean-off, it slid smoothly into the lock of the filing cabinet, which opened on the first turn.

The top drawer was full of personal files. Sorenson's tax records. Bank statements. Utility bills and such like. The lower drawer was empty. Cooper knew he could spend hours poring over Ted's personal papers and find nothing, but he had to start somewhere.

He pulled out a handful of documents. Ted's last five years' worth of tax returns, each year in a separate large white envelope. All of them thick with documentation. If nothing else, he thought, it might give him some idea about who was paying for everything.

Cooper was about to start at the beginning when something occurred to him. He slit open the packet that covered the period when he first arrived in Gainesville. Cooper sat down at the desk and removed the contents, taking care to keep them in order. An accountant had prepared Ted's return, which ran to nearly thirty pages. The bulk of the papers, however, were receipts and supporting documents.

He found what he was looking for in a smaller, buff-coloured enve-lope between a financial statement from Ted's 401K fund and a bundle of airline boarding passes.

One word was written on the envelope.

FOX.

Cooper's hands shook slightly, and he stopped dead, closing his eyes, doing his breathing exercise. Forcing himself to take a whole minute.

The first thing that spilled out of the envelope was his picture. It was Cooper, for sure, but different. He looked both younger and somehow older at the same time. Younger because the head and shoulders portrait had been taken some years ago. Older because in it, Cooper was dressed in a dark suit and tie and wore an even more sombre expression.

His hands were steady now as he leafed through the material inside.

He saw pictures of himself in military uniforms. He had been in the Navy, it seemed, and had left eight years ago. There were other pictures and documents that made little or no sense to him. He looked like a businessman in some. A scientist in a white coat in others. He seemed to have worked for many corporations and had credentials for all of them. There were a dozen or so articles copied from newspapers and printed off websites, but at a glance, he couldn't see any single thread connecting them. What linked a Russian energy company with a Hong Kong bank, a Brazilian beef exporter, or a Chinese movie studio?

Nothing except...him.

Twice, then three times, he saw images of somebody who could have been him, captured in the background of pictures in stories about a German automaker and a few pages on an Australian university announcing a breakthrough in solar film technology.

There was simply no way to synthesise all the information in the limited time he probably had left.

Cooper quickly laid out the contents of the file on the desk and photographed them with the camera on his phone. He returned all the hard copies to the filing cabinet, which he locked before setting the office back the way it had been when he broke in.

Across the hallway in Ted's bedroom, he searched the cupboards, looking for a heavy jacket he could wear against the cold. Most of the cupboard space was taken up by suits and shirts, but there was a good, insulated ski jacket in there. He opened a few drawers and tossed some of the contents, making his visit look like an opportunistic burglary.

Cooper tried on Ted's ski jacket. The fit was good enough, and there was a pocket inside where he could put a handgun. It wasn't ideal, but he'd be able to get to the weapon quicker than he would by digging it out of the backpack. He quickly scoped out the rest of the space, looking for anything that might hide a bigger stash of money. He found nothing.

Less than a minute later, he was gone.

———

"THAT RETARD MOTHERFUCKER just stole my good jacket," Ted Sorenson complained. "And my poker money."

"Yeah, and that retard made you look like a drooling fucking idiot, Ted. Priorities, buddy. And perspective."

Ted and Kristin leaned over a bank of monitors in a secure room less than five miles away. They made no move to go after the man they had been observing via the micro-cams installed throughout Ted's apartment.

"Jesus Christ, do you people intend to clean up your mess at all?"

The third voice belonged to another man.

Kristin Hegel stood up straight and turned away from the multi-screen display.

She smiled, and the second man's confidence appeared to desert him.

"We didn't lose him, Reese. Well, I didn't, and even Ted isn't to blame for this. He did y'all a favour even staying back at Ludgrove's. Our brief was to deliver the package. You guys fucked everything up after that. It's your goddamn mess we're cleaning up, and before I get the mop and bucket out, I need to know just how big a shit show this is gonna be."

18

Getting out of the complex was much easier than getting in. Cooper exited through a mag-locked gate next to the main driveway. He walked out of the cul-de-sac and back to the small retail strip he'd passed through an hour earlier. The foot traffic had thinned out, but most of the drinking and dining spots were busy with the early-evening dinner trade. He tried his luck at the Turkish pizza place and scored a table for two at the back of the restaurant, next to the restroom door. Cooper was okay with that. The restrooms led to an exit, and nobody else wanted to sit there. He could eat with his back to the wall and see anyone who might be coming at him.

He ordered half a Turkish bread and a couple of dips with a bottle of seltzer and a Turkish coffee. He had no conscious memory of ever drinking one, but the tiny porcelain cup in his hand and the pungent aroma of the thick, muddy coffee stirred something deep inside of him.

Cooper ate robotically, putting fuel into his body. Every minute or so, he would stop to scan the room. Between eating and checking the approaches to his table, he flicked through the photographs he had taken on his phone.

The man in the file was him. It was definitely him.

There were even photographs of their home back in Gainesville. From the angle of the shots, he calculated they'd been taken high up in a tree a little way back into the forest on the other side of the road. Cooper ground his teeth as he shuffled through images of Matty and Jess.

There were more familiar faces in the file. Coach Buchner, Doctor Schofield, and Sheriff Andy Briscoe. His temper flared when he saw Sheriff Andy's photograph, but it tapered off when he read the note attached to it. Somebody known only as "K" assessed Andy as a potentially hostile actor who should not be engaged. Deputies Ferrucci and Brown were also flagged as "negative", but Dan Ferrucci was "more easily manipulated", according to "K".

Cooper felt some relief at his rushed decision not to call the Sheriff's office to deal with Buchner and Schofield. This looked well beyond Andy Briscoe's pay grade.

He sat back and sipped at the coffee.

Well beyond the sheriff's pay grade.

That was not a phrase he would have spoken or probably even understood just a week ago. Cooper Fox had been something of a literalist. Nuance did not come quickly to somebody with an IQ of 66 on the Wechsler Adult Intelligence Scale, which was another morsel of personal data he'd extracted from Ted's file.

So much was coming back to him now, though. His ability to reason. His facility for language. A deep and mysterious well of arcane skills and cognitive faculties but...no memories on which to base them.

A waitress approached with a smile to ask if he needed anything. He ordered another coffee to have the use of the table for another ten minutes. There was so much to take in, and he needed to dial in hard on any material that would help him move forward.

Cooper flicked back to the start of the file and resolved to read more deeply into the documents, looking for some angle of approach.

His name, he quickly determined, was not Cooper Fox.

It was hard to know what his real name might be. Before arriving in Gainesville, he appeared to have taken on and shed identities the same way he'd grabbed Ted's ski jacket from the cupboard and shrugged it off when he entered the pizza place. Flicking through photocopies of various documents – driver's licences, corporate ID cards, even a couple of passports – he found eight different names by which he had been known at various times.

His second coffee arrived, and he thanked the young woman, laying the phone down so the screen was hidden. When she left, Cooper flicked back to an earlier image, looking for the extract from his naval records. Surely, the government would have his legitimate ID.

But it was just another name he didn't recognise.

Jarrod Lovell. Chief Petty Officer, U.S. Navy.

It meant nothing to him. He was Cooper Fox. He helped out with the Gainesville Tigers. He loved Mary Doyle. He was not a US Navy officer. A German finance writer. An Australian mining engineer. A Microsoft security consultant. Or a forensic accountant with HSBC.

He was just...Cooper.

And Cooper was beginning to despair as he searched the inch-thick pile of paper for some hook on which he could hang even a basic understanding of what the hell was going on.

He finally found it just as he was about to give up and return to Hampstead Mews to sit on Ted Sorensen's apartment. With a gun to the back of his head, maybe Ted could find the motivation to help Cooper understand.

He was waiting on his check, shuffling through more photographs. One was an apartment with an address in DC. His home address, according to a sticky note.

"Here you go," the waitress said. "Cashier is on your left as you go out. Thank you for dining at Massoud's."

"Thanks," Cooper said absently. "Your tip's here."

He tapped at a five-dollar note held down by the saltshaker.

"Ah, thank you," the young woman said. The uncertainty in her voice made him look up.

He quickly sketched a defensive smile onto his face.

"Sorry," Cooper said, shaking his head. "That's rude of me. I'm a thousand miles away. Heavy day at work, and it's not over." He put the phone away. "I used to work in a bar," he explained. "And sometimes, you know, the staff didn't always get the tip. So, I always leave it separate for the server to pick up."

Another lie. As far as he knew, he'd never worked as a waiter. But the deception came easily, naturally, which was another thing that was changing.

"Oh, that's okay," the woman smiled, understanding. "They're really good here. Massoud's a good boss."

"Well, his food is great," Cooper said. "I'm sure I'll be back."

She grinned and gave her head a little cartoon shake.

"Nothing stopping you. In fact..."

The young woman looked back over her shoulder, saw she was clear and wrote something quickly on her order pad. She tore off the piece of paper and passed it to him.

"If you want to come back about ten-thirty. That's when I get off. I usually go for a drink next door at Marty's."

She winked and spun away.

Cooper stared at her for a full second, his mind blanking.

Why would he...

And then he realised and started to blush. He grabbed his gym bag from under the chair, stood up and shuffled through the other tables toward the cashier, trying very hard not to catch the eye of the attractive young woman who had just given him her phone number.

But that was only part of the reason he was blushing.

Mostly, it was because he realised that he had set up that whole encounter without even thinking about it. He'd laid the five dollars out as bait, and she had taken it.

What on earth would Mary say?

THE WAITRESS DID catch him on the way out, but he just smiled noncommittally and hurried onto the street. That had never happened to him before, or at least not that he could remember. Getting together with Mary had been a long, slow courtship that he had not even realised was happening until it was done. Chances were, he thought, looking back on their unusual, unexpected relationship, she hadn't either. They'd met at Doctor Schofield's and became friends. And then more than friends.

He burrowed deeper into the stolen ski jacket, feeling the weight of Sorenson's handgun in the breast pocket as he put his head down and double-timed it to a cab rank at the other end of the block. The apartment, his old apartment, was in a building called *Tor Millino* – just a short ride away. He could afford to drop ten or fifteen bucks of Ted's money on a cab, but that was not what was exercising him at that moment.

His mind was hundreds of miles away, with Mary and the kids.

He had always thought of Mary Doyle as having a beautiful soul. And she was beautiful with it. At least as far as Cooper Fox was concerned. Until recently, that was a simple belief, strongly held. But Mary was also...

He struggled with the truth of it.

She was not...

He stopped in the middle of the street, almost causing a pileup as a couple of pedestrians had to divert around him quickly.

"Jesus pal, watch where you're going, would you?"

Cooper ignored them. He had been so worried about how Mary would react to the profound changes he was undergoing that he hadn't stopped to think about how those changes might affect his thoughts and feelings about her. She had been his rock for so long. But there was no getting around it. They were very, very different people. And increasingly so. Emotionally, psychologically...intellectually.

He felt his cheeks burning with shame in the cold night air.

What the hell did it matter if she had not finished school? What did it matter if her favourite TV show was the stupid housewives of some place or other? It hadn't mattered to Mary when she was immeasurably smarter and more capable than him. She said she had liked him and fallen in love with him because of his kindness, his honesty, and his gentle nature.

Cooper started walking again.

What they had, that was surely a two-way street? No way was he the kind of guy who would walk out on a girl because he suddenly thought he was...what? Better than her? Smarter than her?

Jesus fucking Christ. He felt disgusted with himself for even thinking it. He was *not* that guy. He was her guy, and she was the only love he had ever known. Cooper reached the taxi rank, took the first cab, and gave the driver the address. Then he fell quiet. The driver took his cue from the self-absorbed, all-but-silent passenger in the back seat and said nothing after acknowledging the drop-off address. He turned up the radio. Some country and western station.

Cooper used the short trip to examine his feelings rather than to interrogate himself any further about what he *thought* might happen between Mary and him. When he put aside everything but how he felt, he found that nothing had changed. She had saved him. He loved her.

But...

But did that mean he would have no choice but to walk away from her?

He understood very little about his life before Gainesville, but nothing he had learned so far gave him any confidence that he would be suitable for Mary or her children. He might have been some criminal or spy.

It might well be that the only human connections he was good for were quick, anonymous hook-ups with…

What? Random waitresses?

"Hey, buddy? This the place you wanted?"

The cab slowed to a halt outside a modern-looking residential tower.

Cooper shook himself out of his fugue state, looking out of the rain-flecked window at the upper levels. It was a striking piece of architecture, like a stack of books piled haphazardly one atop the next, each floor a new volume, and noticeably out of alignment with those above and below.

"I guess," he said.

The singular design did not ring any bells or alarms.

But it was the correct address. Ted Sorenson's file said so.

Cooper paid the fare and got out, the rapidly dropping temperature knifing into him.

19

He could not stand out in the street, scoping the place, for long. It was too cold, even with Ted's jacket. Cooper noted that most of the apartments seemed to be occupied, the lights on and occasionally people moving into view. His eyes dropped to the entry hall. He saw a doorman behind a desk in the foyer.

This place was a step up from Ted's apartment.

Not really knowing what he was doing, he started towards the entrance. A couple appeared from an elevator just as he walked in through the automatic doors. They waved to the concierge, who told them to take care in the cold. Cooper had time to take in the following details about the doorman. He was white, maybe in his late fifties or early sixties. He wore a clean but inexpensive suit and a name tag that identified him as Brian.

Brian waved the two residents out into the night and welcomed Cooper with a neutral smile that faltered and collapsed into a wide-eyed stare, a series of blinks, and finally, into open-mouthed surprise.

"Hi, Brian," Cooper said, unsure of where this might be going. But it seemed evident that he had been made.

"Mr Marston, Sir," Brian said, still shaking his head. "I just...I can't believe it's you, sir. It's been, what, three or four years now?"

Marston, Cooper told himself. My name is Marston, at least to this man.

"I got held up," he smiled, trying out a slight shrug that hinted at all manner of adventures he couldn't go into.

"Okay? You're back for a while, then? It's just, I hadn't been expecting you and...the building management they...they didn't want me wasting money keeping, you know, supplies and stuff in the fridge and...I mean, you're all paid up and everything, no problems there, but..."

Cooper broadened his smile and held up his hands as if in surrender to the situation.

"Brian, really not your problem, man. It's not like I gave you any warning. Fact is I ran into some trouble in Hong Kong. You know, with the Chinese taking over and stuff."

Another lie, one that came just as quickly as before. Maybe even easier. And the hell of it was, he knew not to embellish the story. Just throw the seed of an idea out there and let Brian tend to it himself.

"I saw that on the news, Mr Marston. Not you, of course. Nobody had any idea what happened to you. But I saw that they've been grabbing people up over there."

Cooper Fox nodded.

"Yeah, for a while now," he said. "But I'm home. Or at least, I'm almost home."

He let a small measure of discomfort and strain reshape his expression. "The thing is, I don't have any way of getting into my place. The Chinese, you know they, took everything."

He hoisted the gym bag he was carrying with the small arsenal of weapons.

"I picked up some clothes at Old Navy, and I've been living on snack bars and tap water since I flew in this morning. Got my first decent meal at Massoud's, you know, the Turkish pizza place."

Brian nodded enthusiastically. He patted his tummy.

"I love the cheese and sausage one they do," he said. "But it doesn't love me."

"I'd have saved you a slice, Brian, but I ate the lot," Cooper grinned ruefully. "Chinese prison rations, you know. They're not the best. So, do you have a spare key, or could you let me in?"

The doorman gave him a half-quizzical look and seemed about to ask him a question before answering it himself.

"Oh, that's right, we changed those locks just before you left. You don't remember, do you? Not that I can blame you, I guess, whatever you've been through. You won't need a key, sir. Your apartment still has the Touch ID lock. A couple of people have switched to face recognition," Brian said, leaning forward as if to impart a great secret, "And Mr Leibovitz is even thinking of getting a DNA reader for his place, but you didn't hear that from me."

Cooper didn't need to fake the look of relief.

"Yeah, sorry, I forgot. I've been a little...tied up. Literally."

"Oh, wait," Brian said, obviously remembering something. "You won't have your fob for the elevator. I can get you another one made up. It won't take more than a few minutes, but if you want to get home right now, I'll swipe you up, and you can just let yourself in."

Cooper nodded.

"I would really like that. Thank you, Brian," he said.

The doorman came out from behind the desk and led him over to the elevators. He tried to take the gym bag, but Cooper held it away.

"No, this thing is gross, Brian. It's been travelling with me since Shenzhen. I'm gonna empty out my laundry and throw it away."

Brian opened the elevator door for him and used a magnetic card to swipe Cooper up to his apartment. A sub-penthouse unit.

"I'll get all of your groceries sent up tonight," he said.

But Cooper shook his head.

"No need for that, Brian," he said. "I can sort that out tomorrow. It will be nice to do a few normal things for myself, but thank you. I appreciate it."

"It's good to have you back, sir. I'm really sorry about whatever happened over there."

Cooper waved it away.

"I'm back, that's what matters."

The doors almost slid shut. Cooper stuck his hand out to hold them open.

"Hey, Brian," he said.

"Yes, sir?"

"Have I had any visitors lately? Anyone looking for me?"

"No sir," Brian answered. "Are you worried about the Chinese?"

Cooper nodded solemnly.

"It's silly, I know, but yeah. If anyone does call in for me, could you give me a heads-up?"

"You got it, Mister Marston. I won't let anyone up without your say-so."

"Thanks, Brian."

Brian saluted him with two fingers, and Cooper returned the gesture with a wave. He let the doors slide shut.

The elevator ride was smooth and fast. He rode up eighteen floors in less than half a minute. A soft chime announced his arrival at the sub-penthouse level, and he stepped out into a small foyer with two doors. He moved to the double-wide, dark wood doors to his left. A well-used doormat lay in front of the entrance to the other penthouse.

Cooper walked over and placed his thumb on the small, dark, rectangular pane of glass to the side of the door. A green light appeared, and the door clicked open. He was a little surprised, but he supposed nobody had thought to alter his fingerprints.

Lights came on inside the apartment as he closed the door behind him. It was stunning. A vast open space with views right across the capital. This had been his home, presumably. Every part of it, every square inch, would hold clues to his past and, most likely, to whatever lay in his future. Cooper set the bag down on the floor by the entrance. This would be more challenging than tossing Sorenson's place.

The central part of the penthouse did not have rooms, as such, it was more like zones. There was an obvious living room or lounging zone centred around a huge black and white rug, a series of objects that might have been coffee tables or possibly pieces of industrial art, and at least three expensive-looking couches. None of them matched, but they all seemed to complement each other. Another zone appeared to be something like an open-plan library. There were bookshelves and a long dark-wood writing table of modernist design. The kitchen and dining area occupied one of the far corners of the sprawling floor plan. And a doorway between the massive, commercial-grade refrigerator and a whole wall of double-door ovens and range tops promised access to more private areas.

Following his lead from the search of Ted Sorensen's apartment, Cooper checked out the bedrooms first. But they were simply bedrooms. Whatever he had done in his previous life to lead him to a place like this, he had not thought it necessary to make do with a home office crammed into a second bedroom.

The refrigerator was on; he could hear it humming, and now and then, ice cubes would rattle into a hopper in the freezer. He supposed he was paying somebody to come and empty them occasionally. Or, more likely, he was paying the management company via regularly scheduled direct deposits from an offshore account, and they were paying someone like Brian to come in and maintain the property. If that was so, it meant he almost certainly had access to significant liquid funds. He needed to find them.

But first, he had to search this place, and he had to be quick. He couldn't stay here. They would eventually look for him.

Somewhere inside his head, another small switch clicked.

He could use the waitress, he thought. Pick her up. Stay with her.

It was a simple fact. No frisson of sexual excitement came with it. She was an asset he had acquired and could exploit as needed. It was why he'd developed her.

"Shut the fuck up," he hissed at himself.

He was not going to be doing that or anything like it. He would find accommodation somewhere. In a homeless shelter if he had to.

Cooper searched the library first. There was a safe with a keypad lock, but without knowing the combination, it wasn't much use to him. A filing cabinet built into a wall unit, however, opened at a light press of his fingertips. It was not locked. Probably because there was nothing in it. He searched all the drawers and pulled a random selection of books from the shelf, flicking through them for hidden papers.

Nothing.

It was frustrating as hell. He had lived here. This had been his home, and it should contain everything he needed to piece together the mystery of his life before Gainesville. But even the books in his library were a seemingly random selection of titles and categories. He had one shelf devoted to American political biographies and another to fantasy and science fiction novels. He owned a complete collection of Neil Gaiman's Sandman series and a library within a library that seemed to be composed of the required reading for a couple of MBA degrees. There were travel books, restored editions of Gibbon's *Decline and Fall of the Roman Empire*, and even one shelf devoted to audiobooks recorded on CD. He frowned at that. They were all in foreign languages.

Cooper took down one of the audiobooks. It had been recorded in Italian, and to his shock, he found that he could read the text on the CD case.

He could speak Italian.

He quickly scanned the selection and pulled out another.

He could speak German.

And Russian.

And French.

And...

He stopped, a thought tugging at his mind like a fishhook. Returning to the safe, he took a knee and steadied his breathing. If all those languages had been there all along, thousands and thousands of words...

Then maybe something as simple as a muscle memory could be stored just below the surface of his consciousness, too.

Cooper Fox closed his eyes and emptied himself of clamouring thought and gnawing doubt. He breathed slowly to calm his excitement. After a while, his heart rate dropped below fifty beats per minute. He did not focus his attention so much as set it free. His mind went out into the world, and as far as it was possible, the hand he raised to lay his fingertips upon the keypad of the safe moved without conscious effort.

He breathed in, he breathed out, and he let his fingers do the walking.

He wasn't even sure what number he keyed in. Just that it was six digits. The safe clicked open. He sat back, staring at it, not really believing what he had just done. But it wasn't magic, any more than what he had done to the three men who attacked him in Gainesville was magic. It was just muscle memory, or neural pathways, or something. He was sure there would be a word for it.

Force of habit, maybe.

Cooper shook his head, dismissing the speculation as a waste of time. He pulled the door of the safe all the way open. It wasn't a large unit. Not much bigger than a bread box, to borrow an old saying. But inside was a whole world. He pulled out the contents, spreading them on the polished wooden floor where he sat. Another handgun and two clips of ammunition. Six passports, only two of them American. Five driver's licences from four different states. Why two from California? No idea, but he took the most recent one, which identified him as Tom Hackmore, and slipped it into his back pocket. There were bundles of currency and a small stack of plastic debit cards. He gathered the cash and the cards and put them into his gym bag. He returned the handgun, a Sig Sauer, and ammunition to the safe along with all the foreign currency. The greenbacks and the plastic he put into a zip-up pocket of his ski jacket. The final item from the safe, he sat staring at for many minutes. Long enough that he lost track of time.

A girl, African American, somewhere in her early teens, smiled out of the image at him. She wore braces. He didn't recognise her but...he wanted to. That was what he felt most at first. He really wanted to know who she was or to remember her. The photograph stirred powerful, contrary feelings inside of him. Grief, confusion, anger, and none of it explicable. It was as though she was simply a talisman for unlocking wild, unruly emotions he could not tie to any memories.

Cooper Fox folded the image away and put it safely into his back pocket. He was sitting on the floor of the luxury apartment, his legs splayed out in front of him, his hands shaking, and tears in his eyes when they came for him.

"Hello, Michael."

He jumped at the voice. A woman.

She was holding a gun on him. So was the man who had come in with her. Ted Sorensen.

"Hello, Kristin," Cooper said.

He didn't wonder why Brian hadn't warned him.

He should have warned Brian.

Kristin pulled the trigger.

He heard a thump, and something stung his neck.

Darkness swallowed him whole.

20

Consciousness came first. A thin crack in the blackout which had enveloped him when Kristin shot him. Awareness followed, mute and insensible, but awareness of a sort. He was sitting, manacled to a steel chair. His hands were cuffed behind his back, his ankles duct-taped to the front legs of the chair, which was in the centre of the small room, painted white. Understanding was less immediate.

Cooper groaned and lifted his head. He grunted even louder at the sudden pain in his neck and shoulders. He blinked a couple of times and almost toppled over when he realised his eyeballs were tracking independently of each other. He was cross-eyed. He swore softly. Closed his eyes.

When he opened them again, he still saw double, but not as badly. And there wasn't much to see anyway. The room was small. The walls were made of cinderblocks painted white but dulled by age. There was no other furniture in the room. No people, either. He carefully turned his head from left to right, wary of the stiffness in his neck. He saw no windows, no one-way mirrors, no doors.

The door must be behind him.

As if to confirm this, he heard a latch. A slight creaking noise and the faintest breeze on the back of his neck. A door opening. A woman's heels clicked on the concrete floor.

"Hello, lover," she said.

Kristin.

Cooper caught her in his peripheral vision half a second before he heard the duller footfall of a man in business shoes coming in behind her. Probably Ted, he thought.

But no.

It was Reese Needham, Coach Buchner's lawyer friend. Except that Cooper now understood that Needham was neither Buchner's friend nor his lawyer. He was some sort of co-conspirator. A fixer.

They came around in front of him. His eyes were still moving weirdly, causing his head to wobble and the two newcomers to float in his vision like balloons.

"Dizzy, huh?" Kristin said. "Don't worry, hon, it'll pass in a minute or two. They tell me this new formula they got is a hell of a lot better than the old one. That shit woulda put a feral hog down for a whole day."

"Who are you?" Cooper asked. "What am I doing here? What have I ever done to you people?"

Kristin smiled like a wolf contemplating a newly hatched chick.

"Oh, baby," she said. "What haven't you done to me?"

Needham rolled his eyes.

"Ms Hegel, please," he said. "If we could just get *this* done?"

Kristin Hegel put one hand up to the side of her mouth, play-acting at shielding her words. She pointed at Needham with her other hand and mouthed, *"No fun at all."*

Needham snapped his fingers, and two men dressed in black coveralls entered the room. One of them took hold of Cooper's chair and dragged him back a couple of feet, the metal legs scraping loudly on the floor. The other man carried a couple of fold-up chairs under his arms. He unfolded them in front of Cooper but at some distance.

They clearly thought he was dangerous.

Needham took a seat, placed a briefcase on his lap, and snapped open the locks. He took out a sheaf of papers, closed the briefcase, and laid the papers on top. He looked over at Kristin as though expecting her to sit with him, but she leaned against the wall and smiled at Cooper, looking like she had a secret she was dying to share with him.

"It is a pity we have to meet under these circumstances, Mr Garner," the lawyer said. "Until now, your case has been proceeding without issue."

Needham looked up from his notes and shook his head at Cooper as if deeply disappointed in him.

"What?" Cooper said. "And what d'you mean, Garner? Is that my name? My real name, Reese? Seriously, what the fuck is going on here?"

"Mikey, why so grouchy?" Kristin teased. "Do y'all need another nap? I could tranq' you again. That was fun. Not the most fun we ever had, but still, a girl's gotta take what she can."

She smiled at him again, that same carnivorous grin.

"Garner!" he shouted. "Is my name Michael Garner? My real name?"

He couldn't keep the desperation from his voice. His eyes were slowly coming back into alignment, but the room was still spinning around him. He was unbalanced. Disoriented. And even though he understood that they wanted him that way, it still stopped him from finding his feet. Mentally. Emotionally.

Needham did not answer him directly.

"What do you think your name is?" he said as he clicked an expensive-looking pen and held it over a notepad.

"Cooper. My name is Cooper Fox."

He knew it wasn't. And yet he felt that it was. The only thing he had to hold onto was the certainty that he was who he *felt* himself to be. Cooper Fox of Gainesville, Virginia.

"Interesting," Needham said, making a note. "You know that's not true. Your name, your actual name, is Michael Garner. Do you remember that, Michael?"

Cooper shook his head. His neck was still sore, and he winced.

Kristin disappeared behind him, making him nervous. He turned around as far as he could, looking for her, but she reappeared on his other side, kissing him on the neck where she had shot him.

He flinched away from her hot mouth.

"Don't want to come too soon, huh?" she whispered. "That's okay. A girl can wait."

She moved behind Needham again.

"We retrieved the data from Doctor Ludgrove's final scan," said Reese. "We know that you are no longer medicated. But we understand your recovery will likely proceed in fits and starts, at differential rates on various measures of cognitive and physical competence. That's what's important, Michael or Cooper, if you prefer, that you help us determine these measures."

Cooper stared at him.

"Are you fucking kidding me?"

Needham shook his head.

"Not at all," he said. "You would like to go back to Ms Doyle, would you not? You have become quite close, the two of you."

Kristin Hegel pushed out her lower lip in a burlesque display of hurt feelings. Cooper ignored her.

"Just leave her out of it," he said.

"I'm afraid that won't be possible, *Cooper*," Needham said. "She is as much a part of the trial now as you are. In fact, we may decide to retest the original nootropic serum on Ms Doyle. She would be an excellent candidate."

"What the fuck are you talking about?" Cooper said. "If you touch her, if you go near her, I will kill you."

Needham shook his head.

"That's very dramatic, but no, you won't. You shouldn't concern yourself unduly with her welfare, Cooper. I can assure you that from the results we've gathered so far, Ms Doyle would benefit greatly. You must surely want that for her and the little ones. Matthew and Jessica."

He said the names of the children like a threat.

Cooper turned away from the lawyer. He sought out Kristin Hegel with his eyes. They seemed to have a history. Perhaps he could use that?

"We were together?"

"Oh my," Kristin said, fanning herself as though in danger of swooning.

"Kristin, can you tell me what's going on?" Cooper asked.

"No," she said, not fucking around anymore. "You need to answer Reese's questions. *You* need to tell *us* what's going on."

"But I don't know," Cooper protested. "I don't know who you people are or what you're doing."

Reese Needham nodded, clicking his pen for emphasis.

"Exactly. So, can we get back to my first question? I need to know what you know. I need you to tell me what you remember."

Cooper stared at him and said nothing.

"Mister Garner," the lawyer said, reverting to his "real" name. "I can call an orderly in here and have you returned to the trial. One injection is all it will take. You will forget everything that has happened. You will revert to your previous clinical state. We don't know yet whether you will forget everything that happened during the trial period during your time in Gainesville. We have legitimate reasons for wanting to know that, of course. But nothing can move forward until we establish the new baseline."

He leaned forward and stared at Cooper. "What do you remember?"

Cooper closed his eyes. Shut them tightly. The sensation of the world spinning around him eased off a little.

He was going to have to give them something. He didn't want them injecting him with whatever drug he had been on for the past three years. He knew what it did to him. It would annihilate not just his intelligence and his memory but his entire personality. It would be like dying, but worse.

"I know how to speak German," he sighed, letting them feel both his exasperation and an inkling of surrender.

Needham's eyes went wide, and Hegel stepped away from where she had been leaning against the wall.

"Excellent," Reese said, clicking his pen and writing a note. "Any other languages?"

Cooper shook his head.

"*Nein, ich glaube nicht*," he said. "*Nur Deutsch.*"

Needham nodded, even allowing himself a smile.

"Good, that's very good. What about information? We know you have reacquired a number of deeply scripted skill sets, but we are less interested in pre-programmed physical capacities than in your cognitive performance. We need to know what you know and understand. Not just information, but meaning, if you get what I'm saying."

Cooper tried to look as if he was cooperating. As if he was struggling to recall some detail or scrap of memory.

If they had reason to think they could extract value from him, he judged that he would be safe.

"I can read, and I suppose I can do basic math, but otherwise I..."

Needham shook his head, creasing his brow.

"That's not what I mean," he said. He dug inside the briefcase again and brought out a single piece of paper.

"Let's try a different approach," he said. "Tell me if any of these words mean anything to you."

Cooper shrugged.

"Okay," he said.

"Night Dragon."

Kristin rolled her eyes. "Oh my fucking God."

Needham ignored her, and when Cooper shook his head, he said, "Tangent Blue?"

Cooper shook his head.

"Triple Helix? Chrome Sanction?"

"Nothing."

But that was a lie. The words Triple Helix had blared in brushed metal from the front desk at Ludgrove's offices. And Coach Buchner had said he didn't care how much money "those Helix assholes" spent on the drug Doctor Schofield had been giving Cooper. The words Triple Helix rang like a bell in Cooper's memory.

Needham went on, reading out a seemingly random series of unrelated words for the next minute. Cooper did not have to fake any lack of comprehension. None of them meant anything to him.

When the lawyer reached the end of his list, he folded up the piece of paper and returned it to the briefcase. He sat for a moment, thinking. Finally, he asked, "What is the first thing you remember about Gainesville?"

"That's easy," Cooper answered. "I was..."

He trailed off. He remembered meeting Mary at the doctor's, but he didn't want to give them that.

"It was... I think it was...maybe the school. I think I remember somebody taking me to the school and..."

He stopped again.

"It was you," he said, looking at Needham. "You took me to the school, and I met Coach Buchner."

The lawyer nodded and smiled.

"Yes, I did, that's right. I took you to Gainesville, and I handed you off to overwatch."

"To what?"

Cooper knew what that was, but it was weird to think of Coach Buchner as...what? His handler? His runner?

Another switch flipped inside his head, and the terminology came back.

Buchner was a guarantor. He would vouch for the reputation of SUBJECT FOX within the area of operations. And he would provide overwatch and security as needed.

Cooper blinked at the jargon from another life.

"Jesus," Cooper breathed. "You planted them both? Buchner *and* Schofield? What were they? Sleepers? Or...no..."

He caught his breath.

"I was the sleeper."

Kristin smiled.

"Close, but no. Y'all were just asleep, Mikey."

"My name is Cooper."

"Whatevs."

Reese Needham frowned at the interruption. He leaned forward like a teacher wanting to encourage a promising pupil.

"So, Cooper, your post-dosage recall is excellent. But this is important: what do you recall of your life before arriving in Gainesville?"

"The car crash, you mean? The accident that didn't happen? Because you faked it, I guess."

He looked at Kristin accusingly. She laughed.

"Baby, I've been faking it with you for years."

"Ms Hegel, please," Needham said. "We are very close. Cooper, concentrate. Do you remember anything before your arrival in Gainesville?"

Cooper really did try to search his memory. He felt...no, he *knew* that there was a whole undiscovered world somewhere inside him. A place where he had been born. The parents who had raised him. The path that had led him to this room. But although it was there, and he knew it was there, he could not make out even the merest hint of his past.

Was that what they wanted to hear, or would it result in the sting of a hypodermic needle and the complete erasure of everything he had regained?

"Cooper?" Needham asked.

"I'm trying," Cooper said.

"Try harder," Kristin put in from the other side of the room.

"I don't know what you want from me."

"We simply want the truth," the lawyer said. "We need the truth. What do you remember?"

An idea came to Needham, and he held up one finger. Searching in his briefcase, he produced a photograph.

Cooper recognised it immediately. It was the image of the young woman from his apartment. Or the apartment where an earlier version of him had lived.

"Do you know who this is?" Needham asked.

Again, Cooper was seized by the conviction that he should know, that she was important to him. But of course she was. Her photograph had been in his apartment. He could feel it folded over in his back pocket.

"I don't...I don't know," he admitted. "She's important, I know, but... not familiar. I don't recognise her, I'm sorry."

"Yeah, we're all fucking sorry," Kristin Hegel said flatly.

Cooper shook his head.

"I was in the Navy," he offered.

Reese Needham's expression told him that was the wrong answer.

"Don't tell me what you read in the file, Cooper. Look inside yourself and tell me what you see there. Tell me who the girl is to you."

Kristin Hegel pushed herself off the wall.

"Fuck's sake Reese, he's playing y'all. He's stringing you along. He knows once we get the information, we got no more use of him. At least not like this. He knows he's going back to the short bus."

Needham slammed both hands down on top of the briefcase with a sound like a gunshot in the small concrete box of a room.

"Is there any possibility, do you think, Kristin, that you could put aside your personal feelings and behave like a God damned grown-up about this."

"That's what I'm doing, sweetie, when I tell you this guy is playing y'all. If'n you want to find out what he really knows, y'all gonna have to dig in on his pain points. For reals."

"But I'm telling you the truth," Cooper pleaded.

Her smile was knowing and cruel.

"Yeah? We'll see about that."

Four long strides took her across the room. He heard rustling behind him before she reappeared with his gym bag. It was open. He could see that the weapons were gone. But that's not what she was after. Kristin Hegel reached into the bag and pulled out the burner phone he'd bought at the truck stop. Cooper felt his balls move, a protective response.

She worked the keypad until she had what she wanted.

"Gonna need me some help in here, boys," she called out.

The two men in black coveralls came back into the room.

"Gag him," she said.

"Yes, ma'am," one of them said. A tremendous meaty ham hock of an arm reached around Cooper's face and pulled his head back. He felt a knuckle dig into the nerve point behind his ear, and his mouth popped open involuntarily. They shoved a wadded-up cloth into his mouth, causing him to gag and choke. There was nothing he could do about it.

"Y'all best stay here, just in case," Kristin said.

"Yes, ma'am," one of them answered. Cooper couldn't tell which. They were both standing behind him.

"What are you doing?" Needham asked.

"My goddamn job," Kristin answered. She took a small black puck out of the breast pocket of her suit and plugged it into the charging port of the phone.

She made a call. There was only one place it could be going. There was only one number stored in the burner. Mary.

Kristin Hegel winked at Cooper.

The call connected, and she spoke in a bright, singsong voice with no trace of her cowgirl accent.

"Hi, this is Wanda at the front desk. We were just wondering whether or not you were going to be needing laundry service later today."

She listened to whatever Mary said on the other end of the call.

"Oh, sorry, didn't Mr Fox tell you? We have your number because it's the law. We can't let people check-in without a phone number. I think it's about terrorism or something. It's pretty dumb if you ask me. We don't get a lot of terrorists around these parts. But anyway, your laundry service, do you want fresh linen tomorrow?"

Cooper seethed, mostly at himself. He had exposed Mary and the kids to this woman by leaving that phone with her. He lunged forward, hoping to make such a loud noise when he crashed to the ground that it might alert Mary to something being wrong. She had to hang up that phone. Whatever that device was, hanging from the charging port of his cell phone, it was probably tracing her right now.

Two, then four, massive arms clamped around him and pulled him back.

Kristin Hegel blew him a kiss.

"That's all right then, honey; you just let us know if you need anything. We are here for you."

She cut the call, unhooked the device, and tossed it to one of the men standing behind Cooper's chair.

"Give that to Ted," she said. "Tell him to pull the location data."

Cooper strained against his manacles, the steel restraints biting deep into his flesh. He had never wanted anything more than he wanted to break free at that moment.

But he was trapped.

"Put him under," she said. "And gimme that second shot of Dexi."

He felt a sting in his neck.

Darkness fell as Kristin Hegel advanced on him with another syringe.

21

"There's my bad boy."

Cooper's head came up slowly. The world of real things came into focus even more slowly. But one thing was very real.

Kristin Hegel.

His one-time lover. His partner. His betrayer.

She stood in front of him in her sharply cut black suit, Italian leather ankle boots planted shoulder-width apart, her arms folded, an easy, confident smile on her face. She wasn't alone in the small, white room. He could sense the presence of others behind him. Just guards, he guessed. Kristin was the only one who mattered in here.

He remembered her.

He remembered everything.

The war. The years after. The one-eyed Englishman from his waking nightmares.

"You what, mate?"

Cooper remembered that his name, his real name, *was* Lovell. Not Fox or Garner or any of a dozen other names he had taken on and off over the years. She had lied about that, too. Casually, pointlessly. Why? Because she could. He remembered that now, as well. Casual cruelty and deception were just things Kristin did. It's what he had done with her for many years.

As Jarrod Lovell he had joined the Navy straight out of high school. Passed SEAL selection a year later and served with honour for six years.

But he had been changed by doing terrible things in even worse places.

In the years that followed, he'd sold his skills to the highest bidder, and he'd acquired even more skills. He sold them, too. Most often to a man called Rolly.

Or Sir Roland.

He remembered stealing three years' worth of research into Professor Lianzhou Wang's quantum dots, tiny nanoparticles which could power super-efficient solar skins that would one day cover whole buildings, whole cities.

He remembered sabotaging a BMW plant, setting back the automaker's autonomous car plans by a decade.

He remembered cleaning up a drug trial gone badly wrong. He remembered nine dead test subjects.

"I killed them," he croaked, looking up at Kristin.

She chuckled, a low throaty sound.

"Oh sweetie, y'all gonna have to be more specific than that. You done killed a whole heap of motherfuckers in your glory-ass days."

"The other subjects in my cohort. They weren't just random test subjects. They were... they were like family. And I killed them. You and Rolly, you made me kill them."

Cooper tried to launch himself out of the chair to get to her. He crashed to the ground, hitting the side of his head on the cold concrete floor. Stars flooded his vision. He heard scuffling footsteps and felt himself hauled upright. The two goons from before. Tears filled his eyes, and his head swam with the impact.

"You. You did this to me," he hissed at Kristin.

"Such a disappointingly typical thing for a man to say. Always blaming somebody else. Y'all did this to yourself, Mikey."

"My name isn't Mike."

"And it ain't Cooper neither," she said. "But you'll always be Mikey to me."

He shook his head, ignoring the pain. He swore and struggled against his restraints again.

Kristin nodded to somebody standing behind him.

He heard an electric crackle, and an instant later, his entire body spasmed.

A Taser.

Cooper cried out in shock, but they hadn't zapped him hard. It was just enough to subdue him.

"Y'all remember what happened now, Sweetie?" Kristin asked.

Sweat ran into his eyes, mixing with the tears. Blinding him. He saw Kristin approaching as a blurry, indistinct spectre. A dark ghost floating up to him against the background of the whitewashed cinderblocks. She loomed over him, filling all he could see as she leaned in and kissed him. One long kiss on each eyelid.

"Mmm," she whispered. "Salty."

Cooper did not struggle or resist. He didn't even move. With Kristin, he understood there would be no point.

She stepped away, and he stared at her, saying nothing. He could see her clearly now. She stared back, supremely unconcerned. And why would she be concerned? He was the one chained up in a concrete box with a couple of goons lurking somewhere behind him, wielding a cattle prod.

"How did you do it?" Cooper said at last.

"How did you end up the biggest retard in Feebsville?" Kristin retorted cheerily. "Quite an achievement, given the shallow gene pool down there, let me tell ya. If y'all have recovered your taste for irony, you will surely love the narrative elegance."

"It was Rolly, wasn't it," Cooper said. A statement, not a question.

She snorted, "It's always Rolly. Always was, always will be. Whatever and ever, amen."

The one-eyed man loomed over Cooper in his memory. Grinning.

"You what, mate?"

He heard footsteps. Two sets of them. Not the dull clomp of the guards' heavy boots.

Kristin nodded to somebody behind him.

Reese returned from wherever he had been, this time with Ted Sorensen.

"Our little boy Mikey is back," Kristin told them. "The second shot was the charm. Just needed the chaser to loosen him up, was all."

The two men appeared in Cooper's peripheral vision before moving past him to stand with Kristin. Reese carried the same briefcase. Ted Sorenson made do with an air of grievance.

"Welcome back, asshole," he said. "You're gonna pay for the stuff you stole from my place."

"You're going to pay for the three years you stole from my life," Cooper said in a flat voice.

"He remembers Rolly," Kristin said, cutting across the exchange.

"Mr Garner," Reese Needham said, sounding pleased, "it appears you are recovering your faculties, which is excellent news. Sir Roland will be pleased. He's been asking about you. But it's late, and we're still putting together a team to pick up Doctor Ludgrove's work. This has all been.... very disruptive. I have instructions to collect as much information from you as I can before they get here. So, if you don't mind?" he said, turning to Ted and Kristin.

Needham sat down and opened his briefcase again, taking out a leather binder and opening it.

"Now, Michael," he said, "I'd like to start with what you remember of Munich and Tangent Blue. The BMW operation."

"My name isn't Garner," Cooper said, clearly and slowly enunciating each word. "It used to be Lovell. But not anymore. You took that from me. You took everything."

Needham threw a worried glance at Kristin Hegel, who shrugged and rolled her eyes.

"I said that second jab of Dexi shook a few things loose. I didn't say he was a hunnert per cent. But y'all should be good to go, Reese. If'n he is of a mind to cooperate."

"How about I push a couple of roofing nails through his dick," Ted suggested. "Might put him *in more of a mind to cooperate*," he said, gently mocking Kristin's accent.

"Nobody touches the dick," she smirked. "The dick belongs to me."

Cooper was only half listening to the exchange. Most of him was somewhere else, a long time ago, and far, far away. He was crashing in his drug-addled delirium. Free-falling into memory and deep body shock and moral horror as everything he had done rushed back at him while he slumped, chained to a metal chair in a cinderblock prison cell.

Nine people, nine human beings, confused but trusting, looking to him, looking *at* him from the darkness of the past, imploring him to spare them.

Nine victims, all of them uncomprehending. Because he was supposed to be their protector, not their executioner.

A one-eyed man, standing over them, staring at him.

'You what, mate?'

"I'm not giving you a damn thing," Cooper said quietly.

They argued among themselves until he spoke up again, louder.

"Hey," he shouted. Reese flinched a little.

Ted and Kristin turned toward him.

"I said you can stick it up your ass. I told Rolly I was done with this. I'm not helping you."

Sorensen snorted with laughter. Reese frowned. Kristin raised one eyebrow.

"Feeble tactical reasoning there, Mikey. Which is at least an interesting data point, I suppose. Y'all are reacting emotionally. Getting all rueful and feely. Again. You are really not thinking this through, are you?"

She left the question hanging there long enough that he began to see the mistake he had made. Before he could say anything else, she took a phone out of her suit jacket. Her fingers danced on the screen.

Cooper already knew what she was doing.

She was right. He *had* made a grave tactical error. He saw how grave when Kristin turned the screen towards him. Three faces suddenly came alive. Mary, Matthew, and Jessica.

They all cried out his name.

"Jesus Christ," he muttered.

It was a live stream, not a recording. They were being held somewhere. Unrestrained but guarded by men with batons, cuffs, and guns. He heard Mary crying, asking what was happening. The two children called out his name repeatedly, begging him to come and get them.

Kristin Hegel cut the connection.

"You know, in the olden days, I'd a had one of them shot, just to add a little pepper to this situation we got here. Y'all taught me that, Mikey. Probably woulda been the girl, I reckon. You remember how the only way to get the Hajis to give it up was to threaten their women, especially the daughters? Yeah, you taught me that too. But I don't think we need to be quite so cinematic. Just answer Reese's questions, spend a couple of days debriefing the researchers we bring in tomorrow, and y'all can go on back to them."

Cooper started to say something, but she held up her hand like a traffic cop.

"And before y'all cut up rough. I ain't lying about that. We're not gonna kill y'all and drop your ass down a mineshaft or nothin'. Not like those mouth-breathers probably caused all this trouble, opening that can of whoop-ass upside your head back in Feebsville. Y'all are too important for that, or so they tell me. So you *will* be taking your medicine and going back on the program, little man. Honestly, if it was up to me, I'd just kill the damn lotta ya and throw y'all in the furnace. But who listens to a woman, right?"

22

He agreed to cooperate. What else could he do? They left him handcuffed and taped to the chair. What else could *they* do? He begged them to release him.

"Come on, Kristin, you don't have to undo the cuffs," he said. "Just let me lie down when you go. Whatever that sedative was, it's crushing me. I need to sleep."

She laughed out loud.

"Try harder, Mikey. No. I'm afraid you're staying in the chair until they're done with you. These boys..." She looked at whoever was standing behind him. "...they got no earthly idea of the shenanigans of which you are capable. You mind my words, fellas," she said to the guards, "do not listen to a word this man says. And do not let him out of the chair. If he soils himself, we can turn the hoses on him tomorrow. But you do not come in here without me or Ted. Understood?"

Somebody standing behind Cooper said, "Yes, ma'am."

"Good to hear," Kristin said. "We'll be back in the morning with the guys in the white coats. Don't make me bring a butterfly net to catch Mikey here all over again."

She ran her fingers through his hair as she walked past him and bent down to kiss the top of his ear. He felt himself stirring in spite of his disgust. She bit the top of his ear, hard, and he yelped in pain.

"Oh baby," she purred. "You've changed. You used to like it rough."

Kristin left with Ted trailing behind her, fixing Cooper with a hostile glare. Ted mouthed, "You owe me".

He heard the other guys, the muscle in the black coveralls, shuffling out after them. The door closed behind them, but the lights stayed on.

He closed his eyes and let go of a breath. He was not without hope. He was pretty sure the video Kristin had streamed of Mary and the kids had been shot in this very building. The off-white cinderblock walls behind them were identical to the walls of his makeshift cell. The foldout chairs in which they sat? The same make as the camp chairs Kristin's goons had brought in. And she had said if it was up to her, she would just shoot them and throw them all into "the furnace". It was an oddly specific thing to say. But it would make sense if there really was a furnace. If, for example, they were in the basement rooms of the facility where Ludgrove had put him into the scanner. A medical laboratory is a modern facility that wouldn't need an old-fashioned furnace for heating during winter but would have a need to dispose of biomedical waste discreetly and safely.

Cooper kept his eyes closed and tested the handcuffs behind his back. They were good heavy steel cuffs, not cinched so tight as to pinch the flesh at his wrists but offering no chance of escape. He adjusted his posture, sinking a little lower into the seat, feeling for the chain links with the tips of his fingers. It wasn't easy, but he gradually determined that his captors had looped a length of steel chain around and through the rear struts of the chair. Both of his arms would be asleep by morning unless he concentrated on exercising them with small plyometric movements.

The duct tape securing his ankles to the front of the chair was more promising. He tested the bonds. They were strong and tightly made, but unlike the steel chaining his arms to the seat rest, the tape was at least minimally pliable. It would take hours to loosen it up, but he had the whole night in front of him.

They would be watching. That was fine. He'd been held captive before and was used to working under hostile observation. He made an apparent show of stretching his neck and back and then his arms and legs to stave off numbness and cramps. But while he worked at that, he also strained quietly against the tape, fastening his legs to the chair.

He didn't need to free himself. He just needed to loosen his bonds, and he didn't need all night for that. Just a few hours of concentrated effort.

———

IT WAS impossible to say what time he was done working on the tape, but he estimated that by two or three in the morning, he had degraded the binding sufficiently. He guessed that was the time, given how awful he felt. But perhaps all the chemicals floating around in his bloodstream were messing with his judgement, and it wasn't even after midnight yet. Whatever, he rested.

Closing his eyes, lowering his head as far forward as it would go, he did not try to fall asleep. Perhaps he would sleep, perhaps not. But he would rest after a fashion.

He slept. He may have even snored. But he did not fall into a deep slumber.

Some unknown time later, he heard footsteps and movement somewhere behind him. Not in the room, but nearby. It was time. Cooper Fox brought himself fully awake over the next five minutes. His arms had fallen asleep, and he repeated the muscle tensing and relaxing micromovements of his previous night's exercise. When he was as sure as he could be that he wasn't about to cramp up, he started to spasm.

It was a pretence based on an assumption. Or two of them, really. The pretence was that he was having some kind of fit. He shuddered and jerked with increasing violence inside his restraints. He bit the inside of his cheek hard enough to draw blood, which he spat and drooled on himself. The assumption he made was that somebody was watching and that they gave a shit. If Ted or Kristin was on duty, he was probably fucked. But if one of the goons saw him fitting out and crashing to the floor, as he did just then, they might, just might, rush in to...

As Cooper grunted and twitched, convulsing within his restraints, the door to his cell flew open. A single guard, a man in black tactical coveralls, came rushing in, holding a riot baton.

"What the fuck?"

Deep in his pantomime epileptic seizure, Cooper could see the man was caught at the crossover point between needing to act and heeding Kristin Hegel's order that nobody was to enter the room until she returned. Cooper increased the urgency of his performance. Every spasm and jerk pushed his legs and his feet closer to release. When one foot came free, followed by the other, the guard swore and came at him with the baton raised.

It did not help.

As soon as he moved within striking distance, Cooper turned his improvised fit into an attack from the ground. Both of his feet shot out. One looped around the back of the guard's leading leg. The other slammed into his knee, delivering a shattering sidekick to the vulnerable joint. The man screamed and went down on his broken leg.

Cooper was up on his feet and moving, still chained to the steel chair, before the guard hit the concrete floor. He launched himself as high into the air as he could go, landing on the man's chest and throat with his knees.

He struggled up again.

Another jump, this time driving the leg of the chair into the man's face.

A howl of shock and agony.

Up again.

Another jump.

This time, the chair leg punctured the man's eye socket, and Cooper Fox drove the steel shaft through and into his brain.

The body shook, and the dead man's bowels let loose.

Not knowing how much time he had, or if indeed he had any time at all before reinforcements arrived, Cooper dropped to the floor next to the man. It was not easy to retrieve the key ring from his utility belt and unlock the steel bracelets securing him to the chair. But this was not the first time he had done such a thing. And he had trained for these scenarios many, many times.

Within ten seconds, Cooper Fox was free.

He stripped the man of his weapons and utility belt. He now had a riot baton, a Taser, a handgun, and four clips of ammunition. He dropped the baton through the steel loop at his hip. He drew the gun from its holster and exited the room.

For the first time, he had some idea of his surroundings. There was no natural light anywhere. No sign of night-time darkness either. He was almost certainly underground, in a modern building to judge by the materials and fittings. There had been a small watch room attached to his cell. There was no window between the two, but microlens cameras provided video coverage from each corner. The dead man lay on his back; one leg stuck out at an impossible angle, a dark pool of blood spreading out from his head. A clock on the wall of the small security office told him it was 4:51 AM.

Cooper scanned the room, looking for anything that might tell him where he was or, more importantly, where he might find Mary and the kids.

Nothing.

He moved out.

There were three cells on this level, each with a guard station. He did not waste time wondering what these guys were doing to maintain an underground prison. He had worked for them. He had put people into places like this.

The cell next to his own was empty.

The cell beyond that was occupied. A woman and two children. Mary, Matthew, and Jessica.

They had nobody watching over them, and he almost snorted in derision. Modern business best practice, doing more with less, Cooper thought. Why hire two expensive full-time security guards to watch over your secret detainees when one guy could do it?

A door opened. Cooper heard footsteps behind him and a sudden intake of breath. A second guard stood there, holding two coffee cups and a tray of plastic-wrapped sandwiches.

His mouth dropped open in shock. The food and drink spilled to the ground as he fumbled for his sidearm.

Cooper drew the riot baton and thrust it at him like a sword, catching the man's throat hard in the angle between the main length of the baton and the smaller perpendicular handle. The security guard coughed and gagged, clawing at his damaged windpipe. Moving in a fluid blur, Cooper flipped the baton, grabbing the handle and striking the man five times in less than a second.

A left jab with his fist to the nose.

A right hook with the blunt end of the riot baton, straight into his temple. A left elbow to the other temple as the guard's body started to fall. A hammer fist to the trapezius muscle bundle.

A back fist strike directly into his carotid artery.

The guard was dead before he hit the floor.

Cooper waited three seconds.

Nobody else came. No alarms sounded.

He returned to the monitors displaying video from within the holding cell.

Unlike Cooper, Mary and the kids had mattresses to lie on, and the light in their room was out. The cameras were running in both infrared and low light amplification mode. Matthew twitched and rolled over on four separate screens.

Cooper resisted the urge to charge in and haul them out. He took a minute to sit himself at the console and study the controls. It was an expensive installation but not overly complex. You didn't hire Nobel Prize winners to guard your underground company black site. In less than a minute, he had worked out how to plug into the CCTV network covering the rest of the building. He cycled through all twenty-four cameras.

He was back at Triple Helix, in the blue glass building where Ted and Kristin had dropped him off for his scans. It made sense. A secure facility in a remote location owned by...

He had no idea, but he would bet his life that the listed owners would be some two-dollar shell company, and it would take weeks of registry and title searches to trace the actual beneficial ownership back to Sir Roland Sewell. Cooper was sure that Rolly was behind all of this. He had been working for Rolly just before he woke up in Gainesville.

He had been working with Kristin and Ted on a drug trial gone wrong.

A Triple Helix project.

The building was quiet. No police tape marked the scene of his escape from Doctor Ludgrove's diagnostic suites. The words TRIPLE HELIX stood out in shining metal on the front of the receptionist's desk.

There was no sign that anything had happened there or was happening now.

Satisfied, Cooper looked around the small security office.

His gym bag was lying in a corner.

As soon as he picked it up, he heard the clang of weapons, but that was not what he needed. There was more than a hundred thousand dollars in the bag. It would make everything they had to do so much easier.

He fumbled the zip open.

There was no money. They'd taken it all. And the passports and debit cards, too. He bit down on his anger.

Forcing himself to deal with the situation as it was, not what he wanted it to be, Cooper emptied the bag, piece by piece. They had missed one thing. A Visa debit card for some corporate account caught inside a rip in the lining. He had no idea how much money was on it, but it hadn't yet expired.

He slipped the card into a pocket and repacked the bag before resuming his search of the watch room.

He found what he had been looking for on a corkboard by the door. Car keys.

Time to go.

He left the room and used a magnetic key from the utility belt to unlock the third cell. Opening the door carefully, he whispered, "Mary, it's me, Cooper."

She snored.

He almost smiled.

"Cooper?"

Matthew had woken up. His voice was thick with sleep.

"Cooper, is that you?"

He sounded scared and was inching away into the nearest corner.

"Yeah, Matty, it's me. We're getting out of here. I need you to wake up your mom and your sister. Do it now, but be gentle. Don't scare them. I'm going to check the exits."

While the boy shook his mother and sister awake, Cooper hurried down the short corridor to a heavy steel door. It opened onto a small vestibule, and another door on the far side of that gave onto an underground car park. He pressed the unlock button on the key fob he'd taken. The lights flashed on a Lexus sedan parked in the shadows on the other side of the car park.

He heard a small scream. Jessica. Then Mary's voice telling her not to look. Cooper swore at himself. They had seen the guard he had killed. He should have hidden the body, but as soon as the man was no longer a threat, Cooper stopped thinking about him.

He heard feet slapping on hard concrete and turned around just before Mary and Jessica slammed into him, crushing him with the strength of their hugs.

"Oh my God. My God, oh my God," Mary kept repeating. "You came to us. You said you would come for us, and you did. Oh my God, Cooper, thank you, thank you."

He returned the embrace, kissing Mary and lifting both children off the ground.

But he soon put them down and gave himself some space.

"We have to get out of here," Cooper said. "I have to get you somewhere safe and..."

He went quiet. He had already failed to do that.

"What?" Mary said.

"You were right," he said. "I should have called Sheriff Briscoe."

23

Cooper didn't make the same mistake twice. He drove hard through the darkness before dawn and made it back to Gainesville as the town was shaking off the slumbers of the night just gone. The morning revealed itself with a taste of the winter to come. Wispy clouds in light blue skies and a hard edge on the overnight chill. The Sheriff's Office was still closed, but he knew where to find Andy Briscoe. He'd run past him every morning for the last three years. The sheriff was at the front table of *The Baker's Spoon*, drinking his coffee, enjoying one (or possibly even two) of Sarah McKee's blueberry and white chocolate muffins and reading the *Gainesville Sentinel*.

Cooper parked the stolen Lexus out front.

Sheriff Andy recognised him behind the wheel and performed an almost cartoonish double take. He put down his paper, but he didn't get up and walk away from his muffin.

Next door, at Gooch's Hardware, Wallace Gooch paused at the job, brushing the sidewalk clear of fallen leaves from the park over the street to stare at them. He looked as confused as Sheriff Andy.

"Come on," Cooper said. "Best we all go in." He turned to address Mary. "Take a booth in the back and order the kids some pancakes. They deserve a treat. I'll talk to Andy."

"Is everything gonna be all right?" Mary asked, her fingers drifting up to her face, which was still swollen and bruised from where Coach

Buchner had hit her. She had been using the gels and creams that Cooper bought, but even behind a fresh layer of makeup, she looked like a battered wife.

"You're gonna be safe now," he said, answering her without really answering her question.

"But people will look," she said.

"They will," he agreed. Wally Gooch was still staring. "You can tell them the truth or something else. I'd just tell them the truth, Mary. It's going to come out."

She nodded and checked her makeup in the mirror.

"Can we really have pancakes?" Matthew asked, hope quivering on the edge of disbelief.

"With ice cream?" Jess added.

"Whatever you want," Cooper said. They cheered as they piled out of the backseat.

Cooper reached across and squeezed Mary's hand.

"I love you," he said.

"I love you too," She replied.

A bell over the front door jingled to announce their arrival, and Miss McKee fairly burst with excitement to have finally lured Cooper inside. She did her very best to ignore Mary's injuries, leading her and the children to the booth, which Cooper pointed out. It was close to the rear exit and had clear sight lines on the front of house. He pulled up a chair at Briscoe's table.

"You mind if I join you, Sheriff? It's a work call, I'm afraid."

Andy's eyes went a little wider, and Cooper realised he hadn't seen the lawman since coming off the meds. There was going to be a lot of that.

The park across the street was busy with people walking to work and school. They all knew him as Andy did. As the dummy who helped at the school. As the weirdly gifted savant who couldn't tie his own shoes or read a bus timetable.

"Coop?" Sheriff Andy said uncertainly. He was looking at Cooper, but his eyes kept drifting to Mary at the back of the cafe. "Everything all right, son? That's a fancy set of wheels you got out there."

"Yeah, they're not mine," Cooper said. "I need to report a crime. Not in your jurisdiction, but definitely a crime. You're going to have to notify the Feds. Mary and the kids will need protection and probably relocation under WITSEC. I'd reckon the US Marshals would be your first call, but you're probably gonna need to bring in the FBI, maybe one of the JAGS and a bunch of regulators as well. I'd start with the SEC. Hey, do you mind? I haven't eaten."

He pointed at an untouched muffin lying next to the crumbs of the one Andy had been eating when they came in. The Sheriff nodded, his mouth hanging open. Cooper used a knife to cut the muffin in half carefully.

"Er..." Sheriff Briscoe started. "The Feds, you say. US Marshals?"

"For WITSEC, yeah."

Briscoe turned around in his chair, looking for Mary again.

"We had some US Marshals come through earlier this week," he said, staring at her injuries. "Damnedest thing. They came for your perps. Porter and McClintock."

"Yeah, they weren't Marshals," Cooper said. "And *your* perps, Porter and McClintock, are dead now. You won't find them. I'm pretty sure your Marshals were a couple of private contractors going by the names of Luntz and Merrill. I don't know them, but I do know their boss, a woman called Kristin Hegel. She was a heavy hitter, directorate of operations at the Agency, but she went freelance and feral. She probably gave your third perp a hotshot at the hospital."

Sheriff Briscoe hadn't sat back in his chair so much as he'd fallen back in it. He stared in frank disbelief at Cooper Fox.

"Coop...are you..." he started before faltering to a stop and having to start all over again. "Cooper, are you undercover? Have you been working on a case here? All this time. Because, you know..."

Cooper smiled.

"It's a bit much, isn't it? But no, sir. Like Mary, I'm a witness. But also a victim. And maybe - no, definitely - a perpetrator."

The sheriff blinked.

"Say what now, son?"

Cooper waved that away, a small gesture, like shooing a fly.

"Nothing on your turf, Andy. But I do have a ledger to square."

He looked down the back of the cafe where Sarah McKee was delivering the first fat stack of pancakes, dripping with whipped butter and maple syrup, to Mary's table. The kids were cheering.

They were resilient, he thought. The shit they'd been through.

Sheriff Briscoe was starting to recover his balance, too. He leaned forward.

"Son, I don't have half a damn clue what's going on here, but I am sure as Hell that I do not like it."

"Fair enough," Cooper said. "And I will make a full accounting, but right now, you have to get my family into protective custody. Call in support from Jacksondale or even Richmond if you must. And you *will* have to. These people I'm talking about, they're dangerous. I know. I used to be one of them. Do not make the mistake of thinking you can treat them like common criminals."

Briscoe shook his head, complete incomprehension written all over his face.

"Son, seriously, what is going on? Who are you, really? Cos, you're not the Cooper Fox I know. What's been happening?"

His tone was plaintive, needful. Cooper smiled sadly. He hoped his expression was at least open and honest.

"Long story short, and it *is* a long story, so I'll keep it short, a biotech called Triple Helix has been running illegal human trials on a type of drug called a nootropic and on a new class of drug which...well, I guess you'd called them anti-nootropics. Smart drugs and dumb drugs. A pill to turn you into Einstein. Another pill that'd turn Einstein's brain into a bag of fucking dog hair. There's more. Much more. But that's enough to go on with for now. And it's why I seem so different to you, Sheriff. I was part of that trial."

Sheriff Briscoe added a slow head shake to his performance of open-mouthed incredulity.

"But why? Son, this is crazy talk."

Cooper sat back and looked out of the window. The morning light was clear, and the park where they had celebrated the Tiger's win just a few days and a thousand years ago seemed unusually vivid, as though the lines of everything he could see had been pressed just that little bit harder into reality.

It was so striking he figured it had to be some after-effect of the meds he'd been on. He turned back to answer Briscoe.

"Why? Money."

Andy Briscoe's face had gone the colour of bad cream cheese.

"Goddamn, Coop. This is...this all a bit much to take in before a man's had his breakfast."

He glanced back over his shoulder.

"And you say your guys have seen some of this?"

Cooper nodded.

"Andy, I told you, you've seen it. Doc Schofield works for Triple Helix. Coach Buchner, too, for that matter. Schofield's been dosing me and running observations since I got here, reporting to a Doctor Ludgrove who works out of a facility upstate. Buchner provided overwatch and security. The guy you want to grab up, though, is a Brit. Name of Sewell. Rolly Sewell. Also known as Sir Roland."

Sheriff Andy's expression twisted into frank incredulity.

"I don't know this Sewell guy, but Ray Buchner? Come on now, Coop. I can see you been through some stuff. And Mary, too. She's hiding it well, but she's got quite the shiner under that makeup. And don't you doubt I'll get to the bottom of that," he said, his voice lowering an octave into a growl. "But Ray is our football coach. Our *winning* coach," he added. "He's been..."

Cooper cut him off.

"He's been here just a couple of weeks longer than me. Schofield, too, if you think back on it. They were placed here to run observations. I'll have a bet with you now that neither of them has turned up to work for the last two days."

Briscoe frowned.

"Doc's office has been closed, yes. They said he had an out-of-town emergency. I wouldn't know about Ray, but I could check."

"You can check with Mary and the kids first. Schofield and Buchner came to our place, tried to force me back onto the program. Ray pulled a gun on us. He pistol-whipped Mary and threatened to kill her if I didn't cooperate. But she can tell you all of that herself. I need you to get them to safety. Out of town, to the US Marshals or whatever. The Marshals will be motivated because Kristin's been using them as a legend for some of her guys."

"Who? And what?"

"Kristen Hegel, Andy, remember? Ex-Agency? Went feral. And two of her guys, Luntz and Merrill, impersonated a couple of US Deputy Marshals to get into your office and exfiltrate Porter and McClintock. They did that because any legal case would have exposed Triple Helix to real scrutiny. First thing their lawyers would've done is launch discovery on whatever treatment Schofield was running on me. Soon as they learned about Triple Helix and my treatment, they'd have sued them, too. Way more money. So, Porter and the others had to go."

"But Coop..."

"Porter and McClintock are dead," Cooper said, rolling over him.

"Like Wayne Lubbers. Except you'll never find a trace of them. Call the Marshals, Andy. Track back on the federal warrant. None of it will hang together."

Andy Briscoe stared at him.

Cooper's expression morphed into a sunny, welcoming smile for Sarah McKee as she bustled up with a pot of coffee.

"Freshen that up for you, Sheriff? And would you like something to eat, Coop?"

"I can't stay. I'm sorry, Sarah," Cooper said. "But I will take a muffin and a coffee to go."

The surprise on her face was fleeting, but it was there. She was used to slow, simple Cooper Fox. Even the change in the cadence of his words was enough to unsettle her.

"Okay, hon," she said, her sunny confidence eroded. "Coffee and a muffin to go? What about you, Andy?"

"I think I'll be having a second breakfast, Sarah," he said. "Got a feeling this is going to be a helluva long day."

IT WAS.

Andy Briscoe insisted they all come to the Sheriff's Office with him— or the cop shop, as he liked to call it when he was in a good mood. When Dan Ferrucci and Jamaal Brown got in, they all listened to Mary tell the same story Cooper had just given him over breakfast.

He'd been deeply unsettled at Sarah's by the young man's intelligence and clarity. Not to mention the wackadoodle fairy tale he had to tell. It was as if a giant trout had just ridden up on a mountain bike to recite a bunch of poetry.

But Mary Doyle's story meshed into Fox's with a watertight fit, and then she added a whole bunch of crazy detail that was all her own work. Guys like Men in Black agents grabbing them out of a motel room – and paying the bill! A blindfolded ride to some underground prison. Fox breaking out of his cell and releasing them all. Andy knew she was holding back some details there. They both were. The vehicle was obviously stolen, and neither of them mentioned any guards. Or what might've happened to them. But he could get to that later. For now, this was a hell of a fur ball to cough up on his carpet.

He kept all four of them separate, of course. But as much as you could expect the two little ones to corroborate the grownups' story, they did. The boy had even seen Ray Buchner smash his mother in the face with a handgun. Matty said, blushing and ashamed, that he had wet himself a little bit and run to hide under his bed. Not the sort of detail, in Briscoe's experience, that a young fellow was likely to make up and toss in for the sake of padding out a story.

If Fox and Doyle had coached those children, they'd coached them well.

By the time he was finished taking statements from the Doyle clan, Sheriff Briscoe was not ashamed to admit that he was righteously out of sorts. There could be no doubt something deeply wrong had been set into motion in his town, and he had known precisely nothing about it.

"Those US Marshals," he said to Dan Ferrucci quietly after talking to the Doyle boy, "You got a good look-see at their ID, right, Dan?"

"It was legit, Andy. The warrant too. You looked over that when you got back."

And Briscoe had. He'd been fit to hogtie when he returned from checking on the dust-up over at the Sanewski place to find out a couple of Feds had just grabbed up his offenders and whipped them away into one of their sketchy rendition programs. But the warrant was word-perfect, and he'd recognise Judge Osterman's spiky scrawl anywhere. It was annoying. It was unusual. But it was a long way from being unbelievable. He'd even googled up Duray McClintock and 'Ohio Militia', and sure enough, there was a bunch of stuff online about him getting jammed up in some plot to kidnap the state AG. How had he missed that before?

Briscoe had meant to call Osterman's clerk up in Richmond. Just to check, the feds had dotted all the T's and crossed all the I's, but he hadn't had a chance yet. And Judge Osterman, a Democrat, was a notoriously sensitive and tightly puckered asshole about being second-guessed by the police, so he was gonna have to do all of his second-guessing on the down low.

But now...now he was thinking he might have to drive up to the capital himself to straighten it all out.

Andy sighed.

"We'd better get Coop on tape then, I suppose. Where's he at?"

"He was with Sharon in the kitchen," Jamaal Brown said. "Eating a muffin."

"Alrighty then. Go grab him. When we've interviewed him, I'll call the US Marshals in Richmond. We'll get to the bottom of this. Whatever in hell this is."

But when Deputy Jamaal Brown went to fetch Cooper Fox, Sharon Ferrucci said she thought he'd been with them.

Eating a muffin.

But he was gone.

They never saw him again.

24

Chief Petty Officer Jarrod Lovell had been trained in escape and evasion at the Marine Corps mountain warfare training center, the Air Force's Desert and Arctic Survival Schools, and the SEALs' Survival, Evasion, Resistance and Escape course. As an independent contractor, Mike Garner further polished those skills at courses offered by graduates of the Special Air Service, the Israeli Mossad and even the Russian Spetsnaz. Slipping out of the Gainesville Sheriff's Office when nobody was watching was not one of the standout challenges of Cooper Fox's new life.

He knew Andy would be pissed, and it would lend zero credibility to any future plea that he had used reasonable force to escape Doctor Ludgrove's facility, but he could not afford to get jammed up in the system. Mary and her guys would be okay. As soon as Briscoe made that call to the Marshals Service and discovered that the warrant for Porter and McClintock was bogus, wheels would start to turn. Mary, Matthew and Jessica would be protected because they would suddenly be valuable witnesses in a high-priority case. The Feds would not look kindly upon private operators using them for cover.

But the same wheels would start turning on Cooper, as well. He would be a fugitive. A material witness if not an actual suspect. He needed to get ahead of all that if he was to have the freedom of action necessary to stop Sewell's money and power from winning out. Rolly had so much of both that they created their own gravitational field, bending reality to his will. And if it turned out that Ludgrove's research was being funded out of a black budget somewhere in the ass end of the Pentagon...well, the system would protect itself. Not him.

Cooper slipped out of the back door and across the park to *The Baker's Spoon,* where he'd parked the Lexus he'd stolen from Ludgrove's facility. He smiled and waved to Sarah McKee when she saw him through the front window of the café. He backed out and drove south, looping back a couple of blocks downtown and heading north on the other side of town.

He knew he couldn't keep the vehicle. Even if Kristin hadn't put a tracking device into it, it was a late-model sedan. Tracking technology and even cut-out switches were increasingly common. A signal could come from a satellite at any moment, killing the engine and even locking him inside until Andy or the Jacksondale cops turned up to take him into custody.

Cooper stayed just under the speed limit as he passed through town, but he fed the engine some juice once he hit the state route. He was heading north, returning to the lab and lockdown facility he had twice escaped so far. A new team was due there to replace Ludgrove. Sewell would probably order the whole thing burned to the ground after the security breach. No doubt Kristin would advise him to do just that. But Rolly was a businessman and would not lightly write off a billion-dollar investment without trying to claw something back. The data, for instance.

Cooper flew along the 360, old-growth forest on either side of the car, strobing into a blur of light and dark as the morning sun pierced the gloom with a thousand shafts of sunlight. He guessed the odds of being pulled up for speeding were low. Andy and his guys would be busy back in Gainesville, and Cooper hadn't yet passed into the jurisdiction of the Jacksondale police bureau. Before he did so, he pulled off the state route and lost most of his speed, driving cautiously down an unsealed road just outside of the tiny hamlet of Jetersville. An unincorporated community of just a few hundred souls, it was well known in Gainesville as the place where you could buy a $200 beater for a road trip, for a bachelor party, say, or Spring Break, or a casino run to Atlantic City.

The wreckers' yard was hidden behind a nine-foot fence of rusted iron. Barbed wire topped the fence line, and a sign warned potential customers to park outside the gate. Cooper could hear guard dogs barking when he turned off the engine. He waited.

The owner, a thin, bald, hard-faced man in dirty grey coveralls, appeared from somewhere inside. He wiped his hands with an oily rag, which seemed only to make them dirtier. Cooper rolled down his window as the man approached. The name Vic was stitched into the front pocket of the coveralls.

"Help you with something?" Vic asked.

"I want to trade this vehicle for something untraceable," Cooper said.

Vic stared at him for a long time.

"Is it hot?" he asked him at last.

Cooper nodded. "Smoking."

Vic said nothing, his eyes narrowing. Cooper knew he was being assessed as a possible narc.

"What's in the bag?" The man said, nodding at the gym bag on the passenger seat.

"Weapons, ammunition. They're not for sale."

"Let me see."

Cooper showed him the small arsenal he had liberated the previous day.

Vic nodded and whistled.

"Pop the trunk, get out of the vehicle, and stand away from the door. I'm gonna check whether you got any bodies or body parts or any shit like that in there."

"Fair enough," Cooper said. He did as he was told. Vic checked the vehicle over, pronouncing himself satisfied after a minute.

"This fucking thing is gonna bring the heat like July in Georgia. I got a Chevy Blazer I can trade you for it. Six hunnert on the clock. Rust out the ass. Panel work looks like shit, but it's got clean tags, and I'm gonna guess you don't care about that other stuff. You just need to get somewhere. Or away from someone."

"If it's got another thousand miles in it, I'll take it," Cooper said. "If you're lying, I'll be back."

The two men looked at each other, both experts in their respective fields. Something like understanding and respect passed between them.

Vic called back over his shoulder.

"Roy. Need you out here."

He turned back and put his hand out. It was dirty with oil and grime, but Cooper took it. Both men had calloused palms and fingers. They shook on the deal as Roy, a taller, even thinner version of Vic, appeared. He was younger by half, though, and cursed by red hair.

Vic produced a screwdriver from a pocket and tossed it to the younger man. Who caught it deftly.

"Drive it over to Amelia," he said. "Kill the GPS tracker and put it in with Luke. We'll break her down for parts."

———

COOPER DROVE NORTH, retracing the path of their escape earlier that morning. He nursed the Chevy through a patchwork of forests thick with loblolly and shortleaf pine, the woodlands occasionally giving way to open fields planted with soybean and corn. He drove all the way into the south-western suburbs of Richmond before swinging around to the north-west. He stopped near the edge of town at a Walmart, where he dropped most of his remaining cash. He bought dark winter clothing, thermal underwear, a notepad and pens, five balls of double-strength twine, a flashlight, a hunting scope, three bags of high-energy trail mix and a Thermos, which he filled with hot, black coffee from Starbucks.

An hour later, he pulled onto a fire trail a mile short of the glass office cube where Kristin and Ted had taken him for his scans and where he had later been held captive with Mary and the children. Cooper drove for another minute before pulling off the dirt track. He got out of the car and undressed. The forest smelled strongly of pine needles and sap, and the chilly air already had a sharp edge to it, which made him shiver when he got down to his shorts. He pulled on the thermal underwear and climbed back into his dark outer layers. He put the scope, the Thermos, and the trail mix into his gym bag with the guns. The fire trail looped around behind the Triple Helix building, coming within four hundred yards at the closest point. He approached through the trees and set up an observation post where he could use the hunter's scope to watch who came and went. As he picked his way through the woods, he trailed out the twine behind him, occasionally wrapping it around the base of a sapling.

Just after three in the afternoon, he saw Ted Sorensen drive a red Toyota Camry through the main gate with two men in the back seat. It was impossible to know whether they were medical staff or just more goons. As the warmth and light leaked out of the day, Cooper could feel the chill gnawing at his exposed skin, trying to seep in through his layers, deep into his bones. He was dressed warmly enough for now, but he could not stay out here all night.

He waited.

Nightfall brought one advantage. He could see how many floors were occupied. Three of the four stories were lit up, and occasionally, he would see people moving around inside. He couldn't begin to estimate how many occupants there might be or what they would be doing, but it seemed a fair bet that they were all wrapping up Ludgrove's project.

He waited.

The first vehicle left at 6:37 PM. He noted the make and licence plate number.

Another followed four minutes later. He took down those details, too.

Over the next hour, seven more vehicles drove out of the main gate. He made notes on all of them.

Ted Sorenson left alone at 8:02 PM. It was full dark and freezing in the forest. Most of the building was now lit only by security lights and perhaps a few computer screens. It was enough to observe a couple of figures silhouetted against a corner office window at 8.16 PM. A security patrol, most likely. They stood in the window, looking out over the building's surroundings for a few minutes. Maybe they were the guys who went in with Ted. They would be more capable than the guards Cooper had overpowered.

He was starting to shiver again despite the thermal layers he wore and the hot coffee he sipped. It was time to go. He navigated his way back to the Chevy with great care. Without night vision equipment, it would be easy to get lost in the dark, unfamiliar forest. Instead, he stayed low and used the twine he had laid down that afternoon, letting it run through his fingers and lead him back. The return trip took much longer than the trek to his lay-up point, but the battered, rust-spotted Chevy sat just where he had left it by the side of the fire trail.

Cooper climbed in, started the engine, and cranked up the heat.

He drove out of the forest and onto a state road heading north towards Washington.

IT WAS after midnight when he entered DC. The roads were quiet, and most of the bars and clubs in Georgetown were either closed or shutting down for the night. He couldn't go back to his apartment and he had an unknown amount of money on the Visa. But he did have information.

The license plate numbers of every car that had driven out of Triple Helix.

ONCE UPON A TIME, he would have had networks and infrastructure, too. Human and technological. He could have fed the data he'd collected out in the field—or the forest if you wanted to be literal about it—into those networks.

Now, he had only hunches and partial memories.

He wasn't just rusty at this. He was utterly compromised and vulnerable.

He knew he had dark areas of memory decay and skill loss and that some of those voids were knowable. But some were not.

He was feeling his way through the city and the shadow world beneath it, just as he had felt his way back through the forest. But here, he had laid no trail. He had only the vaguest sense of dangerous shapes in the darkness and how carefully he would have to move around them.

He took Water Street toward the George Washington University Hospital, cutting through West End and jagging a left at Dupont Circle. A police cruiser followed him into the roundabout but exited onto Massachusetts. A few hardy revellers or even hardier office workers hurried along the footpath, their heads bent into a stiffening breeze, scraps of litter and fallen leaves chasing at their heels.

On 20th he swung left into Q Street and drove three blocks north. The great stone and glass question mark of the Washington Hilton rose from a small hill ahead of him, with maybe a third of the rooms lit up. He pulled off the main drive and into a smaller warren of backstreets, looking for a half-remembered spot. It took him ten minutes of driving and backtracking, but he found it.

Kropotkin's.

A Russian tea house in the basement of a colonial-era tenement.

Cooper drove another block past the address and found a place to park on the street in front of a mid-sized office building. He stashed the gym bag in the footwell behind the driver's seat, taking nothing with him but the debit card and the notebook in which he'd written down the details of the cars.

He walked back along the sidewalk, past darkened shops and office fronts, with the hood of his black, fleece-lined top pulled down over his face. There would be surveillance teams in place, probably two of them, two or three floors up, logging the arrival and departure of everybody who visited the tea house.

He tried to walk with the air of a man who had no business in this neighbourhood. He was just moving through.

As he passed the wrought iron gate at the entrance to *Kropotkin's,* he turned and walked up the paved path to the front door.

He could imagine the clicking and whirring of cameras trying to capture his image.

He knocked on the heavy wooden door. A small panel slid aside, and he saw part of a man's face in the dim, red light inside.

Fleshy lips, a five-clock shadow.

"Members only tonight," the lips said in a heavy Russian accent.

The panel started to slide back.

"But, my friend, I would struggle so that all may live this rich, overflowing life," Cooper said quickly. In Russian. *"And be sure that in this struggle, I would find a joy greater than anything else can give."*

The panel stopped moving.

Then it banged shut.

Cooper wondered if he'd messed up the call and response, but he heard a lock turn and a latch click. The door swung open. Not wide, but far enough for him to slip through.

Two men waited for him on the other side. They looked like Soviet main battle tanks disguised as nightclub bouncers.

Cooper lifted his arms to let them pat him down.

When they found nothing to warrant tossing him to the kerb, the shorter one asked, "What is your business here, friend?"

He spoke English, but with an accent from the frozen north of the *Rodina*, with the hard, exaggerated roll on his 'R's.

"Tea and information," Cooper said.

They looked at him.

"We have the best tea here," the shorter man replied. "You may go through."

Cooper took off his heavy, waterproof jacket and hung it on a wooden hook by the front door. He walked through a narrow corridor of white-painted bricks covered in black and white photos. Most were portraits of Slavic-looking men and women. Others were scenic. Locations from the old country to judge by the architecture. A few scenes and buildings even seemed familiar to him.

He ducked his head under a low, dark wood lintel and emerged into a small room thick with smoke and heavy with cooking smells. The space was crowded. A dozen or so small round tables hosted parties of four and five people, mostly men, but not exclusively. They were all speaking Russian. They stopped when Cooper stepped into the room. A man sitting with a party of three on the far side of the room saw him and openly goggled. He scrambled to his feet and left via a small arch leading to another cramped corridor.

Slowly, conversation returned.

There were no tables available, so Cooper made his way to the bar. He took a seat at the end and removed the Visa card from his pocket, laying it on the marble bar top in front of him. A shaven-headed waiter with a barbed wire tattoo circling his neck three times stopped polishing shot glasses and raised his chin at Cooper.

"You want?"

Cooper slid the debit card towards him.

"Piroshki and a shot."

The man nodded, satisfied. He rang up the sale, took the card and swiped it. The transaction went through. He poured a slug of vodka into a shot glass and called an order through to the kitchen for a plate of piroshki. Three of the golden brown, boat-shaped fried buns, fat with pork and mushrooms, came back in less than a minute.

Cooper downed his shot in one go and took a bite from the first bun. It was steaming hot and fresh. While he ate it, he saw another two plates coming out.

He did not have time to start on his second bun before a man took the stool next to his.

"Good evening, Michael," the man said.

"Hello," Cooper said, having no idea who this guy was.

"I must admit I am surprised to see you here," the man said. "You have given poor Dimitri the fright of a lifetime."

"Dimitri must have led a very uneventful life," Cooper said.

The man burst out laughing.

It was the loudest noise in the room. The buzz of conversation dipped momentarily before rising again.

"Two bears cannot live in one lair, no. So, what brings you here, Michael? I hear you are seeking information?"

Cooper reached into a pocket, retrieved his notebook, and tore out two pages, pushing them across to the other man.

"I would like to know who these cars belong to," he said. "And the home addresses of the owners."

The man stared at him.

"That's it?"

"That's it."

The Russian took Cooper by the arm and turned him around to look directly into his face.

"Michael, you disappear, you come back... Why are you really here?"

Cooper shrugged. The truth was often the best option. Or as much of the truth as you could get away with.

"I have nowhere else to go."

The other man said nothing for a moment.

"I see," he said finally. "Perhaps then we can help you. But why would we do this?"

"I would hope to pay you," Cooper said, pushing the Visa card toward him. It really was a gesture of hope. There might only be a hundred bucks on that piece of plastic. Minus the vodka shot and the pork buns.

The other man pushed it back.

"Do not insult me with mere commerce, Michael. For whatever reason, you find yourself in need of help. And I am more than happy to offer what assistance I can. But understand, it would be a friendly gesture on my part. And friendship is not friendship if such gestures are not reciprocated."

It was Cooper's turn to stare at him. He had no idea who this man was. But the Russian obviously knew Michael Garner. He imagined he was treating with Garner because Garner was desperate. And desperation made men vulnerable.

This was not friendship. It was recruitment.

He took the card back and slipped it into a pocket.

"It is only those who do nothing, who make no mistakes," he said.

The Russian smiled.

"You know your Kropotkin very well, my friend. Please. Give me a moment with this."

The Russian took the pages from Cooper's notebook and disappeared into the alcove where the startled man, presumably Dimitri, had fled. The barman started to pour another shot of vodka, but Cooper shook his head.

"I will have tea," he said. "You have the best tea here."

"*Da. Spasibo,*" the barman agreed. He fetched a glass tumbler from under the bar and filled it with hot brown liquid from a samovar, adding a slice of lemon. Cooper sipped at the tea and finished off his plate of piroshki, waiting for the other man to return. Everything about this felt both familiar and wrong. He had obviously been here before. He had memories of a café near the Hilton where he had done business. But to be honest, he had not remembered it as Kropotkin's, just as some Russian place. It was only when he saw the name over the door that he recalled both the venue and the trick of gaining entrance. He knew these people or once had, and they knew him or some previous version of him.

But he felt himself lost.

He felt as though he was swimming against a flood tide, sweeping him out to sea. While he remained outwardly calm, inside, he was thrashing around like a drowning man. At any moment, he knew, this could all go sideways, hard. Hell, it might already have done so, and he just didn't know it.

After ten minutes or so, the Russian re-emerged from the alcove with Cooper's original notes and two sheets of paper, folded twice over and secured with a paper clip.

"You are well, my friend?" the man said, handing him the printout.

"Yes, I am," Cooper said.

The man grunted noncommittally.

"For a man in good health, you seem to know a lot of doctors," he said.

Cooper stood up. He tucked the printout away in a pocket.

"Thank you for this," he said.

"It is just a little thing," the other man said. "Perhaps when you are done with whatever it is you must do, you will come back, and we will discuss some other little things."

"Perhaps," Cooper said.

The man smiled.

"Or I could come find you."

Cooper nodded.

"I don't doubt it."

25

Back in the Chevy, Cooper unfolded the two-page printout. A business card fell out into his lap. The card was expensively printed but simply designed: a name, *Aleksei Kozlov*, and a phone number. Presumably, a contact point for the man with whom he had just...what? Struck a deal? Made an arrangement? Agreed to treason? Cooper wasn't sure, but Aleksei Kozlov had more than delivered on his side of it.

The two-page document was dense with information. Seven names were listed, all of them preceded by the honorific Doctor or Professor, and after each name, there were not just business and home addresses, some with photographs of the property, but career details, too. And high-lighted under five of the seven listings were short paragraphs detailing allegations of serious malpractice. The two cleanskins, a Doctor Vincent Nguyen and Doctor Amy Scuderi, Cooper ignored. His eye was drawn instead to the name at the top of the list. Professor Erhard Schneider.

He'd seen that name on a small plaque in the elevator riding up to Ludgrove's office, where Ludgrove had mentioned working with a professor.

Cooper read Kozlov's mini-profile of the man, fascinated.

In his private practice, Schneider had twice faced disciplinary proceedings before the Medical Board of Maryland and the Ethics Committee of Johns Hopkins. He had been stripped of his medical licence and certification but had taken up a research position with Triple

Helix a week later. The company's website described him as 'the senior responsible executive for neurochemical research.'

Aleksei Kozlov's dossier noted that he was divorced and lived alone.

Cooper folded the paper away. Schneider was his guy. He had already committed the professor's home address to memory when he pulled out and pointed the Chevy at Massachusetts Avenue for the half-hour drive out to Great Falls.

It was only twenty miles in a straight line, but the transition from DC's urban centre to the farms and rolling hills of Great Falls was striking. A favoured retreat for defence contractors and tech executives, it was less a neighbourhood than a collection of five-to-ten-acre principalities. There was no public transport or even mains water through most of Great Falls, but the million-dollar mansions and private estates made do with Teslas and Perrier. Cooper knew his rusted-out beater would draw attention if anybody were awake to see it. During daylight hours, neighbourhood watch types might ignore him as a visiting tradesman, but in the dead of night, he had to be careful. And as comprehensive as the Russian's data dump had been, especially for having had zero notice, it still left him ignorant of what, if any, security measures Professor Schneider might have in place.

He would have alarms and, almost certainly, cameras. They might be tied into a private security service or set to trip a threat board wherever Kristin was holed up. Cooper might have to handle a couple of sleepy, local cops or a ten-strong wet work team dispatched by his ex-girlfriend. Stealth would help, but speed was essential. He had to get in and out before anybody could respond.

Cooper followed the Google Maps printout helpfully included in Kozlov's materials and found Schneider's property at the end of a winding country road that took him down to the banks of the Potomac. The river widened dramatically behind Schneider's property after squeezing through a series of narrows dividing the exclusive suburb from a couple of hundred acres of nature reserve on the far side of the water.

It would have been nice to load a mapping app and get some satellite imagery of the grounds, but Cooper had learned the hard way that carrying a phone was an invitation to be tracked by Kristin. Instead, he parked the Chevy by the side of the road, two hundred yards short of the gated entrance to Schneider's mansion. He removed the MP9 and two ammo clips from the gym bag. He fitted the fat black tube of the flash suppressor, which would serve as a reasonably effective silencer.

Cooper hoped he wouldn't have to use it, and in fact, he would have traded the weapon for a cheap pair of wire cutters. Reproaching himself for not thinking through all the possibilities back at the Walmart, he walked up the road to Schneider's place, listening out for dogs and looking ahead for any sign of patrol vehicles making their rounds.

The quiet neighbourhood slept soundly as a born-again killer ghosted through it.

The wall around Schneider's property was high but fetchingly constructed of river stones and crumbling mortar. Cooper smiled. A break.

He slung the MP9 over his back and tested the grip of his shoes on a protruding rock at the base of the wall. The rubber tread took the foothold securely. He didn't allow himself to worry about everything that could go wrong – disintegrating masonry, electrified wire, a fall, a broken limb. He emptied his mind of all thought but the idea, the certainty, that he was going up this wall.

He went up quickly. An observer watching him might even have gasped at the speed with which he scaled the obstacle.

Going down the other side was more challenging. He was climbing in deep darkness, but his eyes adjusted quickly. He descended with care, dropping the last couple of feet to the soft soil of a flower bed.

Bringing the weapon around, Cooper scanned the grounds in front of him. The house, styled after a Normandy château, sat well back from the street. A small grove of trees stood between Cooper and the three-storey mansion, but an imitation gas lamp at the head of the gravel driveway provided a helpful point of reference for navigation.

A black Chevy Suburban was parked in front of the main entrance. A man in dark clothes, carrying an automatic weapon, sat on the front steps, smoking.

Cooper flicked off the safety on his MP9.

Crouching, he moved forward to the stand of trees, taking cover behind the trunk of an old poplar. He searched the night sky for power lines, finding them about fifty yards to the right of the main gate. The long, drooping cable connected to the corner of the house over a three-door garage. Cooper navigated a path around the edge of the property, getting as close as he could to the garage without stepping out into the open. The last sixty yards he crossed was open ground, protected from the sentry by the corner of the house.

As he reached the fuse box tucked away around the side of the garage, he heard the crackle of a radio. A male voice, tinny and muted by distance.

"I'm taking a piss. Schneider's asleep."

"Acknowledged," another voice replied. It was louder and didn't come through a radio.

The sentry out front.

A minimum of two bodyguards, then. Possibly up to four or even six. He had a couple of minutes while the man inside was on the can.

Cooper worked the edges of the darkness, heading for the corner of the front veranda.

He listened for any sound of movement from the sentry by the vehicle.

Nothing.

Slipping around the corner and up onto the flagstone terrace, he saw the glow of the man's cigarette about thirty yards away. He was still sitting on the steps, mostly scanning the wide expanse of the estate's front garden.

Cooper Fox came upon him silently.

A carotid strangle took nine and a half seconds to black the man out.

Cooper felt that same urge which had seized him when he stood over Ted Sorenson. A cold impulse to murder. A simple adjustment to his grip would do it, shifting the focus of the strangle to the trachea.

He resisted the urge. The sentry had flexicuffs looped through his belt. Cooper quickly secured him with the plastic ties and gagged him with a couple more ties and his own sock.

Crude, but it would do.

He took the man's radio and weapon and tried the front entrance.

It was unlocked.

The door swung open on well-oiled hinges.

A cat screeched at him and darted out between his legs. Cooper's heart rate barely changed. He felt an almost eerie disconnection from everything he was doing. The man he had just attacked. The excellent chance he was about to die.

Cooper moved a few feet into the house and stopped, listening.

Faintly, from a great distance, he heard snoring. And closer, a faucet running.

He ghosted through the house, moving towards the sound of running water. He was a shadow within shadows.

He reached the downstairs bathroom as the tap shut off. The other guard was drying his hands when Cooper found him.

The man lay face down, unconscious and bound with his own restraints when Cooper left.

"GET UP."

The figure in the bed grunted and mumbled before suddenly gasping and scrambling upright.

Cooper Fox took two steps back, keeping the sights of the MP9 on the centre mass of Professor Erhard Schneider, who babbled with a German accent, "Who are you? Please, don't hurt me. I have money. I'll get it for you."

"Shut up," Cooper said. "Get out of bed slowly, and put your hands behind your head, and lace your fingers together."

"Michael? Michael, is that you?"

Cooper aimed the gun at the base of the bed and squeezed off a three-round burst. Schneider cried out in panic.

"Do as I say, Professor. Get out of bed and put your hands behind your head. Your bodyguards won't help you. The next time I pull the trigger, I'm going to put a bullet into your leg. You won't be able to get out of bed, but you will still be able to answer my questions. Your choice."

Schneider struggled out from under the blankets, climbing unsteadily to his feet. He had trouble speaking, he was so frightened.

"Michael, please. We were only trying to help."

"Shut up and turn on the lights. A bedside lamp if you have one."

Cooper covered one eye with his free hand.

Schneider flicked on a lamp. Cooper waited half a second before carefully dropping his hand. His depth perception was affected, but he wasn't blinded as he would have been.

Schneider winced against the sudden light.

Cooper gestured with the gun.

"I want the project data. All of it. You *will* have material here. Or you'll have access to it online. Whatever you've got on the nootropic project, I want it."

"But, but the nootropics…" Schneider started.

Cooper cut him off.

"If you screw me around, I will shoot you in the kneecap. The pain will be like nothing you have ever experienced. But it won't kill you. I will torture you, focussing on that wound, until you give me what I want. So just do it, professor. Save us both a lot of inconvenient splatter."

Schneider wet himself.

"Michael, please, don't do this, let me help you…"

Cooper put another burst into the mattress. The bed looked like an antique. Maybe George Washington slept in it once.

"I'm in a hurry, Professor. I have to assume Kristin or Ted is coming. We have about ten minutes. Give me your project data and any samples of the drug I was on."

"But I don't have anything like that here," Schneider pleaded.

Cooper advanced on him, three strides, and smashed him in the face with the gun. Erhard Schneider tumbled backwards, crying out pitiably.

"You're not used to violence, Professor," Cooper said. "I am. We all have our specialties. Do not make me demonstrate mine again."

He could see the other man's moral collapse. All the scheming and manoeuvring and artful conniving that Schneider might have been planning imploded when he realised that Michael Garner really would hurt him and maybe even kill him if he did not do as he was told.

"I'm sorry, I'm sorry, Michael," he whined. "I have some data here; yes, I can give you that. I'd be happy to give you that. Please, just, please. I can give you the data. The nootropics. The gene sequencing. The accelerants and implants."

Cooper stared at him.

"The what?"

Schneider's hands were shaking. His whole body was trembling. If he hadn't emptied his bladder already, he would have wet himself again.

"I've got it all in secure storage, but it is downstairs."

Cooper kept the gun trained on him.

"What do you mean by gene sequencing and accelerants?" Cooper said.

Schneider was still backing away in fear. He almost tripped over his own feet. He fell backwards onto the bed, flinching as if expecting to be struck.

"Professor," Cooper said, keeping his voice low and level, "I know about the nootropics. The smart drugs. And the antagonist formula they had me on. The dumb drugs. I don't know about any gene sequencing or that other stuff. You better tell me right now. And make it quick. What did you people do to me?"

Schneider's abject terror lost some of its jagged edge. Not much, but enough.

"You don't remember?"

Cooper sighed.

"I remember everything. I know my name was Lovell. I was a Navy SEAL. I got out and went private. I freelanced for Rolly Sewell, among others. The last job I took, cleaning up the mess you and Ludgrove made with your drug trial for Rolly, I remember it all. What you did. And what I did."

His voice was bitter.

Schneider shook his head.

"No," he said. "You don't."

Cooper raised the muzzle of the MP9 a few inches.

"Don't lie to me," he said. "I'm not on that medication anymore. I know what happened."

Schneider gaped at him. "No, you don't," he said. "You have no idea."

"Then make it fast," Cooper said. "Do not screw me around. All I want is the data and the samples. Give them to me, and I will go. But I need to know what I'm looking at. What did you mean by gene sequencing? And accelerants."

Erhard Schneider looked like a man teetering on the edge of a cliff.

He stepped off.

"Your name was not Lovell," he said. "You weren't in the Navy. You didn't even exist."

Cooper shook his head, annoyed.

"I know how it works, Schneider. Ten years ago, Jarrod Lovell *ceased* to exist. They didn't erase him. That's impossible to do. But they killed him, on the record. A chopper crash. A firefight. Whatever. A death certificate and a folded flag for my next of kin. Then Michael Garner appears. A ghost. Deployable, deniable..."

He stopped talking.

Schneider was looking at him differently.

Not with fear now, but pity.

"Michael," he explained. "When I said you didn't exist, I meant that literally."

"What?" Cooper said.

26

"I'm a clone?"

Cooper Fox had lowered the gun. He needed a moment. He wasn't in shock, but he wasn't far off.

"No," Schneider replied. "You're not a clone. You are unique, Michael. All the subjects in your cohort were unique. It was a terrible thing what happened when they had to be destroyed."

"Murdered, you mean," Cooper said. "I murdered them."

He turned the gun back on Schneider.

"Talk. Fast."

"But Michael, there is so much to tell. The program it was years in the making. Decades. An interdisciplinary marvel. Genetics, pharmacology, gerontology, I can't..."

"A synopsis will do, Professor. I have to go. I have to make this right for my family. But I need to know what I'm doing."

Schneider leaned forward on the bed, imploring. The lamp light made deep shadow pools of his eyes.

"Michael, your family was with us. This woman you have been with, I am sure she is a lovely person, but she is not for you. If it were not for your treatment regime of the last three years, these feelings you have for her would not even have been possible. She is beneath you, Michael. Unworthy..."

Cooper's voice came out in a growl.

"Choose your next words very carefully."

The Professor retreated, patting the air in front of him as if to tamp down any spark of offence.

"Please, Michael, I was always on your side," he said, begging Cooper to believe him. "You were my masterwork, Michael. Not just the proof of concept but its very zenith. I always thought of you as the son I could not have. I urged them to take you fully into their trust. First at DARPA and then at Triple Helix. It would have been better for you, for the program. My models proved that."

Cooper exploded.

"Fuck your program and your models. *What. Did. You. Do.*"

"We built you, Michael. From the genome up. We created you, literally. You were a test tube baby of a sort, but a very particular sort. You have a lot of customised DNA in you. You gestated for the normal period, nine months, in a surrogate mother, of course. Unfortunately, we are a long way off building an exo-womb. However, your post-natal development was accelerated by pharmacological intervention and genomic engineering. Some of your abilities, many of them literally inhuman, were designed to specification."

Cooper looked at Schneider without really seeing him.

He was cataloguing all the things he couldn't remember, even as his memory came back. A family home. A family. Anything but the barest details of his life in the Navy. And the more he thought about details, the less they seemed like his true memories and more like impressions and images recalled from someone else's past.

"Whose..." he started to say before pulling himself together. "Whose specifications?"

"DARPA, originally. But they were just reacting to a Chinese program that was much more advanced. Our work there was shut down when idiots in Congress investigated it. Christians, evangelicals," Schneider spat. "Anti-science fanatics and hypocrites, all of them. I had some help from the agency to take the data private to secure the gains of the original program, but the companies I approached did not have the vision or the will to realise the promise of this work. Until..."

Cooper sighed.

"Until you found Rolly. And he did."

Schneider nodded. He was growing less fearful and more animated.

"Sir Roland is not a visionary. He is a thug and a scoundrel, as you well know. But he is also a risk-taker, and he understands the return on investment. This was a large investment, even for him. But the returns, *mein Gott*. Michael, surely you, of all people, can see the potential of this research. Bespoke human beings, Michael. Fully crafted and fit for purpose. Evolution is so slow, so many thousands of generations, and we have the chance to liberate humanity from all its weaknesses and frailties..."

"Shut up now, right now," Cooper Fox said, struggling to contain his anger. This guy was telling some monstrous lie, or he was himself some sort of monster. "Just give me the data," Cooper hissed. "Give me any drug samples you have. I'll figure this out for myself."

"Undoubtedly, you will," Schneider said. "You are more than intelligent enough. That was one of your subject parameters."

"I said stop talking. I've heard enough from you."

The professor fell silent. His nose was bleeding, and his face was swollen from the blow Cooper had given him.

"Just get up slowly and get me the files. Now."

Schneider climbed to his feet. Unsteadily. The German walked with a noticeably bow-legged gait, which Cooper put down to his sodden pyjama pants. The smell of urine was strong.

Schneider maintained a home office downstairs in a drawing room overlooking the grounds at the rear of the estate. The night sky was black with clouds, but Cooper found he had no trouble making out details in the garden. Two fountains, a glasshouse, and a small pond. He thought about asking Schneider whether they had spliced in the genes for his night vision, but he kept the question to himself.

He did not want to believe it, and how could he ever trust this man anyway?

There were several computers on the desk, but Schneider shuffled past them all, heading for a bookshelf. He removed a dozen or more thick hardback books to reveal a hidden safe. He bent slowly on creaking knees and fussed with the keypad lock on the door. A second later, he had the door open and a large packet of documents in his hand as he stood up.

"I don't entirely trust digital storage," he said, offering Cooper the package. "Or Sir Roland, for that matter. That is a hard copy of the most important data, but there are a couple of thumb drives as well. They have more information."

He paused. Turned back to the safe. Cooper kept the gun trained on him, but when Schneider turned around again, he was holding an envelope.

"Money," the professor said. "To help you get away. I would ask you sincerely, Michael, to try to understand. I only wanted the best for you and your siblings. What happened to them was not my fault. I tried; I begged Sir Roland to spare you all."

Cooper almost hit him again, but in the end, he stayed quiet, staring at Schneider. He didn't know what to think or do about any of this. The world seemed tilted off its axis, as though everything might start sliding away and over the edge. Things were bad enough when he'd thought he was just some amnesiac mercenary who'd run afoul of a crooked employer and had been doped up on experimental dumb drugs and put into storage for three years. Schneider's new story was so balls-out crazy that he wondered why anyone would even bother with such a lie.

"Try to *make* me understand," he said at last.

He took the money and lowered the gun. He probably had a minute at most.

"The research, Michael, it was not evil," Schneider started. He threw his hands up as soon as he saw Cooper's expression. "No, no, I understand. It was put to evil ends. That is what happens when the military is involved. Our warmongers, theirs, they all seek the same ends. Destruction. But Michael, my research was about creation. Creating life, extending life. There seemed nothing we could not do."

"So, you just went ahead and did it," Cooper said, his voice flat.

Schneider shook his head emphatically, "No," he said. "I had clear boundaries with Sir Roland. Limits I alone enforced. I told him I would not make the likes of you and your cohort again. I would not make weapons as DARPA had insisted. I would only make and improve upon life."

"What about sense, Professor? Would you like to start making some sense? You can improve on your efforts so far by telling me who this is."

He took out the picture of the young woman he'd found in the safe in his apartment. It was badly creased.

Schneider took it and sighed.

"Subject Raven," he said almost wistfully. "From your cohort."

"We were...like, what? Test tube siblings? She's black," Cooper pushed back.

Schneider shook his head.

"Michael, you must understand you were beyond such foolishness. You were perfected human beings, children of a higher purpose. Such simple traits as skin colour or hair type are easily manipulated. It was the deeper..." He paused, searching for the right word. "The deeper *essences* we sought to...articulate...until the moralisers found out. The straighteners and punishers. *Mein Gott,* they are such contemptible hypocrites," he spat.

Cooper had many more questions, but time was surely running out.

He didn't know whether anybody was coming, but he had to prepare as though they were.

The snake uncoiled inside of him.

That's how he had begun to think of the pitiless instinct he sometimes felt, driving him toward murder. He fought it down.

"I'm going," he told Schneider. "If you're smart, you will too. They'll kill you. You're a witness now, not an accomplice. If I were you, Professor, I'd get out of the country. Somewhere without an extradition treaty."

27

Rolly Sewell owned homes across five cities on two continents. Cooper had no way of fixing his location in real time, but Aleksei Kozlov undoubtedly did. He was already indebted to the Russians; another favour in the bank was just more karmic debt to pay off. And Cooper had so much of that now; a little extra could hardly matter.

He drove back to DC, shaking for the first ten minutes of the trip. He had not killed Schneider or the guards. It was a mistake, he knew, but a tactical error, not a moral failing.

Perhaps Schneider would flee. Maybe he would untie the guards, and they would call up reinforcements. Cooper could not know or control that, but he could control his actions. He could make choices, even poor ones.

His blood had sung with the need to kill everybody in Schneider's house. It was the only way to be sure he would have the freedom of movement he needed. But he knew there would ultimately be no freedom in doing so. He would simply be fulfilling the dictates of his...engineering.

He was not some homicidal robot or cyborg. He was Cooper Fox, beloved of Mary Doyle, and he would make his own choices. Stopping at a roadhouse just outside of Bethesda, he used a payphone to call the number on the Russian's business card. Kozlov didn't answer, but somebody did.

Cooper told them who he was and what he needed.

They told him to call back in fifteen minutes.

He filled in the time by checking over the Chevy. He might have a hard drive ahead of him. The front tyres needed air, and he topped up the gas tank.

When he called back, Kozlov himself answered. It was 3.42 AM, and he sounded cheerfully wide awake.

"Michael, such a pleasant surprise to hear from you so soon. You have been busy with the information I provided?"

"Idlers do not make history, Aleksei. They suffer it," he said, quoting the anarchist philosopher Kropotkin again.

"Indeed, they do, Michael. Indeed, they do. You will find your man at his *dacha* in the Hamptons."

Kozlov read out an address.

Cooper committed it to memory.

"We are informed that Sir Roland repaired there only yesterday with a large security detachment," Aleksei went on. "I'm afraid I cannot be more specific as to his arrangements. Such short notice, you understand."

"I do. Thank you, Aleksei," Cooper said.

"We will talk soon, Michael. Take care."

The Russian hung up.

There was an airport at East Hampton, but it would be another two hours at least before he could hope to charter a flight there, and it was likely that Rolly's security men would have it under watch anyway. He had probably left New York when he heard about Cooper's escape. His next move would be out of the country. He could be on the way now if Schneider had warned him.

The snake uncoiled itself somewhere inside Cooper, hissing at him for letting the German live. He tried to ignore it.

If he left now and drove through, he could get to the Hamptons by mid-morning and choose the best line of approach.

But he was exhausted.

The last time he'd slept had been the few hours he'd dozed while tied up by Kristin's goons. His system had been flooded multiple times by stress hormones and adrenaline, and he'd just come off a three-year-long psychoactive drug trial. He was deeply disturbed by what Schneider had told him, and if he was being honest with himself, he felt as though he was coming unglued.

He had a good chance of falling asleep at the wheel and crashing the car.

He could try to sleep for an hour or two before leaving, but that merely increased the chances of Rolly getting away from him. And he was determined to have it out with Sewell, no matter what. There could be no hope for Mary and the kids if he did not settle up with the old monster, one way or another. He knew that for a cold certainty. Some memories were all too real.

He needed a driver.

The roadhouse, a Texaco, wasn't busy, but it wasn't empty either. He scanned the food court, looking for travellers, specifically hitchhikers. They would be young and hauling backpacks, possibly adorned with stickers or patches from their previous travels.

Nothing.

A tired-looking family picked over a breakfast of fried chicken and hash browns under the flat white glare of fluorescent lights.

Two soldiers with heavy duffels sat in a booth, passing their phones back and forth, sharing videos or stupid memes or something.

A table of half-a-dozen older men, mostly heavy-set, mostly slump-shouldered, looked like truckers to Cooper. Two of them wore Peterbilt caps, and another was sporting a Kenworth. They all seemed to know each other, and they gave off a proprietary air as though they were the traditional owners of this roadhouse, and everyone else was merely here on their say-so.

They would do.

Cooper approached them with a neutral smile on his face, using all his willpower to keep a lid on his simmering cauldron of ill feelings.

"Fellas," he said when he was close enough to have intruded on their space. "Sorry to interrupt. I'm driving through to Long Island, and I gotta get there by midday, but I'm spent. It's not safe for me to push on through. Does anyone know where I might pick up a rider, someone to take the wheel while I rest up?"

A few of them stared at him blankly. One spoke up. The Kenworth hat guy.

"Good thing you know when not to drive, son. Lotta damn fools could do with that sort of common sense."

"Thanks," Cooper said. "It's been a long week."

"Amen to that, brother," one of the Peterbilts said.

"You might pick up a hitchhiker going east over near New Carroll-

ton," the other Peterbilt said. "I seen 'em there looking for rides sometimes just short of the ramp onto Interstate 50."

Another man, black, grey-haired, somewhere in his early sixties,
scoffed at that.

"Fella said he's got to be there this year, Merv."

He looked up at Cooper. The trucker wore a faded army jacket with
an old Cavalry patch on the shoulder.

"What's the rush, son?"

The snake uncoiled, sensing an opportunity.

"My dad's in a VA hospice up there," Cooper said. "We haven't had a
lot to do with each other these last few years, but they called me and said
he doesn't have much longer. So, you know, I been driving."

A few of the truckers nodded in sympathy.

The black man chewed it over.

"A pity you're driving yourself then. I coulda got you most of the way
there. I got shipments for Farmingdale and Maywood, near the airport."

"East Hampton airport?" Cooper asked.

"Ha, no, Republic. Fewer Lear jets, more cargo."

Cooper gave the appearance of thinking it over.

"Okay," he said, "Look, I'm in a jam here. If you're going that way,
I'm happy to pay you for the ride. Leave my car here and come back for
it. She's a clunker anyway. My name is Cooper, by the way. Cooper
Fox."

The trucker waved him to a seat.

"Sit down then, Coop," he said. "I'm Leroy Whitting. You can intro-
duce yourself around or not as you please. My old man is eighty-three
and going strong, but eighty-three is deep in the last innings of the ball
game, whichever way you look at it. I try to call him most days, seeing as
I figure the day's coming soon when I won't be able to. You need to go
make it good with your kin."

Cooper sat down, taken into the magic trucker circle on the say-so of
Leroy Whitting.

He knew he should feel some guilt, perhaps even some shame, for
lying to a good man as he just had. And part of him did. But the part of
him once known as Michael Garner did not care.

They left five minutes later. Cooper's gym bag was heavy with
weapons and Schneider's documents. He unzipped a side pocket and
removed the envelope with the cash he'd taken from the professor,
stashed it in a coat pocket and zipped up the bag. He should have sani-

tised the Chevy or burned it down to the wheel rims, but that wasn't an option.

Instead, he joined Leroy in the cabin of his Freightliner. He pressed two hundred dollars on the trucker, insisting he take it.

"I'm not gonna be much company," Cooper said. "I wasn't lying about needing to crash."

"Then to your rest you go, young man. If you sleep through, I'll wake you when we get to Maywood."

Leroy took the money with a creditable show of reluctance. Cooper put his bag down between his feet and stretched out as best he could. He was asleep within minutes.

LEROY WHITTING DROPPED Cooper off just inside the freight entrance to the small regional airport. Cooper thanked the trucker, apologised for having slept through most of the six-hour journey, and slipped another fifty-dollar note into the cupholder when Whitting wasn't looking.

He felt much better after the rest.

The conversation with Schneider, the whole sequence of events at the house, seemed a half-forgotten dream. The man had been lying. In fear for his life, he'd come up with an unbelievable story and cast himself as the hero of the tale. When small lies will not suffice, tell the biggest lie you can.

He remembered that from somewhere.

Cooper walked to the rental car hut and picked up a grey Nissan Altima. The whole deal nearly came apart when the woman behind the Avis counter asked him for his driver's licence. Suddenly, he was free-falling through his missing years. He didn't drive. He couldn't drive. He was Cooper Fox, whose parents had died in a car accident and...

"Sir? Are you okay?"

"Huh?" Cooper went.

"Your driver's licence, sir? And credit card?"

His hand drifted to his back pocket, reaching for a wallet that wasn't there.

But his California driver's licence in the name of Tom Hackmore was.

"Sorry," Cooper said, giving his voice a softer West Coast lilt. "I'm like a thousand miles away."

The woman took the licence and keyed in the details.

"More like three thousand miles, right?"

"Sure," he smiled, showing no sign of the tension he felt in his neck, wondering what would happen when she fed the licence number into her system.

What happened was she gave him back his licence, his company debit card, and the keys to the Nissan.

A few minutes later, he drove off the lot and turned right, heading for the Hamptons.

Cooper felt refreshed after the sleep in Leroy Whitting's long-hauler. Still, he had an hour and a half's drive ahead of him, long enough to second guess himself and undermine any resolve or confidence he felt and not nearly enough time to prepare for an infiltration, or assault, or whatever lay ahead.

Erhard Schneider's place had been a soft target. Rolly Sewell's billionaire compound would not be. All he had from Kozlov this time was an address and a warning. Rolly had fled to the compound yesterday with a 'large security team'. There would be no climbing the outer walls and letting himself in through an unlocked door. He couldn't assault the place.

Cooper had no idea what he was doing.

Speeding up the Sunrise Highway and across the bridge over the Shinnecock Canal, the morning sun blazed off the white hulls of yachts and pleasure cruisers moored at a marina on his left. The mouth of the canal opened out to the blue-green waters of the Great Peconic Bay beyond.

He eased his foot off the accelerator, just enough to slow his head-long rush towards a showdown with Rolly.

Why was he doing this?

Because he judged Roland Sewell unlikely to let him walk away. Cooper was a threat now.

He eased off the gas even more. Somebody behind him leaned into the horn.

Mary and Matty and Jess.

Sewell would definitely go after them to get to him. Or rather, he'd pay somebody like Kristin to do it.

Cooper turned off the highway and into a beachfront suburb of surprisingly modest houses. It wasn't a poor neighbourhood, not even close. But the grounds of Schneider's mansion could have accommodated a dozen or more of the split-level cottages and modest bungalows.

He pulled over to the side of the road in front of a vacant lot, ankle-deep in red and brown leaf litter from a stand of eastern red cedar and sugar maple trees.

He was overwhelmed by a premonition of doom and a yawning loneliness. He was deeply troubled by everything Schneider had told him and tempted to check into a motel somewhere and spend a day poring over the files. He missed Mary as much as he had ever missed anybody in his life. Or what he remembered of his life. He wanted to turn the car around and drive back to her. Just grab her and the children and keep going. Disappear into the vast anonymous hinterlands of America.

But he couldn't.

While he had breath in his body, he was a danger to Triple Helix and to the billionaire criminal who owned it. If Roland Sewell thought Cooper was out there, he would send killers to find him. Cooper might, just might, have been able to negotiate a return to the program and his life back in Gainesville, but only in the earliest moments of his reawakening.

As soon as he tried to escape, from the minute he threw off his sheep's cloak and reverted to his true self, he was marked for elimination.

If he'd been doing Kristin's job, it's what he would have done.

It's what he *had* done. For Rolly, for sure. And maybe before that for the government. The further back he reached, the less certain he was of his recall.

Cooper sat behind the wheel of the rental car and shuddered as the impossible reality of it all overwhelmed him.

He wasn't a merciless avenger. He was not some reborn killer angel. He didn't know who or what he was other than a guy who'd fucked up and fallen low and, for the last three years, had been a charity case for a small, backwoods high school football team. His hands shook, and his heart raced.

He should turn the car around, drive back to New York and take his dossier, his drug samples and himself to a TV station or a newspaper. He should go to the *New York Times* and tell them he had one of the greatest stories of the decade to tell.

And then he should get ready to spend many, many years in jail.

Because that's where he was going. Into jail or into the ground, probably both and in that order.

Cooper Fox closed his eyes and inhaled deeply.

"Enough," he said. "It's enough. Just get it done. For them."

He restarted the car and pulled away from the side of the road. He drove east, heading for Roland Sewell's compound.

He stopped one more time at a small shopping centre in East Hampton, where he paid a ridiculous amount of money to rent a locker in which he stashed his gym bag and its contents.

28

Sir Roland Sewell's Hamptons estate sat astride twenty-five acres of beachfront land, between the stately homes of a junk bond king and a lesser prince of the Thai royal family. It was protected from the street by high stone walls. And these walls, unlike those of his hireling Professor Schneider, were topped with electrified wire and sharpened spikes. Thick plantings of Norwegian maple and pitch pine soared high over the defences, further protecting the rich man's privacy. Signs warned that aerial drones overflying the property would be shot down. With a week to plan a stealth attack and unlimited funds to equip himself and hire tactical support, Cooper supposed he could have come in from the sea. Rolly enjoyed absolute ownership of the beachfront. Unlike in his native England, the local statutes allowed him to fence off the long stretch of white sand for his use and pleasure.

Yeah, Cooper thought. Come in from the sea. Like he'd been taught. That was the smart move.

Instead, he drove up to the front gate and rang the buzzer. The sound of it acted as a calmative to his confusion and fears. He was committed to action now, and he leaned into that above all else.

A voice crackled out with a statement, not a question.

"Turn around and go. You do not have an appointment."

"No," he said. "Just tell Rolly that Mike Garner is here. I'm not armed."

The connection faded out with a crackle.

He waited.

A minute or two later, a new voice came back.

Kristin Hegel

"Hey, Mikey," she said cheerily.

"Hi, honey," he deadpanned. "I'm home."

"Not even, boyfriend. But come on through. Drive up to the checkpoint and stop. You can't miss it. It is the most delightful little wooden house. Looks like a Hobbit lives there. Stop the car, get out and lie face down on the ground with your hands behind your head. Can you do that, sweetie?"

"Yeah, I can do that," he said.

"Super-duper," Kristin said, sounding ridiculously enthused. "Because if you don't, I got two guys with eyes on you already. One has you sitting in the crosshairs of a Barrett XM500, and he will put a fifty-calibre round through the middle of your pretty face if I tell him to or, you know, if he sneezes. The other guy, he's just got some bullshit spray-n-pray pussy cannon, but he's hiding up a tree near the gate and he won't miss."

Cooper sighed.

"You always did love the sound of your own voice, Kristin."

She laughed.

"That's because it's the only one worth listening to, Mikey. Come on in."

The massive steel gates rolled aside, and he drove through.

Cooper didn't doubt that multiple shooters had him tagged, and he did exactly as Kristin instructed. He drove slowly up the gravel driveway, through the perimeter forest and out into the first of a series of manicured gardens. Giant topiary animals appeared to frolic and play around a large, kidney-shaped pond. A white marble fountain pushed a spout of water high into the air, creating a rainbow effect in the morning sunlight.

The guard post, a small brown wooden shack, sat on the other side of the sculpted hedges.

Cooper stopped the car, climbed out and lay face down on the grass.

He put his hands behind his head and waited. It took a while, but eventually, he heard a strange humming, crunching noise. He lifted his head as far as he dared and saw two golf buggies approaching, each carrying three armed men.

He couldn't help smiling.

It looked like he'd come to a country club for sad guys with a James Bond fetish.

These guys were good at their jobs, though.

None of them got close enough for him to lay a hand on them.

They stood off, kept him under the sights of their weapons, and ordered him to get to his feet.

One of the suits fetched a device from the buggy. A metal detector. The sensor plate was attached to an extra-long arm, allowing him to sweep Cooper from a safe distance. His belt buckle, the heels of his boots, and the metal in his ankles all registered pings. The operator had him remove the boots and his belt.

A quick inspection of his bare feet and lower legs followed.

"Titanium inserts. I got blown out of a chopper in Iraq," Cooper said, explaining why he was still setting off the metal detector.

"All clear," the man announced.

Cooper put on his shoes and threaded the belt again.

"Start yomping, mate," one of the men said. A Londoner to judge by his accent. A Royal Marine once upon a time. Cooper recalled meeting a few of them in the sandbox. Or at least he thought he did. They never walked or marched or hauled ass. They "yomped" everywhere.

The detail climbed back into their golf buggies.

"Hardly seems fair," Cooper said as he trudged ahead of them, crunching up the gravel driveway.

"Money talks and bullshit walks, pal," someone said. An American this time.

Sir Roland Sewell's Hampton pad was a three-storey, mock Tudor mansion with all the medieval Disney trimmings. Whitewashed plaster walls, roughhewn black oaken timbers, half a million hand-carved wooden roofing shingles. It was all magnificently out of place here in the playground of the New World's mega-rich, but it wouldn't have fitted in back where Rolly came from either.

It screamed new money disguised in old-world drag.

Cooper tallied the number of his enemies.

He added the six men who'd intercepted him at the Hobbit house to the sniper and the gunman in the elevated hide by the front gate. Eight shooters, but that wasn't the end of it.

Inside the dark entry hall, two more suits waited.

Ten.

They escorted him through to a large, ornate library at the rear of the mansion. The massive reading room reached up through two storeys of the building and was lined on three sides with floor-to-ceiling book-shelves, all of them filled with ancient-looking volumes. A narrow mezzanine walkway ran around the collection where the second floor should have been.

The fourth wall was a vast expanse of armoured glass, opening the room up to a panoramic view of the Atlantic Ocean. A heavy, antique desk stood at one end of the vista, a full-sized pool table at the other.

No, Cooper thought. It was a snooker table. A larger surface with smaller pockets.

Sir Roland was lining up a shot with his one good eye as the security detail led Cooper into the library. His other eye, blinded in a street fight many, many years ago, was hidden behind a plain black patch.

Ted Sorenson was over by the desk, idly twirling a large globe on a heavy stand.

Kristin Hegel stood with a wooden cue, waiting for her turn at the table.

That made twelve potential adversaries.

Kristin winked at Cooper.

Snapped her fingers.

One of her men disappeared back out of the door through which Cooper had just entered.

Sir Roland gave no sign that he'd noticed Cooper's arrival or that he would pay it the slightest heed when he did notice.

He drew back his cue and executed a crisp bank shot that almost, but not quite, came off.

"Bugger," he said, standing up straight and stretching his back as the balls came to rest in their new constellation.

"Company's here," Kristin said.

Sir Roland carefully placed the cue on the table, folded his arms, and sighed as though reluctantly turning to a deeply unwelcome task.

"So I see, luv. Michael, you'd better come in, son," he gestured for Cooper to come closer. "You too, Prof."

Cooper Fox made a quarter turn back to the door. Professor Schneider stumbled in, his face even more swollen and blackened than before. He had dressed in a suit since Cooper had last seen him, but it was crumpled and spotted with blood. His eyes darted around the room, never settling anywhere for more than a split second.

Cooper regulated his breathing. His heart rate was elevated but not racing away. He opened his senses and let the world pour in. There was so much to absorb, an infinity of detail and possibilities, but he stilled his conscious mind and accepted it all. The saltiness of the sea air, the distant crash of waves on a rocky promontory, the denser thump of the same line of surf punching into the sandy beach directly outside the library. The grip of his shoes on the faded Turkish rug and the grip of the rug on the parquetry floor beneath it. Outside, the late morning sun twinkled off the green-blue depths like a net of gold and silver coins cast upon the seas. Inside, dust motes floated serenely through a shaft of sunlight falling just to the side of the globe, which still turned slowly under Ted Sorenson's fingers. Nine of the solid red balls remained on the snooker table, along with all six colours.

These and a thousand other details lit up the synapses of Cooper's sensory cortex, where something akin to organic algorithms filtered them into binary categories.

Useful data, and the rest.

The rest he dumped without conscious effort.

What remained was an architecture of contingencies.

The chance of grabbing one of those snooker balls and using it as a distance weapon.

The likely force needed to snap a wooden snooker cue to fashion a crude pair of *eskrima* fighting sticks.

The advantages and disadvantages of simply using the whole cue as a quarterstaff.

He noted the disposition of each man in the room relative to the others and Kristin's unique status as the only woman.

She would be the most dangerous of them.

To the inventory of personal weapons he had noted for each man, Cooper added a second armoury of improvised weaponry located throughout the room. Everything from the heavy crystal whisky decanter sitting on a delicate, antique table six feet to his right to the dozen or so silver teaspoons resting upright in a duck egg blue Wedgewood cup on the wheeled trolley set for morning tea. The process, known as priming, was automatic.

"I suppose we'd all best have a bit of chat then, eh," Sir Roland said, strolling over to the trolly set with a teapot and all the fixings. "The fuckin' grief and bother you've given me, Michael. It really makes a bloke think. I've felt legitimate remorse for all the fucking bother I paid you to hand out on my behalf over the years."

Cooper nodded sincerely.

"We could turn ourselves in," he said, turning his hands out to include Professor Schneider. "Make amends to society," he added, with another small gesture, getting everyone used to the idea that his hands might move at any moment and that it was nothing to worry about.

Sir Roland stopped in the middle of his expensive Turkish rug and stared at Cooper with a look of comical surprise.

"Fuck me," he said. "I never thought of that. Do you think that'd work, Mikey? You reckon they'd let me keep all me lovely money and nice things? If I just said sorry for being such a villain?"

"No," Cooper said.

Sir Roland's grin was almost boyish.

"No, lad, I don't imagine they would."

He resumed his journey towards the trolley.

"Tea?"

"Sure," Cooper said, taking a step closer.

"Hey!" Kristin Hegel barked at him. "Back the fuck up."

To Sir Roland, in a much quieter and more respectful voice, she said, "I warned you about him. Do not engage and do not, under any circumstances, get within striking distance. He's already calculated at least half a dozen ways of killing you with your collection of fine China."

Sir Roland paused, but only for a moment.

"Fair enough. No tea for you, Mikey. What about you, Prof? Fancy a cuppa?"

"I...I would prefer a small black coffee," Schneider said.

Sir Roland found that so funny he laughed out loud.

"Oh, dear me. No wonder your mob lost the war."

He performed an elaborate, almost ceremonial pouring of milk and tea before stirring in a teaspoon of sugar for himself. Nobody said anything, Kristin's eyes bored into Cooper. Ted spun the globe. One of the suits deposited Schneider on a couch. The others stood at parade ground rest or shifted minimally from foot to foot as nerves and uncertainty got the better of them.

Cooper noted who remained still and who was prone to alleviate their tension through micro-movements. Ted and Kristin, he filed away separately. They weren't just spear carriers. They were the centurions here.

Sipping from a delicate red and white china cup, Sir Roland closed his eyes to enjoy the moment.

"Marvellous what a restorative cup of tea can do," he said, opening his eyes again.

Another sip.

"Right then, to business." Sir Roland slammed the expensive crockery down.

Cooper noted everyone who flinched.

The same four guys who'd been twitching and fidgeting before, and one other. The metal detector guy.

Ted just kept turning the globe, looking bored. Kristin, like Cooper, remained as still as a cobra.

Schneider looked like he might have wet himself again.

Jabbing a finger at Cooper, Sir Roland advanced on him.

"You have well and truly fucked me, Mikey."

"Rolly," Kristin snapped. "Temper. And distance."

Sir Roland pulled himself up, breathing a little hard. His temper had run away with him, or more likely, Cooper thought, he had imported one of his negotiating techniques from the boardroom. Lull your opponent, then kick the legs out from under them.

"Right. All right then," he said, making an obvious, almost theatrical effort to calm down.

"I came here to turn myself in," Cooper said mildly, cutting across the performance. "To make amends."

Sir Roland blinked.

"You what, mate?"

Cooper froze. The world threatened to yawn open beneath his feet and swallow him whole.

Those three words had haunted him for years, even when he had been trapped inside a waking coma. *"You what, mate?"* The unbelieving response of Sir Roland Sewell when Michael Garner had long ago refused the order to terminate one of his cohort siblings. Subject Raven. A refusal which had, eventually, led him here to this room.

Cooper exhaled a pent-up breath and shrugged helplessly. A small move but expressive of a deep hopelessness that he felt was genuine.

"What else can I do, Rolly? I don't know for sure what Ludgrove and the Professor here were doing for you, and the more I find out, the less I understand. But it's not just you, is it? It's the military. The Agency. Whatever."

Sir Roland turned on the professor. His tone was dangerous.

"How much did you tell him?"

Schneider stared back through watery eyes. He jutted his chin out a little. Defiant.

"I tried to tell him everything," Schneider said. "But time was short. I don't know how much he comprehends."

Sir Roland tilted his head towards Cooper with an unspoken question.

Cooper shrugged.

"He said I was part of a program. Sounded like a breeding program. Genetic engineering or something. Accelerated post-natal development, both physical and psychological. The program raised me. Trained from birth, I guess. And there were others. A cohort."

Cooper stared at Sir Roland.

"The ones you sent me to kill. I remember that. You took in the professor and grabbed up his research, but first, you had to clean up the mess he left behind at DARPA. You sent me to kill my own. And God help me, I did it."

Sir Roland was nodding, smiling, but he did not look happy. His face was twisted into a caricature of a smile.

"It was a little more complicated than that, Mikey," he said, sounding as though he was almost insulted. "I got me start in drugs, you know. Bags of tweed on the old estate. Drugs are a good business if you got the head for it. And the 'nads. But they're even better when the game's legit. Just ask the big pharma companies. So, yes, when the prof here comes to me with a tidy proposition for some legitimate drug dealing, I'm like, good, let's go. No real fuckin' idea what I was getting into."

"You made an informed decision," Schneider protested, arcing up for the first time. Kristin took a half step toward him.

"In the end, yes," Sir Roland admitted. "But you were a bit of a villain, Prof. Giving me a taste like that, appealing to my greedy fucking nature, then pulling me all the way in."

"How, Rolly?" Cooper asked. "How did he pull you in?"

Kristin spoke up again.

"Seriously, Rolly. Do not give this dude your Shakespearean supervillain monologue. Nothing good ever comes from that."

"I'm not fucking King Lear, darlin'. I'm not mad. But young Mikey's not the only one been bent out of shape by all this fuss. It's been a bit bloody trying for all of us, and I'd very much like not to go to jail for three hundred fuckin' years or end up on some bloody CIA kill list. Mikey was always a bit of a champ at sorting stuff out for us. You know, before we had to knock him on the head and stash him away when the inspectors came a calling. I'd like to think he's still got the touch."

Kristin shook her head, mostly glaring at Cooper.

"What did you get into, Rolly?" Cooper asked again. "What did you get me into?"

Sir Roland snorted.

"Mate, I didn't get you into anything. You were part of the package old Doctor von Frankenstein over there was retailing. Isn't that right, prof?"

Schneider did not respond. He was staring at his shoes.

"You know any billionaires besides me?" Sir Roland asked Cooper, his tone appreciably lighter.

"Er, no."

"Fucking lunatics. All of 'em, mate! Fucking barmy on the subject of their demise, aren't they? Can't imagine the world going on without them."

Cooper could tell Kristin desperately needed to facepalm. Ted was grinning, and Schneider simply stared at Sir Roland, perhaps fascinated to hear the story of how he'd ended up in this room.

"Anyway," Sir Roland went on, "all these blokes, they've all got mountain-top lairs and Lear Jets full of baked beans, and they're planning to freeze their brains and stuff. So, when the prof here..." He nodded at Schneider. "...comes to my people about this dodgy government research, all very hush-hush, but he says it absolutely promises absolute control over ageing and such like, well, I'm in. For a new line of business, this sounds almost as tasty as slinging bags of tweed on the Hounslow. Legit anti-ageing pills. Not even bullshit ones. That's a guaranteed earn, am I right?"

Sir Roland stood with his hands on hips, shaking his head.

"Fuck me with a swollen prostate. I had no idea, Mikey, the capers and hijinks these boffins been up to before they got caught out by some God-bothering senators. They had little fucking test tube super-soldiers like you running around. They got these smart pills, and super drugs and tiny, little chemistry tweezers to give your DNA a handy fucking tweak. It's all very unnatural, but a quid's a quid, innit? So I'm in. It's only when I'm neck deep I find out Uncle fucking Sam still has his dick in the pudding bowl, and you, Mikey, you're the reason why. You're a weapon, son. A billion-dollar weapon they should never have built and couldn't bring themselves to give up, even when they got found out breaking all of the laws against messing with innocent little baby embryos and stuff. That's why they let the prof come to me. That's why you had to get rid of those other test tube kiddies. Although, to be fair, they weren't kiddies when you slotted them. They were all grown up into a major bloody inconvenience."

Cooper looked to Professor Schneider, hoping for a clearer explanation. The scientist shrugged.

"It was the only way to secure the project data. I took it private but with approval from DARPA. It was why you were spared when the rest of the cohorts had to be liquidated. You are still in the original program, Michael. Indeed, you *are* the program now, which is merely paused. Awaiting a change in political fortune."

"Oh, I suspect there's a couple of them still running around," Sir Roland said. "Old Mikey here let at least one of his little friends go, didn't he? It's why we had put you in that backwater, son. Wait for things to blow over."

Cooper turned back to Sir Roland.

"But what's in this for you? Seriously. A bunch of drugs you can't take to market? A bioengineering business that you know is gonna be outlawed as soon as you go public? What?"

Sir Roland let him see that twisted grin again.

"It's a decent payday, Mikey. Hiding away the government's dirty little secrets. And I've made real money from some of the prof's side projects. But I'm here for the long game, son. The stuff these blokes have been working on, controlling the aging process, turning it backwards even, that's a fucking trillion-dollar drink, right there. Youth not just eternal, but perfectible. Fuck me, if we get that sorted, I'll be so fucking rich I'll make the Saudis look like toothless fucking street people. And I'll get to enjoy it for fuckin' hundreds of years. But...here you are, pissing on my dreams. What is to be done, Mikey?"

Cooper let his shoulders slump in a convincing display of impotence and surrender.

"I woke up after three years in a coma, Rolly. That's what it was like. Brain death. No idea what was happening. And then I'm awake. I *had* to escape. That's what I was programmed to do. By people like her."

He nodded at Kristin. She smiled.

"It wasn't all work, Mikey."

"But I've had time to think," Cooper added. "To weigh the odds. And we both know how they fall. Look at this place."

He gestured around the room but implied something even greater beyond it. The house, the estate, and the billions that paid for it.

"Look at these goons. You've got an army of them."

He turned slowly, letting his eyes sweep over the security detail, noting any changes in position or attitude.

"I could kill them all. But you'd just send more." He nodded at Kristin again. "And it's not just your muscle. It's the Eye of Sauron. It's on me, isn't it, Rolly? The deep state, the shadow state, whatever you want to call it."

Cooper let his eyes settle on Kristin Hegel. The former Agency operator. She returned his gaze with frank openness. No performative aggression or resentment.

He wondered, just for a second, if she really did work for Rolly.

Whether she had ever truly left the Agency. Or even which Agency it was.

"They don't leave a trace when they clean house," Cooper said, his voice level. "And it won't just be me they clean up. It'll be Mary and the kids, too. So, what's the point? I give up." He raised his hands again. "But I'm doing it on one condition."

He lowered them.

"You cheeky bastard," Sir Roland said, his voice soft. "Go on then."

"Let my family go. I stashed the project documentation I took from Schneider. It's on a dead-man switch. You know what that means?"

Rolly glanced over at Kristin.

She answered the unspoken question.

"If *nothing* happens, it stays in the dark. If *something* happens..."

"To Mary," Cooper put in.

"If something happens to his little sandwich maker, yeah, the data drops into the wild."

"You dodgy fuckin' chav," Sir Roland marvelled. "And what about you? You're not walking away from this, mate. You've given me a lot of grief, and I'll have my satisfaction from you one way or another."

Cooper slowly raised his hands.

A couple of the suits reached for their weapons, but Kristin waved them down.

Cooper could not help but wonder about her.

"I took two vials from Schneider, and I still have my pills from Gainesville," he said carefully. "I don't know what a mega dose of this crap will do to me, but Ludgrove was all set to give me one and send me back to Gainesville. You agree to leave Mary alone, and I will go back on your program. Your pet doctors might get some useful data from the hiatus. Or you might put a bullet in me five minutes from now when I'm too slow and stupid to do anything about it. But Kristin is right. If you go near Mary or the kids, the project data will go out into the world."

"Where is she?" Kristin asked.

Cooper looked at her.

"Are you kidding me?"

"Rolly, we can't trust her," Kristin said. "She knows about the lab."

"Kristin, people keep secrets all the time if they have reason to," Cooper said, talking over her. "You, of all people, should know that. Mary has two reasons to cooperate. Matty and Jess. Keep them safe. Look after them. She'll be quiet."

Sir Roland waved off Kristin's objection.

"By look after them, what do you mean?"

"First, don't hurt them. Second, money. They'll need some. Not much, but enough to be comfortable somewhere like Gainesville."

Sir Roland nodded, thinking it over. The old rogue was thinking of killing them the first chance he had. Cooper knew that. But they were both playing a role here.

"All right then, Michael," Sir Roland said. "Maybe we can pull this out of the shitter. But you're going under, and you're never coming up for air. And you're right, I might decide your care and feeding is too much to bother with, and I might just slot you myself."

"That's what they call informed consent," Cooper said, raising an eyebrow at Schneider.

He pointed at a pocket of his jacket and gestured for permission to continue.

He heard rounds being chambered all around him.

He carefully removed both doses from his pocket.

He tossed one tiny bottle to Kristin, who in turn threw it to Ted.

He held it up to the light, peering at the label.

"Could be lemonade, I guess, but the batch number is good if he did take this from Schneider," Ted said. "I signed these out myself last week. The prof needed the samples for California."

Sir Roland ordered Ted to let Schneider see the dose.

Ted gave Cooper a wide berth as he moved around him to get to the professor. Schneider reached into his blood-spotted jacket to fetch a pair of reading glasses. His hands shook as he fumbled them on. He frowned at the tiny bottle, peering at the label. He looked up and over at Cooper.

"This is the medication I gave him this morning when he broke into my house and crippled the guards," Schneider said. "It is an undiluted dose of the antagonist formula to the original nootropic. A week's worth. It will return Michael to a state of profound morosis. He will be a number of days incapacitated before reaching homeostasis at the previous baseline. But it will not physically harm him."

Sir Roland grinned.

"Time to take your medicine, Mikey."

Professor Schneider struggled up out of the deep leather couch.

"Please, Sir Roland. Is this necessary? Michael is a very valuable subject. He is willing to cooperate. It is a chance to start over again. Our political masters need not find out. Or they might have had a change of heart. The Chinese have made great advances while we have stood still. There is much greater clarity these days about the threat they pose."

Sir Roland didn't even think it over.

"We can sort all that rubbish out when he's safely under. Right now, he's a bloody menace to everyone and everything. He's going back under, Prof. Now."

"Somebody will have to inject me," Cooper said.

"Ha, no fucking way," Kristin drawled. "Nobody gets within arm's reach of you until you're down, staring at your reflection in a puddle of your own drool."

"Fair enough," Cooper said.

He slowly reached into his pocket and removed a syringe.

Ted Sorenson took the ampoule back from Schneider.

"Use that one, smart ass."

Cooper did as he was told.

He loaded the dose and held up the needle for Sir Roland to see.

"I am sorry you have to do this, Michael," Professor Schneider said from across the room.

"Yeah, thanks for that," Cooper said drily.

Without further delay, Cooper jammed the spike into his neck and pressed the plunger. He felt the liquid entering his system, removed the syringe, dropped it to the floor and waited.

They all did.

Kristin's face was a blank mask. Schneider backed away, shaking his head at what he had done. Ted and Sir Roland waited, fascinated, for the transformation. Cooper's eyes were the first to go. They lost focus on the people in the room, drifting out to the vast emptiness of the sea. The muscles in his face went slack, seeming to erase a whole world of hurt. He blinked slowly. A shudder ran through one leg, and he gasped.

"This is to be expected," Schneider said. "I do not want to be here for this. It is unnecessary."

He started moving toward the door.

Cooper's whole body shook.

Somewhere in the library, somebody muttered a curse under their breath.

Cooper's legs folded up underneath him, and he toppled to the floor.

He lay there, shuddering for a moment before stillness crept over him.

"Is he fuckin' dead or something?" Sir Roland asked.

"Something," Kristin Hegel said, but she didn't sound confident. "Stay there, Rolly." She came around from behind the pool table, carrying one of the cues.

Moving closer, she jabbed Cooper in the neck with the tip, leaving a small blue chalk mark on his collar.

Nothing.

She jabbed him again.

He moved, but just a fraction.

Kristin swung the cue hard, cracking the end over the top of Cooper's skull. He groaned, "No, please..."

But his voice was weak and almost empty of feeling.

"This is intolerable," Schneider complained.

"I think we got us a retard," Ted Sorenson chuckled.

"Good. Give me your fuckin' shooter, Ted," Sir Roland said.

"What?"

"I said give me your fucking gun. I'm gonna finish him, and you're gonna find my fucking project docs, and Kristin's gonna bring me that daft cow of his. And her kids. But first, I'm gonna shoot this dribbling fuckmuppet in the head. He nearly fucked everything up for us. He's gone."

Cooper Fox showed no signs of caring about any of it.

Stopping and turning back at the entrance to the library, Schneider stiffened his spine.

"Sir Roland, no. This is a poor choice."

"And you can fuck off too," Sir Roland growled. "But not too far. I'm not done with you. You've got a big fucking mess to clean up, mate, unless you want to help Mikey feed the fish."

Ted Sorenson reached into his jacket and removed his weapon. It was new. The gun Cooper had taken from him was sitting in the gym bag in East Hampton with Schneider's project documentation.

Cooper groaned but did not move.

"Be careful," Kristin warned as the billionaire advanced on his target.

But she was too late.

Sir Roland had taken one step too far.

The mewling, groaning foetal bundle that had been Michael Garner exploded into a whirling blur of sudden violence as Cooper Fox emerged from his pantomime of drug-induced stupor. Everything that happened next happened fast.

Cooper scythed Sir Roland from his feet, and rolling into a tight ball, he launched himself at the falling billionaire. Kristin Hegel discarded the pool cue she had picked up as an improvised prod and reached into her coat for her guns, but the half-second delay in switching weapons was critical.

Ted Sorenson, of course, was unarmed, and he patted at his pockets in a bizarre charade of a man who had misplaced his wallet and keys. The four nervous types whom Cooper had identified as the weak links in the security detail had variously frozen or fumbled their response. The other half of the crew, stone-cold killers all of them, were attempting to target lock onto him for a kill shot.

They were very well trained. Not engineered, like Cooper Fox, but highly skilled and disciplined operators, and they were prevented from firing because their principal, the man paying their fees—Sir Roland Sewell—was now directly in their line of fire.

Cooper had taken his gun and was using him as a human shield.

From behind the relative safety of the half-stunned billionaire, Cooper sent four shots downrange, killing the four most dangerous operators in just over a second. Blood-mist and brain splatter filled the previously pristine idyll of Sir Roland's library.

A single shot answered Cooper's attack, but it flew wide, shattering the teapot on the trolley.

He swivelled his weapon and his shield at the most dangerous of his remaining adversaries, Kristin, but she was already diving for cover behind the couch. He sent one round after her, but his aim was ruined by Sir Roland's desperate struggle to break free.

Dropping into a deeper stance to anchor himself more firmly, Cooper adjusted his hold on Sir Roland to a rear strangle, cutting off the blood supply to his brain. While doing that, he killed another two men.

The final two were moving now, seeking cover rather than shooting at him.

Ted Sorenson, still unarmed, was moving too, charging at Cooper, his arms spread wide to gather him in for a tackle. It would take another eight or nine seconds to black out Sir Roland, but Cooper had nothing like that much time. He pivoted and spun, whipping Sir Roland's body around and throwing him at Ted's feet.

Sorenson tripped and crashed down on top of his boss.

Moving sideways fast, Cooper snatched up the heavy crystal decanter and threw it at the back of Sorenson's head. It connected with a dull thud, and he went limp, trapping Sir Roland beneath his dead weight.

Cooper, unarmed, was moving again, but the two men he needed to kill were already down.

Each of them shot once in the side of the head.

"Kristin," he called out. "You alive?"

Nothing.

"You're the only one if you are," Cooper said.

He waited three heartbeats.

Nothing.

"You can get out of this if you want," Cooper said. "I'll spot you one, for old times' sake."

But she had already gone.

She had killed two of her men and left, possibly taking Schneider with her.

Ted was alive. Cooper dragged him off Sir Roland, keeping the gun trained on him the whole time, the trigger on a half-pull. But Sorenson was severely concussed. For the second time in a week, Cooper Fox stood over him and fought down the urge to murder. He had taken more than enough lives today. They were all men who would have killed him without regret, but he was not like them. He had to be different, or else what was the point?

He tied Ted's hands and feet with a sash he ripped from the curtains.

It wouldn't take much to escape from the bindings, but they weren't meant to secure him forever, just to give Cooper enough time to get away. He searched the room for Kristin again, but she was gone, and the professor with her.

She had saved him, but Cooper did not understand why.

He wrestled the older man to his feet. Sir Roland was conscious but groggy. The choke hold and a significant head impact had rendered him insensible. Cooper gathered up a couple of weapons before returning to kneel over the other man.

He took the second mega dose from his pocket and held it up. Sir Roland's eyes were teary and bloodshot.

"Placebo," Cooper said. "Distilled water. I switched them before coming here. Schneider saw the broken seal. But he said nothing. You should have listened to him earlier, Rolly. You should have told me the truth."

Cooper took a blister pack of tablets from his pocket. "But these? These are the real deal, Rolly. Time to take your medicine, mate."

He pushed the tablets at Sewell and stood back with both guns trained on him.

———

THE SECURITY GUARDS in the foyer of the *New York Times* offices did not recognise Sir Roland Sewell. All they saw was a distinguished-looking older gentleman who seemed to be lost, wandering around clutching a packet of documents to his chest. His suit was finely tailored, his shoes looked as if they cost more than they made in a week, and most tellingly of all, he smelled nice. The guards did not recognise him, but Matt Phillips, a reporter from the business section, did. Coming back from a late lunch meeting with a source, Philips was hurrying through the foyer, mindful of the print deadline that was looming in a few hours. He had a solid lead on a new development in the Archegos Capital Management story, which he had been chasing for months. In fact, he was so intent on getting back to his desk that he almost ran into the two guards who were gently trying to escort a befuddled-looking Sir Roland out of the building.

"Hey, that's Sir Roland Sewell," Phillips said after dodging one of the guards at the last second. "He's..."

Phillips trailed off.

Sir Roland was obviously in some trouble.

"Are you all right, sir? Do you need help? Do you want me to take that while you sit down? We need to get him a glass of water," Phillips said.

"Water," Sewell said in his thick London accent. He passed the packet of documents to Phillips.

"Water," he said.

Phillip fumbled the packet, and the documents spilled to the floor.

"What the hell is this?" he muttered as he gathered them up.

29

The family looked like any other on the beach that day. The man in his bathing shorts seemed unusually fit, but no more so perhaps than some of the young oil rig workers or the army personnel from the nearby base who had leave that day. The children, a boy and a girl looked happy playing in the sand. Anybody who watched them for more than a few minutes, however, would notice that they never strayed far from their parents. And the parents, or at least the father, never stopped scanning the beach.

The Independence Day crowds at Rockport were huge, and the family was lost within them. Yet the man never ceased his surveillance, near and far. They arrived early in the morning and left just before lunch. They washed off the salt and sand at the outdoor showers near the volleyball courts. An older couple, vacationing from Arkansas, commented to the young woman about how well-behaved the children were. She thanked them but did not engage further. The family left the beach and drove back towards the highway, turning left for Corpus Christi, where they would rent a room overnight, paying cash.

They had moved around like this for three months. The children never complained, and the man and the woman rarely disagreed. He was a quiet man who seemed ever ready to do whatever was necessary for his family.

Later that night, when the children were in bed, the man and the woman sat outside in the warm evening air. She drank a beer, but he seemed content with water. The conversation was quiet and intense. The following day, he said, she and the children would have to go with the Marshals. They had held out this long, but the case was looming and there were still people, rich and powerful people, with an interest in ensuring they never testified.

"I'm only one guy," he said. "I can't be everywhere. I can't cover every angle. One day, they're going to get through."

"But I can't do this without you," the woman said.

"It's not safe for you to do this *with* me," the man replied. "Kristin is still out there."

They fell silent for a while. It was not a tense or sullen moment. They'd had this same conversation many times. It had taken some months, but the woman was reconciled to what must happen next.

"How long do you think?" she asked.

"I don't know," he said. "I have a lot to learn about myself and what I did."

"But that wasn't you," she insisted, almost pleading with him. "That was someone else. I know you. You are a good man. A really good, kind man. And you're mine."

He did not push back on that, but after a while, he spoke again.

"I don't even know what I am. Not really. But I do know some of what I've done, and I can't forget that. I promise I will come back for you. But first, I have to know what really happened, and I have to make good on everything I did wrong."

"Where will you go? How would you even start?"

"There was a woman. Her name was Raven. I was supposed to kill her. But I didn't..."

The man fell silent. He heard a one-eyed Englishman accusing him from across the years.

"You what, mate?"

"I'll start with her," the man said. "And I'll find all the others. The ones who are left from the other cohorts."

They said no more about it. After a while, they went back inside.

In the morning, just before the Marshals came, the man left.

The End.

ALSO BY JOHN BIRMINGHAM

The *End of Days* series.
Zero Day Code.
Fail State.
American Kill Switch.

The Axis of Time.
Weapons of Choice
Designated Targets
Final Impact
Stalin's Hammer
World War 3.1
(World War 3.2 & 3.3 coming in 2024/5)

A Girl Time in Time.
A Girl in Time.
The Golden Minute.
The Clockwork Heart (coming in 2024)

The Cruel Stars series.
The Cruel Stars
The Shattered Skies
The Forever Dead (2024)

Dave vs the Monsters series
Emergence.
Resistance.
Ascendance.
A Soul Full of Guns.
A Protocol for Monsters.

CHEESEBURGERGOTHIC

Hi. It's me, JB. If you liked this book and you'd like more of the same, sometimes for free, please join me over at my blog/book club/dive bar on the internet.

At the moment, it's hosted on Substack, but it kind of moves around, and wherever it ends up, it's *always* called CheeseburgerGothic.

Just throw that into el Goog or whatever AI chatbot runs the world now, and I'm sure they'll hook you up. I give away free stories there at least once a month. And my faves—everyone who signs up at the Burger is my favourite—get tasty discounts on new releases.

Everyone else? Well, my friends, don't be like them.

I look forward to seeing you there.